LORD EDGINGTON

BOOK 3

DEATH
ON A
SUMMER'S
DAY

A 1920s MYSTERY

BENEDICT BROWN

COPYRIGHT

For my father, Kevin,
I hope you would have liked this book an awful lot.

LORD EDGINGTON'S GRAND TOUR

NOTE TO READERS

Welcome to the third "Lord Edgington Investigates…" mystery. This is a quick note to say that I've included a character list at the back of the book, along with a glossary of antiquated, unusual and dialect words. You can also read on at the end of the book for a free novella, a list of some interesting historical titbits and an explanation of my inspirations and reasons for writing.

As with all the books in the series so far, this is a spoiler-free story and does not give away the names of the killers in the previous mysteries.

"Bright star, would I were steadfast as thou art…"
John Keats

CHAPTER ONE

I sat in the library with the world in front of me. Well, the British Isles, at least, spread out across the enormous desk. Depicted in incredible detail was one of the largest maps I'd ever seen.

"Cranley is down here," my grandfather explained, more than a little patronisingly. He jabbed his finger at a point in the south of England, as though I didn't know (approximately) where we were. "We'll get to Cambridge in time for lunch with an old friend of mine." His eyes widened as he ran his finger north through the Capital and up to the ancient university town.

"And after that?" I asked.

He gave me a rare smile, and his impressive white moustache curled up on itself. "After that, we'll head to Suffolk, drive on through Norfolk, and all the way up to Yorkshire if we're lucky. England is our large, flat oyster."

I'd rarely seen him so enthused on a subject, which was remarkable as my grandfather wasn't one of those stuffy old fellows who liked to pretend that nothing could impress him. He moved from foot to foot as his eyes roamed the map in front of us. I didn't like to discourage him, but I'd spotted a problem with his plan.

"Grandfather, I don't think you've thought this through. That map is far too large to take in the car with us. We won't be able to see where we're going."

He took the time to deliver a quite majestically unimpressed glare. "This is merely our inspiration, boy. Our *tabula rasa* upon which we will etch a path. With this map, one might imagine we are the first men to explore these lands. Just like Sir Walter Raleigh or Doctor Livingstone, we are setting a course for adventure. Anyone who has ever journeyed forth on a polar expedition or trekked through a jungle must know the thrill we are experiencing at this very moment."

He took in a deep breath through his nostrils and let it out of his mouth, as though he were inhaling the scent of Britain itself – whatever that might be. I, meanwhile, was having trouble following his point.

"I'm not sure that the north of England has quite the same level of exoticism as Africa or the new world, Grandfather." I crumpled up my nose and scratched the back of my head. "And besides, this map doesn't have any roads marked on it. That seems rather problematic considering that we'd be travelling by, well… road."

He sighed and bent down to retrieve a thick leather briefcase, which was so heavy that he struggled to lift it. "I've invested in this set of Bartholomew's maps for the journey. There are thirty-seven in all, charting every road, lane, railway and waterway in England and Wales."

He extracted one of the fold-out booklets and our home county of Surrey was suddenly before us on the desk. It was almost as large as the previous map, and I wondered how fast we'd be able to travel with such a weight on board.

I dared ask another question. "But what are we actually going to do on our trip?" I didn't want to sound ungrateful, as the very fact he was taking me on a holiday was a source of pride and joy to me. The particulars of our voyage still evaded me though.

"We're going to *live*, my boy. We're going to see things you've never seen before, sleep out under the stars, meet fascinating people, attend a garden party and no doubt make plenty of illuminating mistakes along the way." He wasn't looking at me as he said this, but glanced out through the window over the grounds of Cranley Hall's immense estate. His eyes followed a flock of swifts who were performing an aerial display above the elegant gardens.

I gulped down my nerves and tried to be positive. "That sounds… wonderful. I'm sure I'll enjoy sleeping out in the cold and making mistakes."

He narrowed his eyes once more and glanced at me through the side of his vision. "Who knows, we may even find a way to rid you of your crippling aversion to new experiences."

I was about to reply when our footman Halfpenny appeared at the door. He was a stout, upright sort of chap with a grey face and a livery that always looked a little too tight for him – as though he'd inherited it from whoever had done the job before. I was sure he would never do anything so foolish as sleeping somewhere without any beds.

"Milord, Todd informs me that the cars are packed and we are ready to depart."

"Cars? Plural?" I asked, as I'd assumed that it would just be the two of us setting off together.

Lord Edgington did not appear to have heard. He pushed the roadmap in my direction and marched ebulliently across the room. "Jolly good, Halfpenny. Jolly good indeed!"

I had a bit of trouble getting the blessed map to fold the right way. Once I'd finally packed it into its case, and found the strength to lift the burden I'd been lumbered with, I was ready to go. I followed my travelling companion through the house and out towards the barn where he kept his ever-expanding collection of luxurious automobiles. Our dashing young chauffeur, Todd, was already at the wheel of the largest Rolls Royce, which was packed from bonnet to boot with cases, chests and boxes. He wasn't the only one waiting for us though.

"I came to say goodbye, darling." My mother rushed forward to smother me in a hug. Delilah was sniffing about my ankles too, and her canine affection was always appreciated.

"Thank you, Mummy!" I sounded seven years old, at most.

I must admit, I was feeling more than a little nervous about our departure, and it wasn't just the uncertainty of our itinerary that had set me on edge. My grandfather's favourite Aston Martin was already purring in anticipation of the old man's arrival, and I knew how dangerous his driving could be.

"I'll take good care of him." With a truly wicked smile on his face, he pulled on his driving goggles.

"Yes… Yes, of course you will." Mother could not feign that she was overly confident on the matter, and I completely understood why.

It was at that moment that a third car drove out of the barn-cum-garage. Halfpenny was at the wheel, with our cook Henrietta alongside him. My favourite maid Alice and – even more unexpectedly – Driscoll the gardener were in the back seat.

"Didn't you think of inviting the scullery maids, Father?" There was a thick blanket of sarcasm draped over my mother's voice.

I was pleased to see that my grandfather could serve up just as frosty a response to his daughter as he often did to me. "We'll be gone for weeks, Violet. It only makes sense to bring some staff with me."

"*Some staff?* You're taking half the household. While I can just about understand the need for a footman, a cook and perhaps a maid on a cross-country excursion, I don't see what good a gardener will do you."

I noticed that Alice still hadn't looked at me. I'd been in love with her since I was thirteen years old and had spent the time since then attempting to discern any affection she might possess in return. She sat staring into space, like a mannequin in a women's outfitters. While I'm sure you can imagine the pain her inability to cast her gaze upon me caused, that was nothing compared to what I was about to endure.

As Grandfather climbed aboard the ostentatious vehicle, he offered a brief explanation for the size of our travelling party. "I'm taking Halfpenny, as my own butler is otherwise engaged. Todd is driving the supply car and Henrietta will prepare food as we travel. Meanwhile, young Alice and Mr Driscoll requested a day off at the seaside for their honeymoon, but I couldn't spare them."

Honeymoon! In an instant, my world crumpled in on itself, like a piece of paper tossed thoughtlessly into the dustbin. I'd always hoped to accompany my one true love on her honeymoon; I just never imagined she would have married another man.

"Oh, Congratulations!" My mother was a kind and generous human being, without the slightest knowledge of the suffering I was experiencing. "I'm sure you'll be very happy together."

"Thank you, ma'am." Driscoll glanced down at the floor of the vehicle and averted his eyes in his usual anxious manner. I couldn't begrudge the fellow his happiness. He was a lovely chap; he'd once caught me snatching a pork pie from the larder and never told Cook.

"In fact," Grandfather continued with a furtive expression shaping his features, "Mr Driscoll will be most useful if we happen to pass any interesting gardens upon which I might require an expert's opinion."

"It was awfully kind of you, milord," Alice agreed. "I really never imagined…" She couldn't finish the sentiment, as she had become emotional. Luckily her… her… (I'm sorry, but I was finding it difficult to comprehend the new state of things) …her *husband* was there to offer comfort.

Their employer continued his pretence as he adjusted the driver's side mirror. "Come, come now. You're accompanying me in order to fulfil the duties of your roles within this household. And if we happen to stop along the way at a few key beauty spots that are befitting of a post-nuptial voyage, that is merely a coincidence."

My mother was not taken in by his claims. "I've no doubt you'll all have a wonderful time." She gave me one last hug and pushed me towards the foremost vehicle.

I suppose I must have been dragging my feet as a cloud passed over Grandfather's features. "I hadn't imagined that your presence on the journey was in doubt, Chrissy."

Still a little distracted by the intense agony that was ripping through every fibre of my being, I hadn't said anything for some time. Snapping from my stupor, I hauled the case of maps into the dickey seat and walked around to the passenger door. Alice might have peeked out at me as I passed their Crossley, but she soon went back to her joyful crying.

We waved goodbye to Mother, but I couldn't fake any good cheer. My grandfather's golden retriever jumped in alongside me and I hugged her tight, wishing that I was alone in my bedroom, feeling sorry for myself – just as every heartbroken adolescent deserves.

CHAPTER TWO

By the time we'd reached London, I was feeling a touch more human. It's dreadfully hard to remain glum when the sun is shining, and we were about to embark on my first real adventure as a young man. While solving mysteries with my lordly detective-genius grandfather is all well and good, it couldn't beat the promise of the open road.

We zoomed through the countryside – with a little help from my really quite adequate map reading – then shot into the Capital. As soon as we hit Tower Bridge, our speedy journey came to an unexpected halt. An upturned cart in the middle of the road kept us in the same exact spot for half an hour. Some policemen appeared to round up the garden's worth of cabbages that had rolled from the merchant's vehicle.

"I'm not impressed by the officers' work," my former-superintendent grandfather informed me, as he sat in his comfortable car. "Without a commanding officer to tell them what to do, it's bedlam out there. I'm tempted to get out of the vehicle and issue some stern orders." He didn't, of course, and I doubted it would have helped.

Once the path was clear, and we were on the bridge itself, I was able to enjoy one of my favourite sights in the world. The Thames looked beautiful as we passed over its glittering waters. The river was spotted with a flotilla of barges and boats of all sizes. In the distance, St Paul's Cathedral watched over us and the Tower stood imposingly on the opposite bank. Despite the fact I was born in the country, my heart has always belonged to the city, and London is at its very best on a sunny day.

Though he would have denied it, I was sure that Grandfather had chosen a scenic route for the sake of the happy couple at the rear of our convoy. He smiled at me and raised one eyebrow whenever we passed some ancient monument as though to say, *Imagine what those blessed lovebirds are thinking now!* I can tell you what I was thinking; I was thinking, *no one will ever love me and I'll die alone!* I had a rather refreshing sulk until we left the Capital behind.

I always find it amazing how quickly the scenery changes from rural to urban and back again. Just minutes from the terraced houses and factories, we were out amongst the fields. Nonplussed cows gazed at us in mute wonder as my grandfather pressed his foot to the accelerator and we consumed the road in front of us on our way to Cambridge.

Almost everyone in my family had gone to Oxford, but I had some Cantabrigian cousins. To be perfectly honest, I doubted any university would have me as a student unless I suddenly became a lot smarter in my remaining year of school. And, as my plan to marry Alice was now almost completely ruled out, it was time to consider what I wanted to do with my life.

Seeing the golden edifices and perfectly green lawns of that storied city was almost enough to make me want to study my socks off to follow in my cousins' footsteps. I've seen uglier royal palaces than even the humblest college in Cambridge. Much like the puzzled cattle we'd seen, I looked on in awe as grandfather navigated its pretty paved streets.

Sadly, we drove straight past those famous halls of learning, right through the town and ended up in a dingy neighbourhood. Grandfather parked the Aston Martin on quite the most disreputable street I've ever visited. The houses had no gates or grounds, there was a tatty-looking school, which I had to hope the students didn't sleep in, and the people who paraded upon the pavements all looked like salesmen. The most exciting thing I spotted there was an old donkey, on a scrappy patch of grass, who appeared to be eating a tyre.

"Come along, Christopher." Lord Edgington of Cranley Hall disembarked from his vehicle with a spring in his step, and I stayed behind with Delilah.

"You're surely not going inside?" My whole sentence was one appalled question.

"Of course, we are."

"We!" I peered up at the scabrous building we had parked in front of. "But… it's a… *public house*."

He looked a little confused. "That's right. It's one of my favourite taverns in the whole of England. Now come and have lunch."

"We're going to eat?" I had to pause to process this information. "In there?" The place was called The Knacker's Yard and had a picture of a mournful looking horse on the sign, which made me feel even sadder.

"That's right, Chrissy. Now stop being a snob and get out of the car."

When Delilah deserted me to accompany her master, I knew it was a losing battle.

Grandfather tried to soften the blow. "It may not look like much, but I can promise you that the food is wonderful. I've an old friend inside who's waiting to meet you. His name is the Professor, and he's the living embodiment of so many charming characters from your favourite Dickens' novels. I'm sure you'll hit it off like a wildfire." With his part said, he marched away with a forceful air about him.

I certainly didn't mean to be a snob. I simply hadn't realised before that people like us were allowed in places like that. In the end, I thought it was safer to be inside than left to the mercy of the ruffians passing by. Before leaving the vehicle, I hid our case of maps under the seat – just in case some light-fingered opportunist should happen upon them.

"After you, Master Christopher." Todd stopped in front of the door to let me pass.

I tried to pretend I wasn't nervous as I stepped within the bowels of my first ever "pub". Though my heart was beating faster than the Aston Martin's revolutions, I must concede that the world within those dull grey walls was a jolly welcoming one. The low-ceilinged salon we'd entered smelled of roast dinners and warm ale. There was a fire roaring in one corner and a cheerful old chap at the piano was playing a Victorian song. I was surprised, to say the least, when my grandfather went over to accompany him.

"Oh lovely Mary Donnelly, my joy, my only best!
If fifty girls were round you, I'd hardly see the rest..."

The Pickwickian fellow at the ivories played jauntily with a smile on his face, as Driscoll arrived to take the next verse. I'd rarely seen the gardener so animated in front of my illustrious grandfather, and he belted out the lines in a fine baritone, directed squarely at his new wife.

"Her eyes like mountain water, that's flowing on a rock,
How clear they are, how dark they are! They give me
many a shock..."

Standing in the doorway, Alice looked a little reticent, though perhaps that was because of the unconvincing Irish accent my grandfather had adopted. The old man put his arm around his employee, and the two of them swayed and sang the remainder of the song with great enthusiasm. I had to sit down, as I'd never imagined my grandfather behaving so outlandishly before. After all we'd been through together, I really should have considered the possibility.

"Perhaps he's gone mad," I mused aloud, only for Todd to snigger at me.

"I wouldn't be so sure." He looked at the Marquess of Cranley with great admiration. "That's not insanity we're witnessing. It's an old fella making up for lost time."

I could tell that he would have liked to join in with the final verse, but was called to help Halfpenny order our drinks. If I'm honest, I was rather jealous of the freedom that Grandfather showed. To enjoy oneself without fear of what others think is a great liberty indeed.

Despite having to endure the sight of him addressing our cook as "the flower o' womankind", when the song was over, I was rather disappointed that this joyous scene couldn't have lasted all day.

CHAPTER THREE

"The *Enfant terrible* returns!" our pianist stood up to embrace his old friend and Grandfather greeted him just as warmly.

"I'm still terrible," he joked in reply, "though sadly not so much of an infant anymore." The two men bashed one another about the back as though it were a competition. "I'd like to introduce you to my grandson." He paused to peer around the salon and then dashed over to where I was sitting. "Christopher here is shaping up to be something of a protege and I think you'll get on rather well."

The man who I now took to be the Professor was a contrast in every way to my precise and neat forebear. He wore a black waistcoat with a tweed shooting jacket and a pair of wide-kneed breeches, which looked as though they'd been stolen from a pirate. He was messy, eclectic and all the more interesting for it.

The journey across the lounge took him three times as long as it had my grandfather, but he finally arrived to cast a careful eye over me. "Yes, I can see there's intelligence here, though not of a typical kind."

Being a polite sort of boy, I felt compelled to agree with such comments. "My mathematics teacher says that, if I work very hard and apply myself, I might one day graduate to being average."

The two old chaps let out bellowing laughs at this. Yet again, I had the impression they were trying to outdo one another.

"Well, what do teachers know, eh, my boy?" The Professor joked. "I've been one for fifty years and I'm still sure of nothing."

Grandfather stepped in closer, as though he wished to learn a secret. "How many degrees have you completed now, Prof?"

"Oh… Um…. damn near all of them." The tubby fellow turned to me in order to explain further. "You see, I find studying far more interesting than actually teaching and can never decide which subject suits me best." There was a pause then as he considered this dilemma.

I decided to fill it. "I rather like chemistry, though it's by far my worst subject." Even this needed correcting and I soon followed it up with, "Joint worst, in fact. Along with maths, biology, Latin…"

Todd and Halfpenny arrived at the table with pints of amber ale for the men, a glass of sweet sherry for Alice, and some cold, fresh lemonade for me. I was glad they hadn't bought me a beer. I tried some of Father's once and it tasted like stale tea.

We sat down with the staff at one table and Grandfather, the Professor, myself and our presumptuous dog at another. The "buxom wench at the bar" – those are the Professor's words, not mine – served us large platters of food, and I instantly changed my mind about public houses. We all had a ploughman's lunch, complete with great wedges of cheddar cheese, crusty bread rolls and a variety of pickles and chutneys. I suddenly forgot about polite conversation as I plunged mouth-first into those culinary delights.

The Professor, meanwhile, had the ability to talk and eat at the same time. "I was terribly sorry to hear about your wife, old man. She was a kind woman; she left us too soon."

My grandfather nodded his thanks with his eyes closed, and I assumed that he was reflecting on my dear grandmother's passing a decade earlier. "You never married yourself?"

The Professor tittered gently before replying. "No, but perhaps I should have. After all, no one else would have me." This led to some raucous laughter across the tables, and I got the pleasant feeling that we were all in on the joke. "No, no. I had my chance at love, but it passed me by. The only girlfriends I've had are the books on my shelves; the only fiancée I've encountered is the knowledge that I have slowly accumulated these many years." He even spoke like a Dickensian, and I thought he was wonderful.

His eyes caught hold of me and a flash of an idea fired up behind his sparkling eyes. "Christopher, my boy, I don't suppose you know what a terror this old chap was when he was young?"

Grandfather shook his head disapprovingly, and I let out a squeak of curiosity.

"Oh, there are tales I can tell you. The young Lord Edgington was something of a tearaway when we were boys. We used to spend our summers together, and he got up to all sorts of mischief."

Swallowing down a mouthful of green leaves, Grandfather was quick to set the record straight. "Don't exaggerate, Prof. The boy possesses a vivid enough imagination without you putting ideas in his head."

With half of my plate cleared, I found my voice again. "Actually, I don't know anything about Grandfather's childhood." I considered this for a moment. "In fact, I don't think anyone at Cranley does. My parents certainly never mention it."

Grandfather looked across at Alice and Driscoll. They were in a happy little world of their own and I wondered what their employer was thinking about as they fed each other bits of condiment-coated cheese.

"He never told you about Chandos Grove?" The Professor sounded quite shocked by this. "There was a whole gang of us up there each summer. My family is from the north but your grandfather here would join us whenever-"

"Yes, thank you, Samson." His deep voice rose to a frightening level, then descended once more. "Christopher will find out about Chandos Grove in good time. In fact, that's why I stopped here today. I wanted to make sure you'd received your invitation."

The Professor smiled on one half of his face as he reached his hand inside a second waistcoat which was hidden beneath the first. "So you were the one who instigated this little rendezvous! How you managed to convince Bobbie to go along with this is beyond me."

He produced a once-pristine envelope and laid it down on the table beside his plate. The name *Professor Samson Filigree* was written on the champagne-coloured paper in an elaborately looping hand. He tapped it three times and waited for Grandfather to say something.

"Well… are you planning to attend?"

When the Professor smiled, his strikingly white teeth protruded from his garnet lips. They were perhaps the neatest feature he possessed. "I may decide to make an appearance. I suppose it all depends on who else will be there. Have you spoken to Elodie? Do you really think she wants to see you again after all this time?"

Grandfather tossed his cutlery down and folded his arms across his chest. "That is none of your concern."

The Professor remained silent as he considered his friend's response. In fact, the whole room had fallen to a hush. Cook and Halfpenny were frozen in place, with their forks halfway to their mouths. Todd was suddenly primed, just in case he should need to leap into action to protect his employer from a bust-up. And a wizened old chap at the bar put his pint of stout down for the first time since we'd entered.

I was uncertain who Elodie was or what the two men were talking about, really. It was clear, however, that someone in their circle of friends thought badly of my exceptional mentor.

When he spoke next, the Professor softened his tone and seemed to shy away from the confrontation. "Don't you think it would be better not to revisit the past? It's wonderful to see you, old boy, but…" his words faded out and he restarted the sentence. "Don't you think we should let sleeping dogs lie?"

My grandfather picked up a stick of carrot and bit it in two with a resounding crunch. His response, when it came, was resolute and concise. "No, I do not."

A half moment's silence gave way to the Professor's impressive laughter. "Well, that told me." His amusement reignited, and it somehow felt acceptable to laugh at the formidable character who had just silenced the room. "You never were one to mince your words, Reprobus."

Grandfather hadn't quite abandoned the topic. "So, you'll come then?"

The Professor raised his glass and took a long gulp of ale down his throat before answering. "Oh, I'll come, you old swine. I wouldn't miss it for the world."

CHAPTER FOUR

My grandfather left The Knacker's Yard with a smile on his face, whereas I only came away with more questions. I'd never paid much thought to what he had got up to as a boy. My generation tends to think of the past as a musty sort of place where people sat around all day, drinking tea and waiting for the twentieth century to begin, but I knew that Lord Edgington had lived a varied life.

Something must have pushed my grandfather into becoming a police officer. Wealthy lords don't normally turn their backs on status and riches in order to pursue a poorly paid career rounding up villains. I could only conclude that something significant had happened in his life to trigger such an event. I couldn't imagine what it was, but had a feeling I would learn more as the holiday progressed.

When our convoy set off, there was another question weighing on my mind, which I simply couldn't keep to myself.

"Why on earth did he call you Rebus?"

Grandfather kept his eyes on the road (thank goodness) but smiled in reply. He didn't answer immediately, as though considering whether this was the moment to enlighten me.

"Not Rebus; Reprobus. Reprobus was an early Christian, known for his size and strength. When I was young, I was much taller than my friends and the nickname stuck. If I'm honest, I never liked it, but we all had one. There were six of us in our clique. Samson was the Professor – even before he became a teacher, Elodie was known as Lala." He looked at me sidelong, perhaps checking whether I'd followed the logic (i.e. Elodie – Melody – La la la = Lala). "Then we had Bobbie whom you will meet in due time."

We'd left the town behind and were heading east on the recently christened A45. The road wound through a patchwork of farms and fields and the sun beat down upon our roofless car, showing no mercy for my pale skin and sensitive head.

I prodded my grandfather onwards. "What was Bobbie's nickname?"

"His nickname was Bobbie! His full name is Robert. Or rather it's Robert Atwell, His Grace, the fifth Duke of Chandos." He sighed and continued with the list. "I've already spoken to Mimi, that's Philomena to you. She'll be there with her son. Her husband is a member of parliament, though there was no mention of him when we spoke on the telephone."

I performed a simple mathematical equation in my head. "And?"

"And what, boy? I do wish you would speak in full sentences."

"And you've only told me five of the nicknames. You said there were six of you. Even I can take five from six and end up with one." I had a brief moment of panic as I repeated the sum again to make sure I hadn't made a mistake.

He made an uncertain click at the top of his mouth. "Yes? Well, Lala's two brothers made the odd appearance, but our sixth member… Oh, you'll find out about her eventually I should imagine." His tone was open and friendly so that, for a moment, I failed to realise that he hadn't answered my question.

"And what about Chandos Grove?" I didn't expect much in way of a reply. Whenever my grandfather was unwilling to divulge information, there was no sense in pushing him. "That was where you spent your summers, wasn't it?"

"Quite. And it's a lovely place, tucked away in the Lake District. You'll soon see."

"Oh, good." I was struggling to work out whether I had picked up the slightest clue about his childhood from this conversation. Happy with the fact it had not concluded with one of his famously withering looks, I considered it a fairly successful result.

"Now, there's work to be done. We're headed to a place called Henham Park in Suffolk. It's near Southwold on the east coast. See if you can find it on the map and chart a course there."

I rather liked it when he gave me tasks to carry out, and I immediately leaned over the back of the car to fetch our ridiculously detailed selection of maps. I found where we were on map number nineteen, but Suffolk was over on map number twenty. I tried putting the two great sheets side by side, but the wind blew them about and Delilah kept sitting on top of them. In the end, I had to use them one at a time, while she wagged her tail in my face. Being a golden retriever, she wasn't the daintiest creature either, and it was quite the challenge to work out which roads we were supposed to take.

For a moment though, as I traced a line across England – headed off to pastures new – I finally understood what my grandfather meant about the great pioneers who had preceded us. This was a whole unexplored world for me. A land which the Saxons had conquered to create the kingdom of East Anglia. Their traces were still visible in the names of the settlements all over my map. I spotted Saxmundham, Framlingham and Iken, no doubt chosen for whichever chieftain had ruled over them a millennium earlier.

I have to say that it wasn't just ancient history that the odd names conjured up.

"Listen to this, Grandfather. There are areas on this map called Cuckold's Green, Frostenden Bottom and Wangford!" I had a good laugh, but he was not amused. "Oh, come on. That's literally hilarious."

"It's juvenile, Christopher. As well you know."

I wasn't giving in and replied very slowly, stretching out the syllables. "Frostenden *Bottom*!"

He pretended that it wasn't funny, but couldn't suppress a smile as I burst out in hysterics once more.

Grandfather shot off ahead of the other cars to terrify me with his driving. It was fine on the A-roads, but when we got deeper into the countryside, and the asphalt turned to a muddy path, he did not slow down.

"I think we must have taken a wrong turn somewhere," I shouted over the noise of the engine, as Delilah jumped from my lap to cower at my feet.

"There's no such thing as a wrong turn, boy!" the mad chap said, as he accelerated towards the peak of a hill. I swear our vehicle left the earth and went soaring through the air for a moment. "Huzzah!"

By the time I'd opened my eyes again, we were back on solid ground. Grandfather reluctantly slowed the Aston Martin to navigate a stony stretch between high hedgerows.

"You did that on purpose to scare me," I complained. "And if you try anything like that again, I'll get out and walk."

He'd finally found something to chuckle about. "I'll admit that Frostenden Bottom is a funny name if you concede that driving down a crooked country lane at speed is the most exhilarating sensation you've ever experienced."

Whereas, mere weeks ago, I wouldn't have had the courage to

reply so rudely to the redoubtable fellow, I was starting to get the measure of him and had my response cued up. "You recently made me leap from a hydrogen balloon, having provided me with a very limited understanding of how a parachute works. So, no. I'm afraid I cannot."

I'd made him laugh again. "Touché, young Christopher. Touché indeed."

CHAPTER FIVE

By the time we found Henham Park, the others had already arrived. Grandfather and I were still squabbling.

"I told you we'd made a wrong turn."

"Yes, but if we'd taken the most direct route, we'd never have discovered all the wonders that Ipswich had to offer." Only Lord Edgington could make a medium-sized port town in the east of England sound like the Hanging Gardens of Babylon.

We'd entered the Henham estate to pull up in the drive of a Georgian mansion. It was a squat, boxy sort of building with more windows than there were trees in the park, and so I felt most at home there. Grandfather had informed me that the estate belonged to the somewhat ancient Earl of Stradbroke. Though I'd been forced to endure a lengthy description of the family line going back to the sixteenth century, he was less forthcoming with the details of what we were actually doing there.

Propped up against the luxury supply car, our footman Halfpenny was looking typically distressed. "We rang at the tradesman's entrance, milord, but the butler said that they weren't expecting us."

Jumping from the car's running board with both feet, grandfather replied with the same mysterious air that he'd had about him for most of the day. "That's right, man. I neither requested nor would have expected to receive accommodation at the hall. We are here to deliver a message."

"Well that certainly makes the situation clearer." Now that I'd discovered my nerve, I was having trouble passing up the opportunity to deliver such barbs at the old man's expense.

Grandfather did not respond. He rolled his eyes and addressed his staff. "Todd, there is a small lake to the north-east where I fished as a child. You should find it without much trouble. Halfpenny will help you pitch the tents."

"Yes, milord. Right away." Our chauffeur/heroic action man nodded efficiently and returned to his vehicle. I had no doubt that he'd have the camp set up in the time it would take me to work out which way a tent peg goes into the ground.

Grandfather turned to his favourite member of staff. "Cook, perhaps you could start preparing our dinner. We will dine on trout this evening!"

The ruddy-cheeked woman was most excited by this news. "Wonderful, milord. I've got the ingredients to knock up a delicious ox cheek soup as a first course."

Alice and Driscoll were still in their places in the car and looked a little left out.

"I'll do my bit to help, milord," the gardener said. "I'd like to pull my weight."

Grandfather put on a stern expression. "Jolly good, Driscoll. It would be incredibly helpful if you could take a stroll with your beloved in the woods and…" He had to think for a moment to invent an excuse. "…And try to remember what kind of trees you spot. I can't tell the difference between an oak and an elm, so your expertise is essential. I'll be sleeping outside tonight, so you must take my tent of course."

Mr and Mrs Driscoll blushed and mumbled their thanks. I had to wonder what it would take for Lord Edgington to be so obliging to me. The thought of what married people did in tents on the first night of their honeymoon briefly flashed through my head, and I was quite grateful for the fact that I was still hazy on the details.

"With me, Chrissy." Grandfather barked out his order, and I scampered after him while his faithful hound found a shady spot in which to lie down.

"If they're not expecting us, what are we doing here?" I foolishly enquired, as he rang the bell.

A liveried footman swung the huge wooden portal inwards and addressed us with careful diction that did not disguise his deep, country accent. "How may I be of service, Lord Edgington?" He had clearly been briefed on the situation by his colleagues at the rear of the house.

"I have a message for your mistress." Grandfather poked his hand into the breast pocket of his long, grey coat and produced a matching envelope to the one which the Professor had shown us. "This is for Miss Elodie. You must tell her on my behalf that she would be very welcome to join us. Of course, I would not be so presumptuous as to expect her attendance." Grandfather raised his chin as though to emphasise the generosity of his act.

"Very good, milord."

"Oh, and, if it is not an imposition, my staff and I will be camping beside the lake this evening. I have fond memories of my time at Henham as a child and wish to relive one of my very first adventures."

The young chap with the markedly high hairline smiled. "I'm sure that Lord Stradbroke will be only too happy to have you on the grounds, milord."

The two men nodded cordially, and we returned to the car with a whistle for Delilah to join us. I could see what it meant to Grandfather to be back at the scene of so many golden moments from his youth – not that I'd ever heard of the place until that day.

"I can remember countless happy times that I shared here with Elodie and her brothers." He took in the fields and copses of the estate, as though he recognised every twig and blade of grass. "Who would have thought that the same Earl of Stradbroke would be ruling over the place sixty years later, with both his sons killed in different foolish wars? Would you believe that the chap's almost a hundred? There'll be no new Earl to inherit once he goes."

I didn't respond as he chattered on about the family once more. I could see how happy he was to travel back in time.

We followed a winding path across the estate and got to the lake just as Todd was raising the biggest tent – he'd already created a small canvas city, complete with latrine and kitchen.

It was a pretty spot. The lake was long and snaked around the clearing in the woods. It reminded me of the Serpentine in Hyde Park, but with far fewer people bustling about the place. I would like to have taken my book out and continued reading 'Pride and Prejudice' for the first time – it was my mother's recommendation and I was already gripped.

After he'd parked the car, Grandfather had other ideas. "You'll be catching the trout while I sketch the scene. The lake is positively teeming with fish so you'll have no trouble whatsoever."

I didn't know how to respond to such a prediction, so I said nothing.

"Don't look at me like that, Christopher. There's very little to it." I'd heard such claims before from the chap, and they rarely proved accurate.

Along with painting and drawing, another of my grandfather's new hobbies was tying flies for fishing. After poking around in one of his many bags, he produced a fancy case full of brightly coloured lures made of feather and wire. Each one was designed to represent a different insect, and he carefully selected a small dragonfly for my first attempt. Whilst threading the hook onto the fine silk thread, he informed me that, "Fly-fishing is a sport for thinkers." I don't know what this said about me.

Before I knew it, he'd strapped me in waders and galoshes, stuck a rod in my hand and forced me out into the lake. It was cold. I did not like it one bit.

When Todd and Halfpenny had finished their task, they sat on the bank to spectate. "It's all in the wrist, Master Chrissy," the chauffeur explained with a grin.

"That's exactly what I told him." My grandfather had already set up his easel and was registering the first lines of his next masterpiece.

I tried to ignore them and concentrated on casting my line out into the water. I thought about the brief but heartfelt instructions that the ever-wise Lord had given me and pictured his wrist snapping through the air as I attempted to re-enact his technique. Pulling the rod back over my shoulder, I did what I could.

"Ooh, not quite," Halfpenny declared, as the hook and line landed limply a few feet away.

"It's all in the wrist," Grandfather repeated.

"The wrist," Todd echoed, and I half expected Cook to stick her head out of the supply car to say the same thing.

I'm sure my sullen expression told a thousand tales, but not a word fell from my mouth as I reeled the line back in and made a second attempt.

I held my breath, counted to three and tried to visualise the line wafting through the air in a magical loop – like a cowboy's lasso in a travelling show. My rod flashed through space, I released the reel at just the right moment and… and I did it!

"Jolly good work, Chrissy!" Todd clapped his hands and Halfpenny let out a gentle, "Good show!"

Grandfather didn't say anything, as the fly sat prettily in the middle of the lake. He smiled, nodded his head and returned to his drawing.

"I see what you mean now; it is all in the wrist." I was genuinely excited by my success and enjoyed something of the thrill that Lord Edgington must have experienced as a child.

"That's wonderful." He put down his pencil and selected another. "Now, all you have to do is catch a fish."

I'd hoped that the hard part was over, but that wasn't the case. I stood in that freezing water for the best part of the evening and the only thing I caught was a cold.

"This is ridiculous," I sniffled, forty-five minutes later. "We'll never eat at this rate." Cook had already come to check on my progress twice and, though she insisted there was no hurry, I could tell that the rest of the food was nearly ready.

The only saving grace was the fact Alice wasn't there to see me make a fool of myself, but as she was off looking at birds in the woods with her new husband – who, I have no doubt, could tell a peacock from a partridge – it did little to comfort me.

"Come along then." Todd finally took pity on me and rolled his trouser legs up to wade over to where I was standing. "Let me have a turn."

He weighed the rod in his hand, reeled the line in and, with that famous flick, the green and yellow dragonfly zipped through the air.

Twenty-seven seconds! That's how long it took him before he had his first nibble. I know because I counted. Twenty-seven seconds and our dashing driver had hooked his first trout.

"You said it was all in the wrist," I complained, quite reasonably. "I did exactly the same thing as you and nothing happened."

"That's just the casting. The fishing itself is all in your head."

Grandfather let out a little chuckle from behind his easel. "I told you, Chrissy. It's a thinking man's sport."

Perhaps it was the cooler evening after a hot and humid day, but the tension that had been building within me finally broke. I thought I might scream and tell them how thoroughly cruel it was that they'd put the one person who'd never fished before in charge of catching our dinner. I thought I might let out a screeching yell, but instead I just laughed.

"No wonder it's not for me then." I put my head up to the sky and howled. "What's the non-thinking man's sport? Whatever it is, I'm sure to be a whizz at it."

Todd joined in with my amusement, but there was no malice in his laughter. I was awfully glad to be able to see the funny side of things.

"Don't be so hard on yourself, Christopher," my kind, though contrary, grandfather insisted. "You're just as much a thinker as the

Professor. But, like fly-fishing, using the facilities of one's brain is a skill which you must practise in order to improve."

I was unsure whether this was entirely complimentary, but I was willing to give him the benefit of the doubt, especially after what happened next.

"You should never have come here, Reprobus." A woman on a large white stallion was galloping along the path towards us with a face full of rage. Twenty feet from my artistic ancestor, she pulled the horse to a stop and reiterated her initial sentiment. "You should never have come."

"Lala, how wonderful to see you." If he was offended by her anger, Grandfather certainly didn't show it. He beamed up at his old friend, full of grace.

She was a tall, striking woman, who I took to be a few years my grandfather's junior. She had long white hair tied in a plait, honey brown eyes and skin that was almost as pale as the mount she rode. With her high, well-defined cheekbones, I might even have said she was pretty if it hadn't been for the thunder that rolled within her. She took a champagne-coloured envelope out of a pocket in her saddle and tore it to pieces before replying.

"How dare you come here? How dare you bring this to me?"

Grandfather set his pencil down on the easel as his staff tactfully pretended that they were unaware of the very private scene that was playing out between two esteemed members of the English gentry.

Grandfather linked his hands behind his back and began to pick his way through the long grass to approach his childhood friend. "I take it this means you won't be coming to the party at Chandos Grove?"

"No. I shall not be attending the trap you've set for me."

Before he could reach her, Elodie Rous had turned her horse around and gone shooting back off towards Henham Hall. She issued one final shout over her shoulder, as the steed propelled her away from us. "If you're still here in the morning, I'll set the dogs on you."

CHAPTER SIX

I'll always remember that night with great affection.

Grandfather invited his staff to dine amongst us, to celebrate the recent nuptials. Only Halfpenny – who consistently managed to be stuffier than his aristocratic master – found a reason to refuse. Instead of sitting down to the feast, the old footman served the meal and then played a tin whistle he'd brought along for our entertainment. I have to say that he wasn't too dreadful and, once Todd had opened a bottle of Bordeaux and we'd finished the (almost entirely) delicious dinner, we all got up to dance.

Alice and Driscoll went first, of course, and the happiness between them overruled any jealousy I might have felt. Their eyes were locked on one another's as they performed a lively jig and it was almost enough to make me believe that, somewhere in the world, there was someone who could love me in quite the same way.

The lord of our camp was awarded the second dance with Alice, and I got my shoes stepped on by Cook, who apologised profusely. Todd produced a roaring fire, Driscoll sang us a pretty song in that beautiful voice of his and everyone had a jolly good time indeed.

"I haven't had this much fun in decades," my grandfather exclaimed, before toasting the newlyweds.

With them all still enjoying themselves, I decided to retire for the night with my book and the electric torch Father Christmas had brought me. Despite Grandfather's attempt to pull me screaming from the tent to bivouac in the open air, I managed to resist and sought refuge in a world of genteel romance, elegant manners and tight bodices. Admittedly, I only got through five chapters of 'Pride and Prejudice' before I fell asleep.

Though he'd shown no fear at Elodie's threat, Grandfather roused us early the next morning to vacate Henham Park before the hounds came by to eat us. He let me set the itinerary that day, and I knew exactly where I wanted to go.

Ever since I was ten years old, I'd dreamed of retracing young David Copperfield's footsteps to Great Yarmouth on the east coast of England. I longed to meet the fishermen and simple, good-hearted folk of one of Dickens' greatest works, in a picturesque town beside the sea.

How sad it is when the harsh reality of modern existence fails to live up to our dreams. It turned out that David Copperfield's salt-of-the-earth utopia had been transformed by the never-relenting march of progress. In place of pretty little coves with abandoned fishing boats or Victorian tea rooms overlooking an elegant promenade, we found 'The Pleasure Beach'. It was a sprawling monstrosity of coconut shies, artificial mountains and haunted castles. The beach had been eaten away by the stationary equivalent of a travelling funfair, but there was nothing fun about that unholy place.

I stood on the seafront, processing the cries of fear that carried over to us from the attractions. Every twenty seconds, another car would hurtle down the 'Scenic Railway' as a new batch of victims were forced to endure the torment. Dante himself could not have described a more terrifying incarnation of the underworld than I saw that morning.

"What larks!" Alice positively squealed with excitement and pulled her new husband off to suffer in the park.

"I've read about such places of course." My grandfather's eyes were bulging out of their sockets. "But the reality is so much more exciting." Though he didn't quite run along the seafront, he did a seventy-five-year-old lord's best impression of such an act. I was clearly the only sane one amongst us. I followed along after them, if only to witness the madness at first hand.

Three minutes later, I found myself wishing I'd stayed in the car.

"No!" I felt this was a simple enough sentiment, but could see from my grandfather's reaction that he did not agree. "Not a chance."

He was already buying tickets for the nightmarish mechanical attraction and looked at me through the corner of one eye. "Christopher, we've already discussed the matter."

"Human beings are designed neither for rolling nor coasting and I refuse to go on a roller-coaster."

Delilah was barking, as though she would happily go in my stead, and the others had already taken their places on board the counterfeit train. The wooden peak they were about to ascend – complete with painted snowy summit – was about as far from my idea of excitement as I could imagine, and I would not bow to the pressure.

"Ahhhhhhhhhhhhhhhhhhhhhhhhhhhhhhhhhh!" was the noise we all

made as the rickety carriage went hurtling down the wooden track towards certain doom. "Eeeeeeeeeeeeeeeee!" the wheels screeched on the metal rails as we went over bump after bump on our way up the second stretch. "Urrrrrrrrrrrrrrrrrrrrrrrrrrrrrrrrrgh!" a fellow at the front gurgled, as he clearly wasn't feeling too well.

When the ride came to its conclusion, no one moved. Grandfather had turned a shade of green that can only be described as sickly. Halfpenny opened his mouth, but no sound came out, and even Todd looked a little peaky.

"That was wonderful!" I said, clapping my hands together with joy. "Grandfather, you've proved me wrong once again. The next time I refuse to do something that I don't like the look of, you have my full permission to force me into it."

The poor chap clearly didn't have a response. He peered back up the track we had descended, before turning to his chauffeur. "Todd, I may need your help to stand."

Grandfather recovered by taking the sun on the beach after that. I couldn't understand why he was still dressed in his grey woollen morning suit when the thermometer on Wellington Pier had gone past eighty degrees. I didn't have time to worry about him overcooking though, as I soon found myself alone with Alice.

"Where's your... husband?" I asked, just about managing to say the word without choking on it.

"He's gone over to the tombola. He said he'd win me something for our new house."

We were standing on the prom once more, watching the gentle waves come sweeping up the beach. I didn't think I'd find the courage to make another sound, or gaze upon her pretty Irish face ever again, but I surprised myself.

I turned to look at her and, in my most polite, grown-up voice, said, "I'm very happy for the both of you. You deserve all the happiness the world can offer." And then I bowed gracefully and turned to buy myself some candy floss.

My little speech had come off without a hitch. My voice hadn't come out like a young mouse's and I hadn't accidentally called her Mother. In fact, it had gone disconcertingly well, and I was certain I would fall flat on my face or let out a terrible belch at any moment.

But not even those small indignities occurred – though I did make a mess of myself as the sweet, angel-hair confection I'd bought got all over my clothes and face, so that I soon looked like an infant who'd run wild in a sweet shop.

Once I was clean again, it was time to resume our journey. We spent the afternoon driving north-west to Sherwood Forest, which meant yet more maps to consult. I noticed that my grandfather drove remarkably slowly the whole way there, so much so that Todd and Halfpenny were able to keep up with us. He clearly hadn't recovered from his ordeal at the 'Pleasure Beach' and would not breathe a word of the experience for the rest of his days. This wasn't a problem, as there were several more interesting topics I wished to address.

"Are you going to tell me anything more about the woman on the horse who threatened to savage you with a pack of dogs?"

He kept his hands on the steering wheel, his eyes straight ahead and his lips firmly sealed.

I tried again. "What about the rest of your little gang? Are you going to tell me about Bobbie and Philomena and what you got up to with the Professor when you were a boy?"

He checked on our convoy in his mirror, but was not inclined to divulge. "All in good time."

I could have shut my mouth then and kept my thoughts to myself, but I felt as though, for all his reticence, there was something he wanted to tell me.

"Really, Grandfather. You're being secretive even by your standards." I'd raised my voice and sleepy Delilah chastised me from the back seat with a disgruntled bark. I continued to lay out my grievances in a softer tone – for her sake. "You're waving some fascinating chapter of your life in front of me like a sugar lump before a horse, and yet I'm not allowed to ask any questions. It hardly seems fair."

When he replied, his voice was more fragile than normal. "Don't make the mistake of thinking that fairness is ever guaranteed." He paused for a moment, but soon continued in that same gravelly tone. "I was hoping that you could see by now just how cruel the world can be."

I was taken aback by his words. He'd been exceedingly cheerful ever since he'd announced our cross-Britain jaunt, but anger scarred his face now, and I was amazed I found the nerve to reply.

"Tell me what it is I'm clearly missing. Tell me why we're going all this way to see your old friends and why Elodie Rous was so furious."

The scowl on his lips stretched lower, and his whiskers shivered. "I'm not here to do the work for you. That is what you must determine."

I finally got a sense of his thinking. "Is that why we're travelling all this way? Have you done this for my benefit?"

He banged the wheel with his left hand before changing down a gear. "You need practice." The cold look in his eyes gave me no encouragement to hurry him along. "You need to learn to use your brain more effectively. I've told you, Chrissy, I can see great talent in you, but that school of yours has done nothing to cultivate it. It's only too easy for people like us to rest on our good fortune and idle away our lives. For that reason alone, we must fight. We must resist laziness and mediocrity. We must work to keep our wits about us."

We were passing along a shady road with a canopy of trees above our heads that only let fragments of light through. I watched as the shadows danced across his face and, when we emerged once more into the sunlight, I understood what he wanted from me.

"That's why you brought me with you, isn't it? There's a mystery for me to solve."

The bright blue sky seemed to raise his spirits, and his expression relaxed. "Not just any mystery, Christopher. My very first investigation. The crime which inspired me to turn my back on my family and Cranley Hall."

We fell into a contemplative hush, and I turned his words over in my head. For a few minutes, the only sound I could hear was Delilah's snoring and the wind rushing past my ears. Even the noise of the motor and the endless hum of the tyres on the road seemed to fall quiet as I tried to make sense of what little he'd told me.

"You lost someone." I wasn't sure of myself, but this seemed to make sense. "You said there were six of you, but you only told me five names. Did someone die?"

He opened and closed his mouth twice over without making a noise. "Her name was Morwenna Fairbright, and it happened shortly after my eighteenth birthday. As the Prof told you, I was set to head off to Cambridge that summer but her death changed everything for me."

"How did she die?" I hesitated over my next question as, even after the investigations I'd experienced with the famous detective, it still sounded faintly absurd to suggest such a thing. "Was she… murdered?"

He let out a short breath as he steered us onto the wider road which led up to the north of England. "Star."

"I'm sorry?"

"That was her nickname."

"Oh, I see." I considered the logic. "Morwenna Fairbright; bright like a star. Very clever." I laughed a little nervously. "So, are you going to tell me what happened to her?"

He was in an obstinate mood, and I could see it was foolish of me to expect such a simple answer.

"You asked me yesterday what my friends' nicknames were. I was Reprobus – or Reprobate when one of them was angry. Then there was Bobbie, the Professor, Mimi, and Lala who you met last night. The last and the best of us was called Morwenna, but she was known to everyone as Star."

"But what happened? Why wouldn't you-"

He cut me off before I could form the question. "You'll have to work the rest out for yourself."

CHAPTER SEVEN

It felt genuinely invigorating to get out of the car at our final stop of the day. Conversation had not been forthcoming for most of the journey, and four hours in a car is too much for any man.

"Sherwood Forest?" Todd said with disbelief in his voice as he rushed over to the sign to check that his eyes weren't playing tricks on him. "Where Robin Hood lived?"

"The very one," Grandfather replied.

"This is incredible!" He clearly couldn't believe his luck. "He's my absolute hero."

Lord Edgington had failed to notice the excitement pulsing through his employee and continued in a blasé manner. "Though if you read a little into the history, it's really very unlikely that there was one unique person with the name and, if he did exist…" He'd evidently seen Todd's expression by this point and changed his tone. "…he most certainly robbed from a tyrannical ruling class in order to help those most in need. I dare say he was every bit as good as the ballads say."

Our chauffeur was reassured and, with Delilah alongside him, went running into the woods to re-enact scenes from his favourite childhood stories. I was a little disappointed that there were no bandits or men in green outfits about the place, but the trees there were very pretty.

We stayed in the forest that night and, this time, with a little persuasion from my grandfather, I agreed to sleep out under the stars. This did mean I spent less time with Elizabeth Bennet and her lovely sisters, but the night was clear and warm. It was a good place to consider the universe and my place within it.

I couldn't help wondering what those charming ladies from Jane Austen's tale would have made of me if I'd come a courting. Would I have met the level of such suitors as Fitzwilliam Darcy or be dismissed as a mere Mr Collins? The only woman I'd ever loved was asleep in the arms of her new husband. I had never been brave enough to tell Alice how I felt about her in the first place; I couldn't see that there was much hope for me should another pretty girl ever cross my path.

I got cold around midnight and retreated to my tent. It can be awfully chilly in England at night and we were only half way to our destination. I'd spent my whole life in the south and had always imagined the top part of the country to be like some Arctic wasteland. I have to admit that, not only was I mistaken, the beauty of the countryside only increased the further north we drove.

After we set off the next morning, I noticed the land getting hillier and the sight of mountains on the horizon. Taking the scenic route once more, we crossed the Peak District with its crags and elevations clawing at the sky and emerald green slopes as far as the eye could see. It made me want to get out and enjoy them for myself, but Grandfather informed me we had an itinerary to follow.

We skirted the industrial city of Manchester and, after that, it was as though the natural world had fought back against man's best endeavours. Wherever I looked, there was rough countryside and far more sheep than London had human inhabitants. Though I'd expected rain and grey clouds, the sun ruled the skies up there just as it did back in Surrey. It was summer, the nation over.

I longed to explore the wild expanses of the Yorkshire Dales – and perhaps compose a few poems on their beauty or discover 'The Secret Garden' for myself. In fact, as I crossed the country of my birth, I realised that it was one great tapestry of, not just fields and forests, but stories. We'd left behind the land of Charles Dickens and made it as far north as the kingdom of the Brontës. England was an anthology and, for each region, countless fine writers had added to its pages.

And yet it was the Lake District itself which I was most excited to visit – the inspiration for William Wordsworth and Beatrix Potter alike. It was not just the intrigue of Grandfather's ancient mystery which drew me there, but the very idea of such a land. The place had always sounded mystical to me – like some imaginary region within Peter Pan's Never Never land – and I'm glad to say that it didn't disappoint.

We arrived with the sun still high in the sky but the day waning. The road had become far more challenging as we closed in on our destination. We seemed to spend half of forever winding up and back down the fells, snatching glimpses of the famous lakes.

As the persistent wheels of the Aston Martin carried us towards the Chandos estate, I fell in love with a place I had only seen before in books. I fell in love with the colours. Oh, the colours! From the lurid green of verdant valley grass to orange – actual orange – soils which bedecked the mountain slopes alongside burnt red and ochre. There was sun-yellow western gorse, purple foxgloves shouting out a warning for all to see, and the blue – true blue – of the myriad meres, tarns, waters and lakes that gave the region its name. Some men may think of paradise as a sandy beach and a clear sky, but I have been there, and it requires a far more extensive palette to depict.

When we passed through the local village, and I first caught sight of Chandos Grove's sandstone towers in the distance, I wished us onwards, as though that would help the minutes pass any quicker. The elaborate house had been dropped onto a spit of a valley between two violently sloping cliffs. The whole scene made me think that God had come down with a chisel to etch the landscape in the precise way he desired. It was wild and wonderful, but I was glad we weren't visiting in winter.

There were two large wings of contrasting styles which made up the main house. The Elizabethan and Victorian clashed and melded together to paper over the damage some destructive force had wrought upon the old hall. Whether a storm had blown walls down, fire had ripped through it, or an overzealous custodian had decided to leave his mark on the place, the building had a patched-together quality that matched the surrounding landscape.

A ring of hawthorn trees crowned the estate and, perhaps inevitably, a large oval lake reflected a perfect rendition of the mountains back to us. When we finally pulled up the long gravel driveway and parked in the circular courtyard before the house, we were greeted by our host.

The Duke of Chandos fired his shotgun into the air, as my grandfather and I alighted from the car. I was beginning to worry that we weren't welcome after all, when he shouted something in our direction.

"Don't let the cat get away." He reloaded the two barrels and clicked the gun closed. "Whatever you do, you must stop that cat!"

CHAPTER EIGHT

"Bobbie, old chap," my grandfather began, with his hands extended at his side in a sign of amity. "What on earth are you doing with that gun?"

The Duke pulled his head in to his neck, as though he had just heard some wild claim. "I'm not trying to shoot the damned creature, just scare it a little." The fact that the man was dressed in nothing but a string vest and white cotton bloomers added little weight to his claim. "Now where has that moggy gone?"

I considered hiding behind the vehicle just in case the gun went off, but Grandfather wasn't worried and went to embrace our host. "It's awfully good to see you, Bobbie. It's been far too long." He put one hand on his shoulder and stripped the gun free with the other. He passed it back to me, but I didn't want it. I would have given it to Delilah to hide in a bush or something, but she was off sniffing the flowers beside the high wall which hemmed in the estate.

I took a moment to study the wild old gent who'd greeted us. He had a shock of fuzzy white hair on his head and incredibly pale blue eyes that reminded me of Chinese crockery. He was tall but stocky and, from the stains on his clothes, appeared to have gone rolling down a muddy hill that day. Unlike most people I knew, he was forever moving. He twitched and jerked as though he thought there were mosquitos coming to bite him and, even when he spoke, there was a liveliness to him that was most intriguing.

The Duke had not replied to the warm words he'd been offered and was staring at me as though I were trespassing. "Now, who's this then? Not another son, is it?" There was something very unsteady about him. His voice climbed high before falling back down again, and he had one shoulder much lower than the other. "Oh, Reprobus! Don't tell me you got a second wind and re-married some young lovely!"

Grandfather was too busy laughing at this suggestion to correct him and so I did the honours. "He's my grandfather." I probably sounded a little outraged by the idea. "I'm Christopher. My father is-"

He turned away before I could finish the sentence. "No time for that! You're here now."

I was unsure whether he thought this a good thing, but Grandfather hurried to catch up with him, so I did the same.

"Have you heard from anyone else?" the man who definitely was not my father enquired.

"Only the Prof and Philomena. You said that you'd deal with Elodie and she doesn't like me anyway." His thoughts became stuck for a moment, but then he kicked back into life. "Tell your people that the kitchens are at the back of the house and we'll pop inside for an aperitif."

I'd long thought that the esteemed Lord Edgington was an eccentric chap. I was coming to understand that, the higher you went up through the echelons of British aristocracy, the closer you got to all-out insanity. The Duke walked through the entrance of his own home and along the corridor as though some mercenary might jump out from the shadows at any moment to do away with him. His eyes were forever shifting about, and he peered into every dark space. His hands trembled, and there were scars down both sides of his face that looked awfully like his cat had swiped him.

"Dinner will be ready before long," he informed me, as though I'd been complaining. "All we were waiting for was the cook."

"Why don't you have your own?" I accidentally wondered out loud.

He stopped in the middle of the long corridor to have his first proper look at me.

"Do you think I'm made of money, boy?" I would probably have stuttered out an answer, but he spoke again. "Why pay for a cook when I have two perfectly good hands and know how to open a can of sardines?" He blew on his own face as though he were hot. "That's why I'm angry with the damned cat, you see?"

I assumed that he would expand on this topic, or that my highly amused grandfather would step in to explain, but I had no such luck. "Ummm, no. I'm afraid I don't."

He spun back around and continued walking in that odd, jerky manner. "Keep up, boy. Keep up. The cat nabbed my sardines at breakfast and I've been trying to catch him ever since. I thought I had him before you arrived, but he bolted through a window."

"Ahhh…" This was the most intelligent sound I could produce just then. "I'm not allowed cats as my mother is allergic."

"Sensible woman."

The hall we were walking along was incredibly dusty. The curtains were all drawn and very little light penetrated the space, but I could see that it was still bright outside as we occasionally passed a tear in the fabric where a beam broke through like a spotlight on the London stage.

I had never imagined visiting such a wealthy and luxurious estate that was quite so poorly kept. There was no sign of any servants and it wasn't until we walked through a boarded-up lounge and out into a once white conservatory that we saw another living soul.

My grandfather hadn't uttered a word since we entered the house, but I was the one who was now speechless. Sitting in a wicker chair, staring up through the cracked glass ceiling at a small selection of clouds, was a girl my age.

She had hair the colour of Cornish ice cream, a serene smile on her face and was dressed in a blue and white sailor's outfit with a pleated skirt. She must have been at least fifteen but looked like a small child from the early days of Victorian photography. She wouldn't have looked out of place in a large pram or playing with a stick and hoop.

It took her a while to notice me, but when she did, she did not hide her feelings on the matter.

"Oh, you're delicious!" she growled. I had to take two steps backwards, as I was afraid she would bite me.

"Ariadne, stay calm." As soon as the Duke spoke, the young girl stood to order and stopped glaring at me.

"Sorry, father, but he looks just like a sausage roll."

"Evidently so, child, but we don't eat the guests." The Duke planted himself in the chair which the girl had vacated and pulled a dressing gown around him back to front. "Now, be a good girl or I'll lock you in the airing cupboard with the cat."

"I thought you lost the cat?" Grandfather finally pronounced.

"There are two felines at Chandos Grove, Reprobus. A mummy and a daddy. Occasionally they have babies, but we sell them to pay for sardines. Isn't that right?" He looked at the girl for confirmation. She nodded unconcernedly, then turned back to me with a lick of the lips.

"And this is your…" Grandfather began, "daughter? Please tell me you didn't get a second wind?"

"No, no," the Duke coughed out. "She's just a stray I took in. Adopted her as my own, in fact. No one else seemed to want to her, so

I thought it was a good idea."

"And you never had any…?" I was surprised that my grandfather was too modest to utter the question in full.

"Children of my own, you mean?" The Duke tucked his chin into his chest in surprise once more. "Come along, man! That's hardly a polite enquiry to put to a chap. And as there aren't any around here, begging for money, I clearly don't know a thing about them."

He reached out to seize a bell, which he rang for approximately two minutes until a lethargic maid appeared. She was stick thin, had mousier blonde hair than the Duke's adopted daughter and spent the whole time looking out through the door as though there was somewhere she'd rather be.

"What do you want?"

The Duke did not seem concerned by her poor manners. "Dinner, Mabel. What's happening about that? It's been hours since lunch and I'm starving. Especially after the cat-"

"Took your sardines." She emitted a sharp burst of laughter. "Yes, I heard about that. But I'm afraid that the cook has only just unpacked her equipment in the kitchen. She says the place isn't fit for chopping wood, let alone meat and veg. So she'll need time to prepare."

The Duke let out an unexpected cry, which his adopted daughter quietly mimicked. "Very well. Bring me another can. With the arrival of our guests, I was hoping to economise today, but it looks like that's off the cards."

Mabel hurried off to the garden and knelt down beside an ornamental pond. She returned a moment later with a dripping wet can of fish.

"It keeps them cool," the Duke snapped, when he saw the puzzled expression I wore. "Why pay the upkeep on an expensive ice house when we have cold water for free? Such luxuries will bleed a man dry, I tell you. Dry!"

"You're richer than the Bank of England, Bobbie." Grandfather took a white metal chair, placed it in front of his old friend and sat down upon it contemplatively. "You could probably afford to buy Iceland, let alone an ice house. What in heaven's name has got into you?"

"He's quite mad, I'm afraid," Ariadne answered on his behalf, and

I expected her adopted father to disagree.

"That's right." The Duke actually smiled. "Quite mad. The doctors don't know what to do with me. Not that I'm interested in paying another penny to be poked at and prodded. Damn quacks will bleed a man dry, I tell you. Quite literally in some cases. Dry!"

The conversation continued like this for half of the evening. I was relieved that my grandfather had found his tongue; I don't know what I would have said in his place. Ariadne spent her whole time winking at me and, on our way to dinner, she hung back from the old men to pin me against a stretch of tattered wallpaper.

"I meant what I said, you're a tasty little pastry." Her face was inches from my own, and I really thought she was about to eat me. "You may kiss me, if you like."

CHAPTER NINE

"I… I don't know how!" I ducked out from under her arm and chased after my grandfather into the garden.

Halfpenny had laid out a table for us on the scraggly lawn overlooking the lake on one side and a blackened metal structure on the other that, like most things so far at Chandos Grove, I could make absolutely no sense of.

"It's still there," Grandfather exclaimed, coming to a stop with a sudden intake of breath. "You never had it removed."

The Duke didn't wait for us to sit down. He grabbed a piece of bread from the basket, ripped it in two, and pushed both pieces into his mouth. "Why should I? I've no reason to be ashamed."

I could see that Grandfather was struggling with memories from days long past, and so I gave him my arm to lower him into his chair. He had no particular need of physical assistance, but something told me it was necessary. He patted me on the back in thanks, and I took my own place. I noticed that there were four spare seats at the table, even after Ariadne had joined us.

The three of us watched as the Duke devoured another piece of bread. That curious girl was poking me with her foot under the table, so I pushed it away and tried to maintain some decorum. I felt a little silly for running away from her, but… Well, I had never imagined romance being conducted in such a manner.

I'd always assumed that, before a kiss, one was required to spend several months gazing lovingly at a young lady. The next step was to suggest a chaperoned stroll in public together and finally, once a suitable amount of time had elapsed, one could ask her father for her hand in marriage. Jumping to the end like that was terrifying.

I'd been distracted by Ariadne's hungry stare and had failed to notice that our elders had fallen silent. Grandfather hadn't taken his eyes off those strange metal spikes that rose from the ground like they had grown in place. I felt that I could finally make sense of them. Though some had bent and others broken, I could see that they traced out the structure of the building which had once stood there.

"You still blame me, don't you?" For the first time since we'd arrived, the Duke's voice was subdued. He sounded quite fragile, and his eyes studied his old friend's features.

Grandfather shook his head, but could not deny it. "You were the only one there, man. If it was just an accident, you should have confessed."

The Duke seized his napkin in order to throw it back down. "I've lived with this my whole life. I thought you more than anyone would realise that things aren't as simple as they seem." He stood up from the table, scraping the metal chair back on the stone. "I thought that was why you wanted to come here in the first place."

I imagine he would have walked away from his own dinner just then, but someone arrived to interrupt.

"How rude of you to start without me." A severe-looking woman, with a long red travelling cloak and her hair pulled back tightly on the top of her head, made herself heard. She had appeared from the house as the two men were arguing and come striding across the grass towards us.

I was rather surprised that I recognised her from the papers; it was Philomena Fontaine, the Home Secretary's wife. She was a well-known political firebrand, and I'd heard my father declare that her husband would have got nowhere without his wife's influence. Though Mr Fontaine was the famous name, she was a force to be reckoned with in her own right. She was a champion of popular causes of the day and was a leading light in the Primrose League. I was scared of her from the very first moment she spoke.

"I haven't travelled all this way to hear old men arguing. If I wanted that, I'd have visited the public gallery of the House of Lords."

"Mimi," my grandfather pronounced with great fondness. "You haven't changed a bit."

She held out her heavily ringed hand to him. "Well, I hope that's not true. I should like to think I'm a little wiser than last we met. Now what's all this nonsense I read in the paper this morning about you running about at the seaside like some tearaway child?"

Grandfather blushed then. I don't think I'd ever seen him look embarrassed before and it made me respect this fierce character a little more.

"It was just an excursion with my grandson here." He waved his hand in my direction. "Say hello, Chrissy."

"'Say hello, Chrissy.'" Ariadne mimicked, as I greeted our new guest with a bow of the head.

Philomena inspected the young girl as though she were checking her for lice. She didn't have time to deliver her judgement as a pale young man carrying a large case arrived to speak to her.

"There's the first of your luggage, mother. Where would you like the rest?" He dropped it on the ground and bent over to catch his breath.

"Obviously not here, Stuart. We're about to eat dinner and that does me no good whatsoever."

The man who, from his grey eyes and chiselled features, was quite evidently her son, let out a sigh and hid the item behind a large, dead bush before taking his place beside his mother.

The meal was a strange affair. The powerful old lady talked continuously, whereas her two childhood companions could no longer raise their eyes from the table. As a result, in her brusque, businesslike manner, she transmitted messages between them and kept the conversation going for some time before even she grew bored. Her son only spoke when she barked an order for him to fetch her something, thus depriving Halfpenny of his duties. Like his politician father, Stuart Fontaine was a meek sort of chap, and I wouldn't have swapped places with him for the world.

There was no time to think about that, though, as my brain was still awash with the memory of a kiss that never was. As Ariadne rarely took her eyes off me, it was dreadfully difficult to sneak a look at her. I was beginning to suspect that, despite her feral manners and unusual appearance, she was really quite beautiful. Stunning in fact; with her bobbed blonde hair – the colour of corn at the end of summer – and her perfectly rounded lips that kept repeating the same words over and over again in my head. "You may kiss me, if you like."

"Why is your house such a mess?" Philomena replaced the awkward silence with a far more awkward discussion. "Why don't you have a maid?"

The Duke snorted a little. "We do have a maid. A girl from the village is here somewhere. She just doesn't enjoy cleaning."

"I've seen vagabonds with better clothes than yours, Bobbie. What is wrong with you?"

"It's obvious what's wrong with him," my grandfather interjected. "He's a killer, and he's never lived it down."

The word he'd chosen made me sit up and pay more attention. Though I had already reflected upon the various elements of the mystery with which he'd acquainted me, I was yet to land upon a suspect.

"Say one more word, Reprobate and I'll throw you out." The Duke was furious.

Philomena ignored their squabbling. "You can at least tell me why you invited us."

"This wasn't my idea." The Duke stared up at the dramatic cliffs that fenced in the Chandos estate. "Reprobus called and said it was time we brought the old gang back together. I told him it would be a waste of time, but he persuaded me it was the right thing to do."

Philomena thought for a moment before delivering her verdict. "I agree. It's been too long."

"Precisely." Grandfather nodded with a hint of pride.

The Duke's voice soared again. "He told me I could clear my name."

"I never said anything of the sort. I said we could get to the truth at last, and you heard what you wanted."

I was less shocked to see my grandfather lose his temper than by the fact he was so petty about it. Having spent the last months getting to know his fine methodical mind, it was unfathomable to see him sniping at the others. I'd always imagined that he'd been born with his steely demeanour, but that clearly wasn't the case.

"Enough bickering." From halfway across the untidy lawn, the Professor spun his tweed hat through the air so that it sailed above the table like a discus. "I'm here now and the real party can begin." There was an attractive young lady with him, but no one paid any attention to her as there was an argument to be finished that had started decades earlier.

"Fabulous," the Duke yelled. "You can get me a glass of whisky!"

As the accusations flew about the group and the younger generation grew disinterested, I wondered whether this was another part of Grandfather's plan. Had he instigated the scene for my sake? By inviting me there to witness these unusual characters in their natural habitat, was he hoping I would learn something?

There was a mystery to solve – I knew this much at least. A mystery which could still enrage all those powerful figures nearly sixty years after it had occurred. Until then, I'd assumed that any understanding of it was beyond me, but perhaps it wasn't so complicated. Grandfather had already given me plenty of clues, and it was my job to make sense of them.

Morwenna Fairbright was dead, and the Duke of Chandos had been blamed for it. Judging by my grandfather's reaction to the charred remains of the building, which was set apart from the main house, the two things were connected. With my detective's cap on, it seemed fair to assume that the girl they called Star had died in a fire. With my limited resources, I was rather proud of myself for getting this far.

After all, I couldn't even say how this unusual group of friends had come together. I knew that, as a child, my grandfather spent his summers in the north of England but he hadn't told me why. Where had his own parents been while he was up in the Lake District? Had they simply abandoned him there?

When Halfpenny served the first course, everyone fell silent, and it didn't look as though I was going to get any answers. The Prof had been the jolliest of the pack, but even he had begun to look nervous. In fact, his hesitant expression was mirrored on the face of his younger companion. She was in her mid-twenties with a fair complexion and hair so blonde it was almost white. She had eyes like sapphires and the kind of alluring smile that I'd seen on the heroines of so many films at the cinema. Instead of a glamorous ballgown or gauzy chiffon dress though, she wore the clothes of a middle-aged geography teacher.

"And you are?" Philomena asked without hesitation.

"I'm Professor Filigree's research assistant." She wasn't quite so well-spoken as the rest of us and there was a warmth to her which I found intriguing. "My name's Deborah Fisher."

Philomena Fontaine glanced between the two new arrivals and did not look impressed. "Samson! She's young enough to be your granddaughter."

He huffed a little, but clearly enjoyed the attention. "Really, Mimi. Must you always dream up such scandals?"

Deborah blushed a little then, and I wondered if we'd heard the whole truth.

My grandfather had recovered from his outburst and furnished a question of his own. "So why did you bring her here today, eh, old chap?"

The professor was not deterred by their questioning. "Miss Fisher is a geologist and is interested in studying rock formations around the Lakes. I thought she might enjoy the company on the journey up here and a bed at Chandos Grove. Though looking at the place now, I think she would be happier in a hotel."

He glanced around the gardens and back to the house. It was quite a contrast to Cranley. The once neatly arranged flowerbeds were in a bad way, with weeds and brambles choking the few remaining flowers. If it hadn't been for the beauty of the lake and the multi-coloured slopes it reflected, the whole place would have seemed dead and sinister like a modern-day Satis House. Could that explain the decay? I wondered if, like Miss Havisham in 'Great Expectations', the Duke had spent his life mourning a broken heart.

Conversation had died away once more, and, as I've never been comfortable at such moments, I started to blather. "I'm so looking forward to the party tomorrow," I began. "I hope the weather holds out for it. There's nothing quite like a garden party and-"

To be honest, I was relieved when the Duke interrupted me. "I should never have agreed to any of this. Half a century later and nothing's changed. I was guilty in your eyes the moment that Morwenna died. I was a fool to think that anything could have changed."

My grandfather's rage had not abated. "Exactly! More than half a century has gone by and the only thing that makes sense is that you killed her." Oddly, it was only Deborah and I who seemed shocked by his accusations; the others had clearly heard them all before. "That poor girl burnt to death. Our Star died, and you were the only one there. You were the one covered in soot and yet you persist in denying your responsibility."

"I tried to save her and you know it." The Duke's voice came out in one drawn-out cry. "We had this exact same argument when it happened. But you're so stubborn, Edgington, so sure of yourself as ever, that you won't let the possibility of my innocence enter your impenetrable skull."

"Because I know you did it!"

If the Duke had been on his feet right then, he would have had to sit back down. The energy had drained from him and he was a shell of the lively chap who had received us. For the first time that I'd noticed, Ariadne looked a little concerned and went to stand at his side.

With the Duke's sky-blue eyes still resolutely fixed on his rival's, a frosty hush had consumed that warm evening. Philomena excused herself, and she and her son stood to leave in unison.

My Grandfather's iron gaze had not left the Duke's. Ariadne put a small hand on her adopted father's shoulder, but the stalemate continued.

"All right, both of you, that's enough." All the joviality was gone from the Professor's voice. "We'll get nowhere rehashing the same arguments. I've got a much better idea."

Almost back at the house, Stuart Fontaine spilt the case of papers he was carrying and his mother cut through the quiet evening with a stinging rebuke.

"Really, Stuart. You're as clumsy as a three-legged ass. Pick up every last thing you dropped and bring me a cup of tea."

As her voice faded away, she stepped inside the building, leaving her friends to return to their conversation.

"So we should forget all about it then?" My grandfather's voice had a vulnerability to it that I wasn't used to hearing. "Forgive and forget, is that what you're saying?"

The professor cleared his throat and raised his chin appraisingly. "Not at all. What I suggest is that, tomorrow morning before the party, we should go through every shred of evidence of what occurred on the night when the fire ripped through the orangery. It's time we determined once and for all how Morwenna died."

CHAPTER TEN

The maid had disappeared and there was no one to show us to our rooms that night. Grandfather and I re-entered the sprawling house to take our pick of the lodgings. I was tempted to suggest we sleep under the stars again when I saw what Chandos Grove had to offer.

My room was a huge, draughty affair which would once have been quite luxurious with its French Empire furniture and curtains in fine brocade. The spiders who had been living there for the last few decades had done a little redecorating though and, as Mabel the maid didn't like cleaning, the dust was thick as a carpet on every surface.

Clearly not himself, Grandfather left me to find quarters of his own. I wondered how many more times in my life I would have to re-evaluate the old chap. Having stashed himself away like a fossil for ten years, he had confounded my every last expectation when he'd come flashing back to life so dramatically two months earlier. But now his light was fading once more. The wise character I had come to admire was in hiding, and I wasn't sure what to think of his sneering replacement.

I lay in bed, unable to sleep. This was partly because I was terrified that Ariadne would seek me out and devour me, but I had other things on my mind as well. I tried to remember all the clues that Grandfather had provided on Morwenna's death. It was clear that, soon after the fire in the orangery, his path sprang off in an unexpected direction. He renounced his fortune and shocked his family by joining the police. Whatever else happened on my stay in the north, it would be fascinating to find out what had led him to the decision.

By the time I'd made a summary of the case in my head, pushed a small chest of drawers against the door to prevent errant young ladies from entering, and cursed myself for not eating more at dinner, I finally felt tired.

When I woke the next morning, the sun streamed in through a gap in the old curtains to fill me with positivity. For all the sadness and drama of the day before, there was nothing like a party to raise the spirits. I just had to hope that the Professor's plan would help clear the air. At the very least, I knew that Cook made special pastries whenever we had a garden party and, though turbot and onion might not be everyone's cup of tea, I thought them rather exquisite.

When I got out of bed at the positively indulgent hour of half-past nine, I spotted my grandfather through the window. He was sitting at the table where we'd had dinner, alone but entirely at ease with himself. I took a moment to enjoy the scene with the mountains and lake in the distance. Philomena was sitting on a bench by an old greenhouse staring into space, and there was no sign of anyone else.

The world seemed a happier place to be that day with the sun glinting on the lake and a few cheerful larks flying about the place. I quickly got dressed and, by the time I made it outside, Grandfather had been joined by two younger members of our party.

"People overlook the joys of British wildlife, but places like this help you remember just how wild a world we live in." The Professor's pretty student, Deborah, was clearly just as passionate about nature as I was.

"Quite right, my dear." Grandfather took a moment to sip his tea. "We may not have the vast vistas of America or even the high peaks of the Alps, but what we lack in scale we make up for in detail."

Stuart Fontaine let out a hearty laugh. "Have you travelled a great deal, Lord Edgington?" He had his politician father's pale complexion and was already turning a little pink in the rising heat.

Lord Edgington looked serious for a moment before replying. "Oh, yes, young man. I have travelled extensively, to nearly every nation on this beauteous planet. I have scaled the tallest mountains and swum deep in the seven seas, all from the comfort of my library, mind you. There is nothing like a good book for expanding one's horizons."

His audience gave a polite giggle before Stuart spoke again. It turned out that he was a nice chap without his mother standing over him. "I long to travel. Even coming up here for the weekend seems quite the adventure, but I'm certain there are places on this earth to which books and photographs can't do justice. Did you know that, in this very century, they have discovered lost cities in Peru that have lain untouched for half a millennium?"

"Machu Picchu!" My grandfather pronounced most excitedly. "I would love to go there, though I doubt I'd survive the ocean crossing."

We laughed again and I'm sure the old man would have revealed any number of fascinating details on that ancient settlement, if it hadn't been for an interruption.

"Have you seen my father?" Ariadne enquired as she arrived at the table in an even flouncier outfit than the day before. She was all frills and crinoline and looked like Little Bo Peep.

"Not this morning, child."

Deborah Fisher was like a sponge and soaked up the girl's apprehension. "Where would you expect him to be at this time?"

"Right here!" The poor girl's voice went higher. "He has a can of sardines every morning in the garden, then goes to his hut to write."

I was curious to discover what the Duke wrote about, but there was no time for that.

"Perhaps he's gone on ahead," Stuart suggested as Elodie Rous appeared from the conservatory. She was obviously not on her horse today, but looked just as angry with my grandfather as the last time I'd caught a glimpse of her.

"Oh, you came, Lala." I have to admit, he did sound rather smug. "How wonderful to have the whole gang back together."

"Except that Father isn't here," Ariadne reminded us, her fear still apparent.

"You're right, my child." Lord Edgington rose from his seat and put one hand on the girl's shoulder. "Now, where's this hut you mentioned? Perhaps Bobbie went to work a little early today."

Ariadne looked even paler than usual. The sunshine was so bright that morning, it almost cancelled her out and I suddenly felt great concern for the unusual creature. It made me wonder whether I should have been nicer from the beginning.

Without replying, she nodded and jerked away from us. There was something very wild about her. She was like a stoat or perhaps a badger, free to root about those wild northern lands. Leaving behind the formal gardens, she led us towards the lake. I was once more filled with a lightness as I contemplated the reflection of the sky on the water and spotted a peregrine falcon (well, a bird of prey of some description at least) high above us. Pretty rowing boats in seven different colours lay upturned on the shore, and I was reminded of an old painting that I unfortunately couldn't name.

The sight did little to ease Ariadne's mind, and she continued on her quest. In the distance, I caught sight of a large wooden building, which I assumed had once been used as a boating shed. It was painted in cheerful blue and white, like a beach hut, and was in noticeably better condition than the other buildings on the estate.

"He calls it his office," Ariadne explained, as we moved away from the water to reach the door on the opposite side. "He's been writing in there for years."

We were only feet away when we heard a cry ring out and rushed forward to see what was wrong. I threw the door open, but there was no one inside. The unsurprisingly messy space looked like the retreat of some crazed author, with papers and books strewn everywhere.

"Not in there." Grandfather raised his arm to block the door.

I heard a loud plop, plop, plop and some frenzied splashing, and the three of us set off around the building to reach the water once more.

Ariadne was breathing in and out in short, feeble breaths, and so I took her hand to comfort her. It was cold and seemed to throb like a beating heart. A little way along the waterline, there was a figure bending low to retrieve something. From the unusually paired smoking jacket and bright yellow slacks, I rightly assumed that it was the Professor.

"Come quickly," he yelled over to us. "He's too heavy for me. You'll have to help."

I don't think any of us doubted what he was referring to, but the sight of the Duke of Chandos floating face down in the water still came as a shock. Grandfather waded into the shallow water without hesitation and, with the Professor's help, hauled the rather corpulent Duke onto the shore.

"He's not breathing," the Professor announced and quickly got to work raising the Duke's arms above his head, before pressing them on his chest to aid in respiration. It looked as though he was doing the butterfly stroke on land.

Grandfather decided to offer tips on the technique. "Doctor H. R. Silvester recommends sixteen cycles per minute in order to resuscitate a patient. I'm afraid to tell you that I very much doubt it will work this time."

The Professor was not a lithe fellow and was quite out of breath himself from his exertions. "Have some faith, Reprobus," he said as he extended the arms once more. "This technique has been used to bring any number of drowned men back from certain death."

There was something hesitant about the way the Professor spoke that didn't connect with his actions. Ariadne was crying out jets of tears by this point.

Grandfather bent down to look at the supine body of his old friend. "It may work in cases of drowning, but Bobbie has a rather large hole in his breast pocket and I believe he's been stabbed." He reached one hand out and placed it on top of his friend's. "You'll have to give it up, man. He's already dead."

CHAPTER ELEVEN

The sounds of nature rushed in around us. No one moved a muscle and Ariadne's gentle crying was muffled as she buried her head in my shoulder. I squeezed her tightly and listened to the gentle lapping of the water in the wind and the screech of the possible falcon on high.

Grandfather moved closer to reassure his old friend. "You did what you could, Prof. Some things are beyond the best of us."

The Professor collapsed down onto his knees. He was physically and emotionally depleted. And yet it was fear that I saw cut into his face. Pure, unmistakable fear.

Grandfather soon switched to his professional persona. "Christopher, you'll have to call the police. Try to remember exactly where everyone is as you enter the house."

I listened to his instructions, but something else had caught my attention in the water.

"Tea, Grandfather!" I should probably have chosen my words more carefully.

"Not now boy, a man has been killed and there's no time to waste."

I turned him around by the shoulder. "It wasn't an offer, look over there." I pointed across the water some twenty yards to where a china cup and saucer and a small silver teapot were bobbing about. "Perhaps the killer threw them away."

"Well spotted, Chrissy. Now all we're missing is the murder weapon."

I was about to say something stupid along the lines of, "perhaps the tea was poisoned," but he foresaw my idiotic conclusion and nipped it in the bud.

"For goodness' sake. He wasn't drowned, and the tea didn't kill the poor chap. It looks as though he was stabbed with a short-bladed knife. But if the killer threw the weapon into the lake, I suspect it would have floated to the surface."

"Might he not have used something to weigh it down?" The Professor asked, rising to his feet so that all four of us were standing in a line attempting to extract understanding from the water in front of us.

"It's possible. Though judging by how far he was able to throw the tea set, it shouldn't be too difficult to find." He clicked his tongue three times at the top of his mouth as he considered the predicament. "Chrissy, you'll have to swim in to get them."

The only thing I hate more than running is swimming. My voice barely squeaked out a reply. "You just said that the police would be able to find anything he'd thrown in there."

He pursed his lips together, unimpressed. "Time is of the essence, my boy. We must not leave anything to chance."

I would probably have complained and made a fuss, but Ariadne was looking at me hopefully and I couldn't let her down. I took my shoes off, rolled up my trousers, and splashed into the water. Luckily, there would be no swimming necessary as the lake was shallow for some way out. I collected up the evidence in the tails of my shirt so as not to get any fingerprints on it – I had learned something from my more experienced grandfather after all – then returned to shore, dripping from the waist down.

"Wonderful work, my boy. Now you can call the police."

Ariadne refused to let me return to the house on my own. She clamped her fingers around my arm and wouldn't let go. I must say that I felt more than a little self-conscious. As much as I thought that practically all members of the opposite sex were really top-notch sorts, I'd rarely spent time with any girls my age. I'd been to a boys' school my whole life, and Father never let me go to public social events as he thought they were a corrupting influence on a young man. When you think about it, it's really no wonder I'd fallen in love with a maid from Cranley Hall.

On our way back to Chandos Grove, I should probably have been focused on the case at hand. Sadly, I was distracted by the fact that, whenever that lovely girl touched me, my whole body started buzzing like a bee. To help me focus, and because I was worried she might notice and report me to the police or some such, I opened my mouth to speak.

"I don't suppose you have any idea who killed your adopted father?" I could definitely have chosen my words more carefully.

When her answer came, I had to strain to hear it over the crunching pebbles beneath our feet. "Oh, yes. All sorts of people wanted to kill him. The Prime Minister, for one, and several of the king's courtiers too. He was forever talking about plots that had been carried out against him." She stopped to let out a sob before adding a relevant point. "But don't forget that he was entirely mad."

Something in her voice told me that she didn't actually believe this, and a thought came into my mind. "Do you love him?"

We'd reached the side of the main house by now, and I could hear voices floating over from the patio. Elodie was telling Philomena how angry she still was about my grandfather, which was hardly a revelation considering what had happened the last time I'd seen her. I counted my blessings that she hadn't brought any dogs with her.

Ariadne took her time to consider the question. "I suppose I must, though he wasn't exactly an ordinary father." She shook her head quite violently then, as if to dismiss some dark thought. "No, I did… I do love him. He took me in when my mother died and I don't like to think what would have happened if he hadn't. He could be quite bizarre and had a temper like an old bear, but he was awfully kind to me. He always tucked me in at night and sang me a funny old song each night. Oh, and he was awfully generous with his tins of sardines. He only ever ate three a day, but I was allowed as many as I wanted."

"That's nice." I had to think about my own father then. Instead of a hug or a pat on the back, Daddy preferred to express his affection through a nice, firm handshake. I suppose that we all have different ways of showing our love. Some hug, some call you "old chap" and some share their tinned sardines.

"The telephone's in here," she said, as we nipped into the house, then cut off the main corridor into a spacious lounge with impressive Renaissance portraits covering the four walls. The room was lighter than most, but that was only because the curtains had been torn down at some point. Despite there being holes in several of the windowpanes and a generally tatty look to the place, a shiny black telephone had been installed in one corner and we'd soon informed the police of that morning's developments.

I heard voices just then, and some dramatic instinct forced me to seize Ariadne and pull her behind a small bureau against the wall. It wasn't as though we weren't allowed to be in there – it was Ariadne's house after all – but wouldn't it have been wonderful if my quick thinking had allowed to us overhear the savages who'd committed the crime? We could have had the case sewn up in time for lunch.

Sadly, that wasn't to be. But it was terribly romantic; just the two of us pressed together in the dark. If she'd offered again, I might have had the courage to take her up on that kiss. It probably wasn't the right moment though, so soon after she'd discovered her father's bloody and lifeless corpse.

"Isn't it strange to be back here after all this time?" I heard Elodie Rous ask, and the voice that responded could only have been Philomena's.

"One old house is much like any other to me." She didn't sound as though she'd recently murdered someone, but she didn't sound very happy either.

I couldn't actually see them, though they were standing really very close to us. Elodie paused before replying. "It's just that, after everything that went on here – the good and the bad – this place has always felt haunted to me…"

"Since Morwenna died, you mean?" Philomena showed little compassion for her friend and spoke in her usual matter-of-fact tone.

"Yes, that's exactly what I mean. It's as though she's still watching over us. Blaming us for what happened."

I don't know if Elodie was more shocked than I was by her companion's transformation, but Philomena's tone hardened and her voice shot louder. "What utter nonsense. That girl's death was an accident and, whoever says otherwise is a damned fool."

I must have started a little as, when her words died away, she took a few steps forward and said, "I heard something. Who's there?"

Before I knew what to do, Ariadne had grabbed me by the wrist to go running past them.

"Welcome to Chandos Grove," I blurted, as I really don't like to appear rude.

"Dratted children," Philomena shouted after us.

"That girl's a horror," Elodie declared. "She's a leech and a brat. I knew it the moment I saw her."

CHAPTER TWELVE

We shot along the corridor and only stopped when we were both out of breath and the coast looked clear. Sadly, I've never had the best eyesight, and the infamous maid who didn't like to clean stepped from one of the salons to catch us.

"What are you two imps doing running about the house?"

I was intimidated by her sudden appearance and pointy face. Her long blonde hair was tied up in a bun, and she had a rather vicious manner about her. Instead of answering, I froze and pretended I wasn't there. It was not a particularly good stratagem, and she looked at me as though I were a scarlet fool.

Fortunately, Ariadne knew just how to deal with the girl. She stared her straight in the eye and told her the truth. "Someone killed Daddy. We found his body floating in the lake."

I was amazed that she could tamp down all that emotion and find her confidence at such a moment.

The maid put her hand to her chest in overacted dismay. "What are you saying, child? I were in the hut to see him not twenty minutes ago."

In a frankly ridiculous moment of synchronism, all three of us turned to the grandfather clock that was handily placed alongside us. It was ten minutes to ten.

"That's right. I saw you fetching his sardines from the pond." Ariadne thought for a moment and took a step closer to the woman who was at least ten years our senior. "How did you know he'd be in his hut at this time of day?"

"Oh… I…" She waved her hand through the air once more. "Miss Ariadne, you've flustered me. I don't know now… I suppose I just went looking for him when he weren't in the garden. I found him snoring away in his chair."

Ariadne offered a pensive, *hmmm,* as my grandfather so often does when dealing with a suspect. It was quite impressive. "The police will need to speak to you when they get here."

"Yes, miss. Of course, miss."

Though I approved of Ariadne's radical intervention, I had to feel a little sorry for poor Mabel. She let out a comical shriek and ran off to collapse on a dusty sofa.

"She's a silly creature," Ariadne told me once we were back outside. "She never lifts a finger to help. I've no idea why Daddy kept her around."

With the brief interview concluded, she appeared to rediscover something of her sorrow, and so I sat her down on a bench in the garden to comfort her. "I'm so sorry for everything that you're going through. I lost an aunt recently... and an uncle in fact... and actually, my grandmother... Well, people keep dying around me and so I know how it feels. The Duke seemed like a really..." I kept having to pause to search for my words. "He seemed like a truly unique sort of fellow."

I'd managed to provoke at least half a smile from her. "Oh, he really was. He's the only man I've met who ate just one type of food – as sardines are more difficult to poison. The only man who believed that moustache growing should be a sport, and the only man who loved me as a daughter."

This raised the question of what happened to her real father, but I could tell it wasn't the moment to upset her further.

"Will you be all right here?" I looked deep into those gorgeous cerulean eyes of hers and realised I was almost certainly in love (again). "I have to tell my grandfather what we discovered, but I won't be too long."

"Yes, of course," she responded in a manner which implied, *I'd really rather you didn't.* There was little else I could do though, so I nodded and rushed away.

Urghhh! I detest running! It's like a stupid man's walking or a poor man's driving. But Grandfather said that time was of the essence and I thought I had better be quick. I was starting to wonder why none of the murders we'd investigated occurred in nice small houses. I'd spent the last two months sprinting about England like a hare. I was seriously worried about the weight I'd lost; no girl was going to regard me as a delicious sausage roll if I kept running everywhere.

When I got back to the lake, Grandfather and the Professor were nowhere to be seen, though the Duke was still lying motionless upon the shore. I thought it really rather careless to leave him alone like that. While I'm aware that vultures aren't native to Britain and wolves were wiped out centuries ago, in such wild surroundings, you can never be sure what might turn up to nibble on a corpse.

"We're in here, Christopher," a voice informed me from within the long wooden building.

I peeked through the door to find my grandfather standing in the middle of the room looking around in quiet contemplation. The Professor, however, was a little more vocal.

"I really haven't the faintest idea why anyone would have hurt the old coot. He has no heirs except that young girl, and she surely couldn't be behind something like this." As he walked about, he picked up items off the shelves in front of him as though they would give him a clue to our mystery.

"I've already told you, Prof," my grandfather erupted. "Will you please stop touching everything?"

"Oh, sorry!" The cheerful old chap laughed rather guiltily before continuing with his analysis. "Bobbie was as mad as a drunken mule, so it's not as though he could have held some dark secret over one of us – no one would have believed a word he said. Perhaps he upset some jealous husband in the village. He always was one for the ladies. But then, wouldn't we have seen someone entering the estate?"

He'd come to the desk at the end of the room and stopped to read from a thick pad of paper which was open at the last used page. I didn't know what else to look at, so I decided to join him.

"'…it's all coming to a head,'" I read aloud. "'The players from my youth have returned and I will clear my name once and for all. I have no fear of death nor malady, but dishonour is a punishment I cannot endure.'"

"The poor fool, he really believed his own story." He paused to flick through the book, which was covered over with the same scrawled handwriting.

"Prof!" my grandfather shouted once more. "Would you please keep your hands off the evidence?"

"My apologies, my apologies," the Professor shook his head, apparently unable to believe his own carelessness. "Criminology is not a subject to which I have had the time to devote much attention. Still, it's one to add to the list."

I examined that great, leather-bound pad and could see at a glance that there was a chunk of the book missing. A number of pages near the beginning had been torn out, and I had to wonder whether it was the Duke himself or his killer who was responsible.

It didn't look to me as though our experienced detective was doing a vast amount at that moment. He hadn't moved from his spot in the middle of the room and was eyeing his old companion through his typically unimpressed gaze. It felt rather wonderful not to be the source of his ire for once!

"Why do you think the tea things were thrown into the water?" The nice chap moved on to peep at a few loose papers, this time without his hands interfering.

"I haven't formed any conclusion on the matter just yet," Grandfather replied noncommittally. This surprised me as it was the opposite of his usual attitude. "Now, Prof, perhaps you'd be so good as to wait outside for the police."

"But, Grandfather, the police won't-" I began, before the old man raised his hand to silence me.

In response, the Professor gripped the back of the desk chair he was standing beside and bowed his head obligingly. Once he had left, my favourite detective untethered himself from the spot he'd been stuck to and came over.

"Now, tell me everything you've discovered."

I thought for a moment before replying, as nothing in his behaviour quite added up. After three investigations together, I was long past the point of dismissing his eccentricities as the actions of a fading mind. There was a reason behind every last thing my grandfather did, though it was rarely apparent what that reason was.

"You suspect the Prof, don't you?" I eventually declared.

He straightened his back and looked a little put out. "Of course I do. He discovered the body and couldn't give me a good reason for why he was over here. He said he'd gone for a stroll by the lake but, to my knowledge, he's never been one for even the lightest physical exercise. Add that to the fact he seemed determined to smear his fingerprints on every piece of evidence and we have a likely suspect."

I was stunned that he could speak so harshly of one of his oldest friends. It must have shown on my face, as he immediately continued. "Which isn't to say that he's guilty of course; there are all sorts of innocent explanations to even the most alarming circumstantial evidence. I'm saying that we mustn't eliminate him from our suspicions just because he's an amiable sort of chap. Now, tell me what the police said."

"Well, the local police won't be here for some time. They say they only have one car, and it got a flat tyre coming back from somewhere called Broughton-in-Furness."

"Ahh, the English wilds." He took in a deep breath to savour our distance from civilisation. "A fine place to visit, though not necessarily the ideal location for investigating a crime."

"I saw the maid too. She says she came in here to give the Duke his breakfast at around nine thirty and that he was dozing in his chair. Perhaps that will help you rule out some of our suspects."

He walked up to the table and skimmed the passage I'd read aloud. "Perhaps. But one can never be too sure with such details. Now what else did you see?" He spoke with a cynical detachment, which was at odds with the facts of the case. We were looking into the death of his childhood friend, and yet he'd shown no sorrow. Even if he believed the Duke responsible for Morwenna's death, I expected more humanity from him.

"Well Elodie Rous certainly doesn't like you. I overheard her singing your... what's the opposite of praises?"

Grandfather knelt down to look at the chair where the Duke had sat to write his memoirs. "Yes, thank you, Christopher. I'm principally interested in information that's relevant to the investigation."

Not allowing his self-importance to get in the way, I took him up on the matter. "How do you know it doesn't have anything to do with the investigation? Elodie arrived around the time that he was killed. Perhaps she's responsible." An idea shot into my mind. "Perhaps she did it to frame you!"

He looked up at me disapprovingly. "Well, she hasn't done a very good job. I can find no evidence of my involvement and, if Bobbie was alive at a half-past nine, I was out on the patio with Philomena's son around the time that the murder was committed."

This raised a significant question. "What about the student who the Professor brought with him? Deborah? When did she arrive for breakfast?"

He had paused his inspection and considered the point. "A few minutes after Stuart, which would have just given her enough time to run back from here."

"That's a shame, so we can't rule her out either." I was disappointed at this. Deborah seemed like a perfectly lovely person, and I was hoping she couldn't have been involved.

Too often in our investigations, I'd been won over by a pretty face or a gentle manner. I'd been sidetracked and hoodwinked a number of times by such superficial considerations and I vowed to myself then that I would not dismiss any of our suspects just because they seemed nice or made an effort to be friendly. I had no reason to suspect Deborah of the crime, but, based on this logic, was fairly certain she must be to blame.

While I was having this argument with myself, Grandfather had been busy examining the evidence. "Of course, to identify the killer, it will be important to understand why he dragged Bobbie outside."

He'd managed to surprise me, which was one of his many talents. I looked about the room for evidence of his claim, but knew I'd have to give in and let him dazzle me. "How the deuce do you know that the body was moved?"

He turned to the soft-backed swivel chair he was kneeling in front of. "A small tear in the fabric and the faintest hint of blood." Rising, he pointed to a mark on the desk that I hadn't noticed before. "And here, another stain and more on the floor beneath, as though he slumped forwards before he died. Either Bobbie was murdered here, and the killer moved him, or, with his dying breaths, he stumbled outside to die in the open air."

My voice went a little squeaky. "Oh... Ummm. I see. And which do you think is more likely?"

In response, he performed a little dance. I don't think that was his intention, but there was a rhythm to the steps he took as he circled the desk and directed my attention to a stain on the thick Chinese rug.

"You can see that the bleeding increased as he was dragged from the room. This, along with the smudging we can see, suggests it happened soon after the attack. Had the killer seen Bobbie stumbling away, there would surely have been more stab wounds on the body. I am convinced therefore that he died here, before being moved to the lake."

"But why?"

His face came alive with excited curiosity. "And that, Christopher is the essential question we must answer."

72

CHAPTER THIRTEEN

I fell into the trap of actually doing what he'd just suggested. "Perhaps the killer thought they could wash away any evidence in the water. Or maybe…" My voice died out as he raised a hand to silence me.

"I didn't wish to imply that you should wildly search around for a solution to our puzzle. I meant that, in the course of the investigation, I believe it will be essential to understand what happened here this morning if we hope to identify the guilty party."

It seems odd to suggest that my grandfather was ever anywhere but at the top of his game, but I noticed a marked improvement in him that morning. It was as though he had set from his mind the arguments of the night before and could focus on the case at hand.

"And what about the tea things?" I felt this a safe question to put to him.

He peered around the room, and I noticed that the space still held traces of its original use. There were old ropes tied in knots hanging on the wall, and two crossed oars displayed at the far end. There were a number of touches that must have been more personal to the Duke as well. A small amateur painting of a young girl was visible in one corner, some old-fashioned plates hung on one wall and there were a number of interesting antique figures dotted about. Such irrelevant details were not what my grandfather was looking for, though.

Retracing his path past the desk, he located a Swan brand electric kettle near the door. The Duke didn't like to spend money on food, though he clearly had a taste for the latest technological inventions. Even Cranley Hall hadn't purchased an electric kettle, and I was sure that Cook would be most jealous.

"It appears that he made his own tea with the facilities here and wouldn't have needed the maid to deliver it. And there!" He turned once more to examine a small table beside where the Duke had been killed. "There's a second cup which, going by the fact it's still present, suggests the killer never touched it."

"So he threw the other in the water to wash his prints off. Does it tell us anything more than that?" I was still secretly hoping that the tea had been poisoned. Poisonings are far less messy than knives and guns.

"It tells us that the killer likes tea." He had a little laugh then. I didn't quite grasp the joke. "But more importantly, it tells us that Bobbie was willing to sit down with the man who murdered him. I think that's rather an important piece of information, don't you?"

I wasn't sure how to answer. I made a vague, *hmmm,* then waited to see if it would do the trick.

"Yes, indeed," he continued, happy to hear his own voice laying out the latest suppositions. "We can rule out some jealous chap from the village, as the Prof suggested. And the chances of that old dog Bobbie tempting young Deborah in here to have his wicked way with her seem less likely when they took the time for a nice civilised cup of Earl Grey."

I was about to question whether he could really know the type of tea they'd drunk when he anticipated the question by darting his hand out across the room. Inevitably, a box of Earl Grey sat on the shelf beneath the kettle. "And, what's more," he said, to continue his rebuttal, "there is no method of refrigeration here in the hut. Earl Grey is the obvious choice to drink without milk… unless you're a total savage."

It was frankly odd how much he was enjoying himself, but I thought I knew why. "This is fun for you, isn't it? It's just a game you're playing."

He shook his head seriously and opened the large double doors which gave onto the water. "Really, Christopher, how could you think so poorly of me? Murder is a serious business. The fact that the victim was a cruel, selfish character who never owned up to his crime is neither here nor there."

I didn't believe him, not least because, whilst trying to disprove my point, he'd put forward a convincing explanation for it.

"You're not as clever as you think, you know," I said in reply. This was probably a shade arrogant coming from the boy whose last geography report card simply stated, "Christopher couldn't find the ocean on a map of the earth." While there is a caveat to my teacher's claim, it would take too long to explain and I still wouldn't look particularly clever. Suffice it to say, the map was upside down at the time.

To my surprise, he was rather amused by my retort. "Oh, really?"

"Yes, really. You think that the Duke has had his comeuppance, don't you? You think that, just for a change, you're investigating the murder of a victim who got what he deserved. But I'm not so sure."

"Now who's reading minds, Chrissy?" he fired back at me, but I noticed that he didn't dismiss the idea outright.

"What I want to know is how any of this is connected to the events that occurred here fifty years ago."

"Actually, Morwenna died in 1868. So that's fifty-seven years ago."

"Fifty-seven then." I took a step forwards to drive my point home. "I want to know how the Duke of Chandos's death is connected to Morwenna's. What do you think?"

He turned statue still for ten seconds and I thought I might relent and apologise for being so rude. In the end, he was the first to flinch. He clapped his large, lined hands together, and the noise echoed about the boat hut.

I remember sitting with him in the Cranley Hall library when I was a very young child. I would trace the veins and wrinkles on the back of his immense hands as though it were a board game. I remember wondering if my own hands would take on those miraculous patterns when I reached his age. As he clapped them together, all those thoughts amalgamated in my head and I felt I was reliving the scene from a decade before.

"Good for you, Chrissy. Now, let's get back to work."

He turned and disappeared through the door. I can't tell you how thrilled I felt at that moment. It was as though I'd won some grand award, the Olympic medal for grandfather wrangling, for example, or perhaps the Nobel prize for family interrogation. The experience was rather intoxicating, until I realised that he hadn't answered my question and I was standing alone in the hut, staring into space.

"Grandfather, wait for me!" I shouted a little pathetically and ran after him.

He was already some way off along the shore by the time I caught up and I worried once more what would happen to the body.

"Don't be foolish, boy," he replied without me actually speaking. "There are few wild animals around who feed on carrion – though perhaps Bobbie's cats might seek revenge for being locked up in the airing cupboard."

"Then what about the-"

"Again, that's ridiculous." He was clearly just showing off his superior facilities. "The killer has already had the chance to interfere with the body and will be looking to distance himself from the scene of the crime. Still, when we see him again, we'll send the Professor back to keep an eye on things until the police get here. An old fellow like Samson could use the exercise."

I considered reminding him that he and the Professor were the same age, but thought it rather obvious. Instead I plumped for, "So, what's next?"

"One of my favourite parts of the investigation." By this point, he wasn't even hiding the joy he was experiencing. "It's time to break the bad news."

Once we got closer to the house, grandfather sent me ahead to gather up every last suspect and even those who he doubted were involved. "The conservatory should do the trick, don't you think?" he suggested. "Let's make them sweat in the sun whilst they await my arrival."

I might have pointed out that he'd be making me sweat too, but then that was already the case what with all that running about. "If you say so, Grandfather."

"Oh, and Christopher?" He came to a stop at the wall that surrounded the estate. "Make sure you listen for anything significant. Just because they're my friends, that doesn't mean I trust them for a heartbeat."

I thought this a rather sad statement, but he was busy rubbing his hands together quite contentedly. I soon left him behind and, like a good sheepdog, rounded up the various parties. I also rounded up our own dog who'd been asleep in the kitchen all morning, completely failing to sniff out clues or find the body. Delilah was warm-hearted, generous and fiercely loyal, but she also spent a lot of her time sleeping.

"Anyone been murdered today, Christopher?" Cook asked as she attended to her morning's tasks. She'd got the place looking rather presentable. Todd and Halfpenny were busy with the preparations for the garden party – as Grandfather had sent Alice off to a cottage somewhere to enjoy her honeymoon. I was very impressed by the speed at which Todd could peel a potato. I doubt that they'll ever invent a machine faster than him.

Cook looked too busy to be burdened with the truth, so I let out a shy giggle and continued to the sweltering conservatory with Delilah at my heel. It was a little embarrassing when everyone arrived and I couldn't explain why we were there. Ariadne and Mabel had apparently made up their differences and were consoling one another on the white, wicker loveseat, Deborah had that nervous look about her and everyone else appeared mightily peeved that I'd called them together.

"If this is another excuse for Reprobate to play silly tricks, I won't be having it." Elodie's complaint was met with a stir of approval.

It wasn't the first time one of them had made reference to my grandfather's troublemaking, but this was only a minor mystery compared to the great number of questions I had accumulated in my mind. To make the most of my time, and because Grandfather clearly wanted us to sweat a little longer before he arrived, I attempted to start the investigation without him.

"If you don't mind me asking, madam," I began most courteously. "Why did you come here today if you were so offended by his invitation?"

Despite my good manners and the fact that women of a certain age usually found my chubby cheeks and reduced stature utterly charming, Elodie let out a snort. "Impertinent child. I see you take after your grandfather. If you must know, I thought it would be pleasant to see some old friends. It's been a long time since Mimi and I crossed paths and I thought we were due for a reunion."

She glanced across at the politician in our midst. Philomena might have answered then but for a figure in the doorway.

"I foolishly assumed that you'd come to see me." Still dressed in his long woollen morning coat, despite the thermometer in the conservatory teasing ninety degrees, Grandfather displayed no amusement as he said these words. He hung in the entrance, as though unsure whether to enter, and, when he did, it appeared that his voice had deserted him.

Everyone was there now. There were the four remaining members of the once-youthful gang, in my grandfather, the Professor, Philomena and Elodie. The next generation was represented by Philomena's son Stuart and the Duke's adopted daughter, though I suppose Deborah the geologist and Mabel the maid fitted into that category well enough too.

"I have an announcement to make," Lord Edgington began.

"Is it that there was a problem with your luggage and you left all your summer clothes at home?" Philomena suggested in her usual superior tone.

"Very droll." The old chap was clearly unfazed by the interruption and happy to wait until their mockery had run its course.

Elodie was up next. "Or perhaps you and Bobbie have called us here for a round of apologies. They're certainly overdue."

"No, I'm afraid that won't be possible."

"Oh, no? You've never had any problem exercising your vocal chords before." She wore a peacock blue, ankle-length dress that was covered from collar to hem in long, beaded tassels; I remarked to myself once more what an unusually beautiful old lady Elodie Rous was. While that might sound a terribly odd thing for a sixteen-year-old boy to notice… well, in fact, I suppose it is.

Grandfather replied in the same mournful tone. "I'm sure that's true, but you see…" I knew he was only acting, but it was terribly convincing. "You see, Bobbie's dead."

The smile didn't immediately disappear from Elodie's face. She looked around the room and it was only when her eyes rested on the Professor's troubled countenance that she realised the truth. "He can't be. How is that…"

"He's been murdered." Each word he spoke seemed to land upon his friends like a ton of iron. "And it seems awfully likely that one of you is to blame."

"Steady on now, old boy." The apprehension which the Professor had displayed turned to fear. "Don't go dashing off accusations like that."

Stuart hadn't said a word until this moment, but suddenly came to life. "In fact, I'd like you to take that back this instant." He turned to his mother and jabbered out the next sentence as a mess of panicked thoughts. "Mother, this isn't going to help you get to Westminster. If anyone-"

"Keep your mouth shut, boy," Philomena responded. "This needn't concern you. And I'm sure our dear Reprobus here would never want any harm to come to his old friends." The tall, bony figure of Philomena Fontaine walked across to stand beside the aging detective. She evidently wished to suggest that they were on the same side.

"So you're thinking of following your husband into the House of Commons?" he asked without taking his eyes off the rest of the group. "It's about time we had more sensible people haunting the halls of parliament." They both smiled then, but not everyone was happy with the digression.

"Can we get back to the topic at hand?" Stuart ignored his mother and raised his voice once more. "Who killed the Duke, and why?"

"Calm down, boy," she tried again.

"No, Mother. The sooner we get to the truth of what happened, the less chance there is of you getting muddled up in something untoward." He turned to the former superintendent. "Lord Edgington, are you sure the man was murdered?"

"Well, yes. Unless he stabbed himself in the heart, hid the knife somewhere and dragged himself out to the lake, I'd say it was highly likely." Stuart was stunned into silence by this unexpectedly direct response.

Deborah took a half step forward and, in a crisp, careful voice, asked a question of her own. "Do you have any idea why he was killed?"

As if he had all the information he could possibly need and was just about to deliver his verdict, Grandfather took a slow walk around the room. "I believe I do."

Reaching the wall of tall, curving windows at the far end, he turned to address us. "Fifty-seven years ago, a beautiful, kind-spirited young woman died on this property. There was no explanation for the fire that killed Morwenna Fairbright and the only man present denied he was responsible."

He paused to let these words have their effect. "I called you to Chandos Grove to get to the truth of what happened on the terrible night when the orangery burnt to ashes, but I believe that someone has beaten me to it. Bobbie Atwell was a killer, and he has finally been punished for his crime."

CHAPTER FOURTEEN

There was some murmuring at the announcement, but the others appeared unconvinced by the old man's presentation.

"How many times have we heard the same story from you?" Elodie jumped down from the window ledge she'd been perched upon and took the centre of the room. "There was never any evidence of foul play. The magistrate at the time concluded it was an accident, and Bobbie had no reason to have caused her any harm. They'd been friends since they were children; he would never have touched her."

She slowed her pace then, as though trying to reason with him. "We all miss Morwenna. God knows I think about her every day, but you have to accept that she's gone. Throwing blame around won't bring her or Bobbie back."

"I'm telling you, beyond any doubt, Star was murdered." Gone was the ever-confident former officer with his air of authority and the quiet assumption that he knew more than the rest of us. In his place was a frenzied creature who could no longer hide the obsession that was running through every cell of his being. "Bobbie lied about so much that went on that night. As for the magistrate, he would have said whatever the previous Duke of Chandos told him."

"Very well." Philomena stepped between them and attempted to mediate, much the way a defence counsel might coax the truth from a witness. "Let's say that you're right. Let's say that Bobbie killed Morwenna and someone finally found the time to serve up the punishment he deserved. Who was responsible?"

Grandfather's eyes were wild. His fingers twitched like he'd been plugged into a wall socket. "I don't know that yet."

He crashed down in a chair of his own. But it wasn't just the emotion running through him that made him so nervous; Philomena was controlling the scene.

"The way I see it, Reprobus, you were the one who wanted him dead. You were the one who convinced him to host this party. You brought us up here and, if anyone killed him, it was you."

Rather like Stuart rushing in to protect his mother, a feeling of familial anxiety came over me and I realised that it was my job to stand up for my beloved grandfather.

"That's nonsense. He was out in the garden with your son when the Duke was killed." I turned to the maid to support my story. "Mabel, tell them the last time you saw the Duke alive. Tell them just what you said earlier."

She was as nervous as anyone else in the room, and her eyes flashed up to the heavens for help before she found her answer. "I were in there with him at nine thirty. I brought him breakfast, but I didn't wake him as he don't like it when I wake him. I left the tin on the table with the kettle and left him be."

"I can confirm that," Stuart said, choosing his words carefully. "I left the house shortly after to have breakfast in the garden. I saw Mabel returning from the direction of the lake."

Elodie hesitated for a moment and then stepped forward to deliver her own alibi. "And I had just arrived and was with Mimi in the ballroom at the time when he must have been killed."

I didn't pay her much attention, as I already had what I needed. "At half-past nine, Grandfather was out in the garden. He wouldn't have had time to get to the hut and back in order for Stuart to join him there at…" I looked to the young man and, when he didn't answer, I pointed one shaking finger at him until he replied.

"A few minutes after that. Nine thirty-five at the latest, I'd say."

"Thank you." I nodded my appreciation and moved on. "My grandfather, Ariadne and I arrived at the Duke's hut at approximately nine forty-five, which means that there's only a fifteen-minute window when he could have been murdered."

Still panicked, Grandfather had a question of his own for the Duke's drowsy domestic. "Mabel, what exactly did you see in the hut when you entered?"

Looking no more at ease, she answered the question. "He were sleeping right there with his head down on his desk. Snoring away, he was. It wasn't the first time I'd found him like that. He always said he went over there to write but, more often than not, he spent all day drinking whisky. He must have started early today."

Clutching the side of his chair, Grandfather took a deep breath. "Did you see any glasses? Any bottle of drink?"

She looked to Ariadne for help, but she had slumped in her chair and was staring at the floor. "No, milord. Nothing like that. Just a teapot and a couple of cups, but he were never one to stand on ceremony. He might just as well have filled a teacup as a whisky glass if he were thirsty."

"What does any of this prove?" Philomena's low, creaking voice captured the room once more. "Perhaps this is one case too many for our *legendary* detective." Her gaze ripped through him and I felt terribly sorry for the old chap.

For all that I had said that week – for all the times I'd felt inferior to my grandfather and worried what he really thought of me – I would have done anything to protect him from such accusations.

I stepped forward to put things right. "As it happens, former Superintendent Edgington has amassed a large amount of evidence on who killed the Duke, and he has already determined that the culprit was known to the victim." I stopped short of revealing that *the culprit* was almost certainly one of them. "Until the local police arrive, my grandfather will be in charge of investigating the murder."

"Oh, I don't think so." Philomena launched a patronising smile in my direction. It was no longer any wonder that my grandfather could come across as arrogant when he'd grown up around such characters. "If anyone knows how to hide his involvement in a crime, it's dear Reprobus here."

"He is the only one with any experience as a police officer and I've already proved he wasn't involved."

"So you're suggesting that we could be?" The Professor was outraged. "I don't like your tone, young man." He glanced across at his student in search of support, but she was quieter and more cautious than ever. Deborah couldn't watch the argument that was raging around her and I very much doubted she'd heard a word we said.

"You were the one who found the body!" I muttered, and my words set off a wave of repercussions. The Professor slapped one hand through his closely cropped hair in despair. Philomena went to support Elodie, who was clutching her cheeks as though she was struggling to make sense of the news, Ariadne let out a cry, Delilah yawned, and Stuart took it upon himself to speak to our main suspect.

"Did you do it?" When the Professor didn't reply, he rephrased the question. "Did you kill Bobbie?"

"That's enough." I shouted out the warning and the brief, chaotic storm died down just as quickly as it had arisen. "Grandfather will talk to each of you in his own time. Until then, no one is to leave the estate."

The old man still didn't look at me. He'd barely moved since he'd sat down.

Perhaps the reality of the Duke's murder hit Elodie at that moment as she started to cry and, in a broken voice, demanded, "Well, what are we supposed to do now?"

Philomena threaded her arm through her old friend's and moved her gently towards the door. "The invitation said that there'd be a lunch in the gardens at noon. There's no reason to change our plans."

Stuart immediately picked up a case of her papers and hurried out after them, but the Professor hesitated in the doorway.

"If there's anything you need, old boy…" His polite offer was at odds with the anger he'd just shown, and I don't think he expected an answer.

"We need you to wait for the police by the lake." I was surprised at how readily such orders leapt from my mouth.

I could see this was the last thing he wanted, but he motioned for Deborah to follow him and they vanished through the door.

Mabel was the next to go, which only left poor Ariadne. Though normally a bright azure, her eyes looked like two hollowed-out woodpecker nests in the trunk of a dead tree. Between her and my grandfather, I didn't know who to comfort first.

I went to put my hand on his shoulder but, instead of the fear-stricken look I'd been expecting, a great smile beamed back at me.

"That's the stuff!" he said, tipping his head back so that his long silver hair fell off his shoulders. I punched him on the arm – a little harder than I'd meant to – and he stopped laughing and rubbed the new bruise. "Ow! Why did you do that?"

"I should be asking you the same question." I crossed my arms over my chest in a perfect demonstration of my displeasure.

"Oh, you mean my little piece of theatre?" He laughed once more. "Well, I might not have spent a lot of time with them over the last few decades, but I know my friends. It will be a lot easier to get what we need from them if they think I've lost my mind."

He was clearly terribly impressed with himself, but I did not like being kept in the dark. "*I* thought you'd lost your mind. And what's more, I'm tired of only knowing half the story. I've done my best to join the fragments together, but it's high time you told me the rest. I need to know exactly what happened on the night that Morwenna Fairbright died."

CHAPTER FIFTEEN

"We'll stretch our legs as I tell you the story." The old man set off without waiting for my opinion on the matter. "There's something I'd like to confirm."

We left the conservatory behind and filled our lungs with the fresh air of the outside world. Grandfather led us on a path through the diverse though wildly unattended gardens as he recounted his tale.

"Our parents were all friends. That's the first thing you must understand. Bobbie's family never minded having a few more at the table, and so we'd all troop up here. Whenever my parents wished to be free of me, they'd take me to the railway station and wave goodbye. I remember the trip up from Surrey like it was yesterday. It took forever to get here. I can still-"

"Grandfather, focus on what we need to know." I was getting a lot better at reining in his flights of nostalgia. I was really quite proud of myself.

When Lord Edgington had found his voice, Ariadne appeared to have lost hers. She trailed along behind us, making nothing but the odd whimper as we left the borders of the estate and began the march up the side of the valley.

"Very well, boy. Yes, of course." He took deeper breaths as our path got steeper. "We used to come up here every summer from the time I was eleven. Before that I spent my time with my governess, or one of the many nursemaids my parents paid to do their job for them. But, when I turned eleven, they decided I was mature enough to spend two days on a draughty train surrounded by strangers and criminals." He did not hide his distaste for his parents' decision, and a note of anger occasionally emerged.

"Ultimately – I must confess – it was the making of me. I experienced things here that would change the path my life took."

"You mentioned that on our journey," I puffed out, as I was feeling a little winded from the climb. "Was it the reason you joined the police?"

"All in good time, boy. All in good time." We both had to stop then, but Ariadne sprang onwards through a bracken-bordered path that went straight up the slope. She must have spent years exploring those wild environs, while I had grown up among the plains and gentle hills of southern England. Delilah was in an equally energetic mood and kept her pace.

Grandfather motioned for me to go ahead of him, then continued his story. "Bobbie, Philomena, Elodie, Star and the Professor weren't like any of my friends from Oakton Academy. They were loud, opinionated and really rather wild – except Morwenna, of course. She was as sweet as a mint imperial and we all loved her. She was different from the rest of us. Rather than coming from a rich family, she was the daughter of the Chandos Grove gamekeeper. Bobbie's family treated her like one of their own, but the other girls could be cruel nonetheless."

He took in another breath. It sounded more contemplative than exhausted this time. "By our last summer here, we were the best of friends, but things were more complicated than they'd once been. As we grew up, tensions formed in the group. Impossible conundrums emerged that none of us could resolve."

He paused again, and I decided to prompt him. "How do you mean, Grandfather? Jealousy and that sort of thing?"

He chuckled to himself before replying. "Well, yes, I suppose that was part of it. The Professor and I were forever trying to get one over on one another. We longed to be the brightest in the group and show just what scholars we were, though that wasn't the biggest problem. You see, as so many young people do at that age, we started to fall in love. Elodie had claimed me as her own when she was only eight years old."

It was my turn to laugh. "Oh, Grandfather. I never imagined you to be one for cradle snatching."

He was not amused. "Very witty, my boy. I did not say that the feeling was mutual. Many years later, when I was set to go to university, she was fifteen. I admit that I entertained the idea that we might be in love, but after Morwenna died, I knew there was nothing in it. Sadly for Elodie, she didn't want our summers together to end."

"Hurry up," Ariadne shouted from the false peak of a rocky outcrop she'd scaled. There was no warmth in her voice now, but she called us forward nonetheless. "The view from here is the best." Delilah confirmed the sentiment with a rather impressed bark.

We attempted to increase our pace, but Grandfather needed my arm for support as the path became rockier and the stones beneath his feet slid away.

"The Professor, meanwhile, had eyes for Morwenna alone – not that he would ever admit such a thing. It became another challenge between us; he did all he could to win Star's affection – without much success, I have to say – and I showed off by courting Elodie. We were incredibly competitive, and our once-solid friendship suffered as a result."

"But what has any of that got to do with Bobbie and Morwenna? Were they suitors?"

He shook his head. "No, no. Bobbie was engaged to Philomena. It had all been arranged by their parents when they were young. The Atwells were an industrial institution and owned half the factories in the north of England, whereas Philomena's line had influenced British politics for over a century. Everyone thought it was the perfect idea to marry the two together."

"And how did Bobbie and Philomena feel about it?" I asked a little cheekily. I would not have made such a comment to most men of my grandfather's generation. I knew that such Victorian types considered familial duty to be far above issues like love or personal tolerance.

"I don't think they ever questioned it. Philomena certainly adored Bobbie, until that night at least. And Bobbie was a character. He charmed his fiancée from their very first meeting. He could outdo a Frenchman for poetic sentiment and turn of phrase. Girls have always loved him, and perhaps that was his biggest problem. I've heard all sorts of stories about him over the years, even though we'd largely lost touch."

We drew level with Ariadne, and she offered a cold stare as I helped Grandfather up onto the great sandstone boulder that stuck out from the slope at a diagonal. None of us spoke as we looked down over the estate and the lake beyond. The sun was high in the sky by now. Its harsh light turned the surface of the water black, though up close it had a bluish sheen.

Chandos Grove looked quaint in apparent miniature. The crumbling stones and broken window panes were impossible to see from so high up. The one thing that clearly wasn't right about the place was the rectangle of blackened ground in the middle of the garden. Even from halfway up the mountain, I could see the remnants of the orangery where Morwenna had died.

"It was quite the most luxurious part of the estate," Grandfather revealed when he saw where I was looking. "Bobbie's mother had commissioned it and spent her days in there enjoying every available beam of sunshine. It was built like a Roman villa with elaborate tropical plants and mosaic tiles in every room. The doorways were covered with long, velvet curtains and that's what the police believe caught alight first. They found the traces of an oil lamp on the floor, but there was no table there or ledge it could have fallen from."

His manner had hardened, just like at dinner the night before. "Bobbie said it must have been an accident. He claimed that he was in his room asleep and heard the blaze. He always insisted that he had gone to see if anyone was inside, and, when he dragged Morwenna's body out, she'd already died from inhaling the smoke."

He'd told this tale without worrying what the man's own adopted daughter might think, but she clearly already knew the whole sad episode herself.

"So why didn't you believe him?" She trembled as she spoke, despite the warm breeze swirling around us. "Daddy was as mad as an old duck, but he was never cruel."

"Because none of it made sense," he replied in the faintest breath. "He couldn't have heard the fire from his room on the other side of the house. And, if he hadn't known she was in there, why would he have gone inside? There was never normally anyone in the orangery at night."

"It hardly proves he's a murderer." I felt obliged to defend Ariadne's guardian for some reason. "Perhaps the Duke knew Morwenna was inside. Perhaps he even dropped the lamp, but that doesn't make it an intentional act."

I expected Grandfather to display the same level of anger he'd shown his friends in the conservatory, but he maintained his gentle tone. "If you'd been there, you would think the same as me. Bobbie was all in a mess. He lied and contradicted himself ten times over. He couldn't explain what had happened, and I could tell he was terrified of the scandal it would bring him. He would go on to lose everything."

"So it was Philomena who broke off the engagement?" I asked.

"Yes, at her parents' behest, of course. Even if he was cleared of any criminal wrongdoing, the stories got out about Bobbie's involvement and it would have brought shame upon her family if they'd gone ahead with the alliance. They hoped he would go into politics, like the chap she eventually married. There was no way that a man with such a murky past could win favour in Westminster."

"Who was Morwenna?" that same little voice spoke up. "Why do you think my father would have wanted to hurt her?"

Grandfather turned to Ariadne and took a moment to examine her. The rougher edges she'd exhibited the previous day had been smoothed out, and her face was a picture of innocence. She stroked the soft fur around Delilah's floppy ears as she awaited the old fellow's answer.

"She was a good person; everybody's friend. She was the one in our group who healed wounds and resolved arguments. Her only failing was that she was too trusting by half."

"So you think-" I started to say before he broke in.

"Star didn't have the advantages that the rest of us had. She was easily taken advantage of and really quite poor. I can only think that, to Bobbie, she was just another conquest. I believe that he seduced her and then made sure that she couldn't tell the story of their night in the orangery to anyone else." This was the moment that brought Ariadne to tears. "I'm sorry, child. But you must know what sort of person he was. You must have heard the stories of Bobbie's liaisons."

"That doesn't make him a killer," she snapped.

"I'm afraid it does in my book." He didn't look at her then, but traced a line with his finger around the long wall that divided the estate from the valley road which led to the village. "But now I have another murder to solve and I will give it just as much attention and commitment as if it were Morwenna's own."

Stepping closer to the edge of the rock, he bent down to look her in the eye. "I promise, on my word and my honour, I will find your father's killer."

CHAPTER SIXTEEN

"What did you see up there?" I asked when we were back in Chandos Grove. "You must have made the climb for a reason."

He nodded with an appreciative look on his face. "That's right. I wanted to see whether someone from the village could have accessed the hut beside the lake without being seen from the garden."

"It's impossible without a ladder. The wall goes all the way along the estate and halfway up the mountain."

"That's right. But while it would make sense for one of my old acquaintances to be involved in the killing, we must take nothing for granted."

I could see the logic in his statement, but I also wondered how closely he was following his own advice. Though he may have been exaggerating his distress and playing up to expectations, he clearly didn't have the same detached attitude he normally possessed during our investigations. Even when we'd been hunting for the killer of two members of our own family, he hadn't seemed so conflicted by events. It was no longer apparent what was real and what was an act, and my sense of confusion was only enhanced when he walked over to the burnt-down orangery and set up his office there.

He took a chair and a small garden table and sat facing the U-shaped wing of the main house.

"Would you like a drink... or something?" Ariadne asked with her eyebrows raised.

"No, child. I'm not here for refreshments. I'd like one of you to bring me my first witness. I think Philomena would be a good choice to start with. She certainly seemed combative this morning and I always like a challenge."

"I'll go," I said, but Ariadne put her hand out to stop me. She smiled with a hint of trepidation as her fingers brushed against mine.

I'd never met anyone quite like her before. I could see now that she was as wild as the hills that surrounded us, but she was fragile too. Her sorrow at losing the man who had raised her was apparent in everything she did, and I couldn't take my eyes off her as she wandered back to the house with her shoulders hunched and her head low.

"Be careful, boy. You do know she could be the killer." My grandfather's abrasive comment snapped me out of my contemplation.

"What would drive you to say such a thing? Of course she couldn't have killed her own father."

"Her adopted father. And it wouldn't be the first time such a wicked act had occurred. There's a word for it, you know? It's called patricide. If you don't believe me, ask the ancient Greeks."

"They also had a word for one-eyed monsters. It doesn't mean we come across them very often." I was incensed by his aspersion and tried to show him just that. "Not everyone is a criminal. Your mind has been warped by the decades you spent dealing with savages."

"No, but we cannot rule out suspects just because they seem like pleasant souls."

"She's not a suspect!" I shrieked, but it did nothing to win him over.

"Then we'll call her an interested party. The fact remains that we don't know where she was when the man was murdered and she's seemed awfully interested in sticking with us as we investigate the crime."

I would have shouted straight back at him, but wasn't sure what to say. When my answer finally came, it escaped from my mouth in a weak, throaty murmur. "She hasn't got anyone else. Perhaps she needed companionship and didn't expect you to be so mistrustful."

He glanced back up the mountain path we had just descended. "Oh, please, Chrissy. If anyone has a motive for the killing, it's her." I must have looked rather blank in reply, as he continued in an unimpressed voice. "Who else do you think will inherit the Atwell family fortune? Bobbie was the last of his line. I'm not saying that Ariadne is guilty, I'm merely–"

It was bad timing on my grandfather's part as, once again, one of our suspects had approached without us noticing. You'd think that, with his years of experience dealing with sensitive cases for the Metropolitan Police, he'd have learnt to avoid such occurrences.

But, no.

Ariadne had already made it to the scrubby lawn, which was easily close enough to overhear the old man's words. She stopped in her tracks and turned to run away, looking thoroughly let down by the pair of us.

"Excellent work," I said, and I rather missed the cases where I was the one who made all the mistakes.

I considered going after her, but she had escaped through the garden gate before I could make up my mind. By that time, Philomena had come from the house and was bustling over to us in a long, high-necked dress which was covered with tiny, sparkling sequins and matching black beads. She looked as though she were dressed for a royal soirée.

"Oh huzzah!" she said in her usual, slightly bored tone. "I'm to go first, am I? Christopher, fetch me a chair."

I might have found the courage to put my grandfather in his place, but that didn't mean I was about to speak rudely to a lady. My parents had brought me up too well for that, and so I ran off to do as requested. I soon returned from the conservatory with one of the wicker chairs, which I placed in front of the table. Without taking her eyes off the former officer, she took her seat as a queen would before a private audience.

To begin with, neither of them said anything, and it gave me the opportunity to take in the steamroller in our midst. Lady Fontaine – as the press always called her, though she held no title – was intimidated by nothing and no one. She sat with her hands folded in her lap, perfectly at ease with herself and her surroundings. I very much doubted that Grandfather could do much to shake her confidence.

"Which of us is supposed to begin?" she enquired after a good minute of mutual silence had passed. "Only I believe that lunch will be served before long." She wore a considerable amount of makeup, and the thick black lines around her eyes made her look quite diabolical.

"Oh… but I was so enjoying the silence," Grandfather retorted.

She somehow laughed without making a noise. "Come along, Reprobus, there's no need to play your games with me. We're old friends, we can talk this through without any of your tricks."

Grandfather crossed his legs at the ankles and leaned back in his chair. "Very well then. I'll jump straight to the point. Did you kill Robert Atwell?"

She actually laughed this time. "Oh, Reppy, you always did amuse me. It's charming to see that you haven't lost your unstinting belief in the world. I sometimes wonder if you should have been born hundreds of years earlier, in the time of the knight-errant. People like you think that everything is neat and moral, but I'm afraid to tell you that life isn't so simple. In fact, this world is swimming in sin."

They were clearly happy to talk at cross purposes and, just as Philomena had ignored Grandfather's question, he would ignore her response. "It's not the most ridiculous idea that you could have killed your former beau, is it? After all, you were engaged to him when Morwenna died. You were the one whose life transformed as a result of his deeds. And while the man you married may have scaled the political ladder, you wouldn't have had to make such an effort to rise so high if you'd married a duke in the first place."

"Well put. You always did have a way with words." She batted her painted eyelids and waited for him to continue.

Her acquiescence surprised him. "So you're not going to deny it?"

"No, I will not deny that Morwenna's death had a profound impact on my life or that I regret it occurring. But the fact remains that, at the time Bobbie was murdered, I was greeting Elodie at the front of the house."

Grandfather raised one finger. "Elodie said you were in the ballroom together."

Philomena was unflustered and replied with a growl. "The ballroom is at the front of the house."

I knew from my mother's regular and passionate proselytising that women had not been allowed to stand for parliament until just seven years earlier in 1918. But the more Philomena spoke, the clearer it was that she was a born politician.

"Yes, we all regret what happened to Morwenna," Grandfather pronounced in a graver tone. "And yet, none of you would support me when I presented my view of the case to the magistrate. None of you helped. Can you tell me why that was?"

"Bobbie had been punished enough. You saw what it did to him; look at this place." She waved her hand around the decaying estate. "Was it really necessary that he should go to gaol to increase his suffering?"

"Yes, I very much think it was." The sentence rocketed across the lifeless space, where I could still make out fragments of stone and tile beneath our feet. "You see, you were wrong about me. I don't believe that the world is such a wonderful place. I've seen evil and suffering that would turn you from a conservative to a fully fledged socialist. What I believe in is justice – in the punishment fitting the crime. But where was the justice for our little Star? Bobbie's father hushed everything up and her killer was free to get on with his life."

"But that's just it. He didn't *get on with his life*. His whole world collapsed in on itself." Philomena changed her approach. "You know, I'm genuinely sorry that he was killed in such a manner. Believe it or not, I was looking forward to bringing everyone together."

My grandfather's voice broke from him like a siren. "Not everyone. Morwenna couldn't be here. She died when she was seventeen years old on this very spot. She was poisoned from the insides out. Her lungs filled with carbon monoxide and cyanide, but no one was particularly upset about it."

"You're wrong there," she continued in that same even tone, no longer attempting to score points or bait her opponent further. "We all cared. But we didn't lose our heads the way you did. A girl died; such things happen and no one was to blame. Bobbie let that single night define his whole existence, and so did you."

"I made a difference." Grandfather paused to let the words echo about us. "I saw how little the law did for anyone but the richest in society and that's what drove me to change my life. I joined the police so that, if I ever came across a case like this one, I would be able to avoid the injustice that befell Morwenna Fairbright."

I stood beside my grandfather, fascinated by their tennis match of wits. He'd hinted at his reasons for becoming a policeman, but never told me outright.

"No, Reprobus." Philomena took her time and turned her head to one side to regard him. "That's not quite true. You let Morwenna's death consume you. Even now, fifty years-"

"Fifty-seven!"

"Indeed, fifty-seven years later; you still can't see past what happened. One of the wealthiest men in Britain has been murdered and your only consideration is that his death was brought on by an event that happened when we were all but children."

Halfpenny and Todd had appeared with stacks of crockery from a door on the other side of the garden. Taking in the scene before them, they looked uncertain whether to continue. Finally, like all good staff should, they fulfilled their task in a quieter, less noticeable manner than they otherwise would have.

As Grandfather hadn't responded, Philomena continued. "Did you know that I've followed your career? The great Superintendent Edgington, scourge of London's criminals, defender of the underprivileged. I heard about what happened at the Cranley Spring Ball, and at Christopher's school. I'm sure that, for all the other cases you've investigated, you considered every last option and sought out even the most miniscule thread of evidence. Yet you decided the motive for Bobbie's murder the moment he was dead. Do you really think that is the behaviour of a detached, rational detective?"

"I know how to do my job, thank you."

She didn't give him a moment and fired straight back. "Then ask me about my family's dealings with the Atwells. Ask me why I dropped everything and came up here yesterday. Demand to know whether Stuart's father really is the staid, milksoppish fellow I married when Bobbie threw me off. Do something!"

Grandfather clenched his jaw and ground his teeth together. I could almost hear the enamel wearing off. "Very well, is Stuart Bobbie's son?"

She made no attempt to hide her distaste. "No, of course he isn't. He is the spit and image of the honourable member for Holborn, and I hadn't seen Bobbie for ten years when my son was born. But at the very least you should be considering such questions."

Grandfather allowed a ripple of joy to play across his face, and he turned her words back onto her. "Did you know that I've followed your career, too? Oh yes, I was most fascinated by your early adult life in London, winning friends and gaining influence. I was positively enthralled by your efforts to boost your husband's political career and the speculation over your own potential run for parliament."

He slowed his speech down and I could tell that he was building towards something. "I noticed that you supported universal suffrage without ever getting your hands dirty, helped female candidates to stand without standing alongside them. In fact, you cleared the way for your own career to take off, whilst managing never to get too close to the radicals who wished to change the system."

She did not look happy to fall under the great detective's magnifying glass. "And what of it?"

"You are a woman of singular determination. A woman who would let nothing stand in her way. And I put it to you that you went to see

98

Bobbie this morning because of the memoir he was writing. I imagine that he hoped to publish it and that you feared it would have shown you in a less than flattering light."

"I have an alibi!" The loose skin under her chin trembled as she emitted this furious statement. "This is preposterous."

"No, it isn't." He pronounced each word in a crisp, matter-of-fact manner. "The protection of one's public reputation is a very good reason to stab someone through the heart with a dagger. I have come across a number of cases with a similar motive."

"Oh yes, and from where would I get a dagger?"

"You know as well as I do that old houses, such as this one, have more dangerous weapons than the armoury at the Tower of London. How we continue to let children grow up in such death traps always amazes me."

She turned her head to one side to regard him at an angle. "So, you're saying that I woke up this morning, pocketed a knife on the off chance that I might need to stab someone and then went for tea with Bobbie?"

"No, I'm saying that you woke up this morning already knowing about the book he was writing and went to deal with him as you saw fit. I'm saying that you've spent your life hating the fellow, and you weren't going to let him get in the way of your future success."

"Preposterous!" she said once more, and rose from her seat. "You're a foolish man who thinks he knows more about the world than anyone else. So very little has changed there."

She turned to go, but still had more to say. "Heed my words, Edgington. Treat this like any other case or you'll come to ruin. I'll see you both at lunch!"

CHAPTER SEVENTEEN

"I do so love a worthy adversary." Grandfather was full of life as we walked to the front of the house to meet the police.

"But did your interview actually get us anywhere?" I was a little confused about exactly what had occurred.

"Well, I got under her skin, for one thing. She only ever calls me Edgington when she's peeved."

"I mean, does it help us get any closer to proving who murdered the Duke?"

He stopped at the side of the house. "In fact, yes, it does. For whatever reason, I caught dear Mimi in a lie." He immediately shot off again, and I thought I might have to beg to find out what this was. "She said that it was Bobbie who called off their engagement and I happen to know that isn't true."

When investigating a case with my wise old grandfather, I have sometimes had the tendency to speak without thinking. To avoid accusations of idiocy, I took my time to consider the impact of this revelation and, when nothing came to mind, returned to my original question. "Does that mean she's the killer?"

"Really, Chrissy. I'd hoped you would have learnt by now that the fact a person is lying merely implies that he has something to hide. We all have things we'd rather not air in public. I once denied enjoying light operettas when, in truth, I find them quite delightful." He spoke as though he had disclosed a great scandal.

I hesitated for a moment and tried to put Philomena Fontaine's role in the proceedings into context. Why would she have lied about ending the relationship with the Duke? If anything, it was worse for her to be thought of as the jilted party; so why would she have invented such a story?

By the time I'd thought up an explanation, we were standing with the local bobbies in the front courtyard.

"Afternoon, guvnor," the rounder of the two men said in a cheerful voice. "We hear there's been a spot of murder."

"Don't get too many murders around here, do we, Jim?" his tall, skinny colleague commented. They reminded me of a cartoon I'd once seen in Father's newspaper.

"None in fact."

"That's right. None at all." He moved in closer, as if he had a secret to share. "I did once have to deal with a case of sheep rustling. Though it turned out that the sheep weren't stolen in fact, so much as a little bit lost." The smile returned to his face. "We rounded them up, and no harm was done in the end."

"That's wonderful news." My grandfather was the king of the dry rejoinder. "Now perhaps you'd like to see the body?"

"Right you are then." They both said at once and, like a music hall double act, put their hands out in unison to usher us forward.

They chattered happily the whole way to the lake about the various cases of criminality that had occurred under their watch and the disgraceful characters they'd apprehended. "I charged one chap for permitting his flock to wander onto private land, when he knew it weren't allowed."

When addressing one another, they switched to the local Cumberland dialect. I must say I found it quite beautiful, though I struggled to understand a single word.

"Hasta iver deeked a cuddy loup a five bar yat?" one reflected or perhaps lamented. It was hard to tell.

We caught sight of the Professor. He was sitting on the shore, with his knees up to his chest and his head down. He looked as if he was mourning the departed soul who was laid out beside him.

"We found him in the lake," my grandfather explained as we grew nearer.

The two officers laughed and big Jim took the lead. "'T'in't a lake, guvnor. Did ya hear what he said, Phil? He called it a lake."

Grandfather was struggling to understand the issue. "This is the Lake District, is it not? Surely that would make this large body of water *a lake*."

They looked at one another in astonishment, apparently unconcerned by the dead body at their feet. "No, it's not a lake, guvnor. That there's a mere!"

The Professor stood up to help bridge the gap in his friend's understanding. "A mere is a local word for a shallow lake."

"'T'in't a lake," P.C. Jim repeated. "Lakes are deeper than meres."

Phil had a caveat to this statement. "Except Windermere, of course."

"Aye, 'cept Windermere. Too deep to swim t' bottom is Windermere."

"They say it's the largest lake in Britain, in fact," the Professor added.

"T'in't a lake," Jim said one last time, and I was afraid we'd have to repeat the whole conversation again.

"How fascinating." Grandfather cast his gaze around the glistening sheet of water, then addressed his old companion. "I don't suppose you know anything about the type of rocks we see at the top of the mountain there? I've always been interested in geology."

Phil raised one finger to say, "T'in't a mountain. That's a fell." but the two men ignored him.

The Professor humbly bowed his head. "I concede, geology is not my forte. I'm sure Deborah will be only too happy to give you the details though."

"I'm sorry," I interrupted, quite on impulse. "But couldn't we get back to the matter at hand?"

They shuffled about guiltily and it was the skinny officer, Phil, who replied. "So this is the body, is it?" He looked down at poor Bobbie, who had developed a purplish hue in the midday sun.

"That's right." I was impressed that my grandfather managed to keep a straight face. "We found him in the… water and dragged him to the shore."

"Right you are," Jim replied. "So he was… drowned?"

"Stabbed."

"Stabbed. Exactly. That would have been my next guess."

Phil knelt down to examine the corpse. "And, from the look of his clothes, I take him to be some sort of wandering vagrant?"

"He's the Duke of Chandos." Grandfather did not sound impressed by their skills of deduction. It made me feel better about some of the uninspired conclusions I'd come to over the last two months.

"Well, I never," Jim muttered. "I'd always wanted to meet the Duke. Kept to himself, he did. Not one for leaving the valley and, sadly, we've never had a crime reported in Chandos Valley until today."

The two men fell to silence whilst they considered the particulars of the case. They looked back and forth at one another, as though arguing over who should speak next.

Phil lost. "So, who do you reckon stabbed him then?"

"Isn't that your job to determine?" the Professor suggested.

"Oh, no, no, no," Jim began.

"No, no, no," Phil agreed, or perhaps disagreed. It was hard to tell.

Jim helped his colleague back up to standing with a heave. "You'd have to wait for an inspector to come from Manchester if you wanted to find out who killed 'im."

"And how long would that take?" I asked, having the creeping suspicion that I was the most sensible person around. It was a strange sensation and I can't say I fully enjoyed it.

"Couple o' days?" Phil guessed.

"Aye, a couple of days if they're not too busy. You see, we can record evidence and secure the scene of the crime, but detection and investigation really aren't part of our day-to-day duties."

Grandfather looked oddly pleased by the turn of events. "Oh, that is a pity. Well, I'm Lord Edgington, formerly of Scotland Yard. I imagine you've heard of me."

They chattered in the affirmative and looked even more delighted than they had when encountering the dead body of the Duke of Chandos.

"Jolly good. So if you 'secure the scene of the crime', I'll deal with the investigation. That should save those poor overworked inspectors in Manchester the trouble of heading up here."

"That's awfully kind of you, sir."

"Awfully kind." Jim was quite surprised by my grandfather's generous offer.

"So we'll stand here and make sure no crows spot the body until the coroner arrives?"

Grandfather nodded his thanks. "Yes, that would be wonderful."

The officers exchanged another uncertain glance before speaking. Jim lost. "There is one question we have for you, guvnor."

Jim gave up, so Phil had to take over. "You see, we haven't had a drink since first thing this mornin' and... Well, we were wondering whether there's any tea?"

His patience finally running out, Lord Edgington rolled his eyes. "There's a kettle inside, but make sure you dust everything for fingerprints before you touch it. And, if you find any that don't belong to the victim, no tea!"

They relaxed a little and Jim said, "Right you are, sir. Phil you get the equipment from the car and I'll look for some clean mugs."

CHAPTER EIGHTEEN

It was strange to see how much the Professor had transformed in the space of a morning. He'd changed from the chirpy, lively fellow we'd met in Cambridge to become nervy and distant. I thought it most important that we discover the reason why.

"Terrible business," Grandfather began.

"Terrible," the Professor agreed. "It makes me think about my own mortality when faced with the death of a friend."

As we walked back through the garden gate, which gave onto the wider valley, Grandfather eyed his childhood friend contemplatively. "Is that what's been upsetting you?"

The Professor put on a laboured smile. "No, it's a selfish way to think when poor Bobbie is lying there dead. It's just that the whole situation we're dealing with is an awful mess."

"Coming here brings back memories, doesn't it?" My grandfather was supremely talented at fishing the truth from our suspects.

The Professor needed no more prompting and coughed out his story. "Indeed it does. You know I've only been here once in fifty-seven years?" I noticed he was the first person after my grandfather to get the length of time just right. "When I was a boy, Bobbie was the world to me. He was everything that I wasn't. Funny, charming, beloved by every girl. I longed to be just like him from the very day we met. But it all fell away when Morwenna was killed."

I could see now that, compared to Philomena, his views on their past were more closely aligned with my grandfather's.

"It's funny that we could both be so affected by the death of a woman we might never have known if we hadn't spent our summers here." Lord Edgington spoke in a wistful, tender voice, as the two men came to a stop just within the limits of the estate. "I have often reflected that our little Star was simply better than the vast majority of people I've known since."

"That's right." The Professor looked quite heartbroken in that moment and struggled to pronounce these two simple words.

I could hear our party convening in the walled garden, but the two old gents appeared quite unaware of the world around them as they broached this sensitive topic.

"You loved her, didn't you, Samson?" Grandfather reached his hand out without touching him. "I suppose I always knew it, but I would never have pushed you to confess. We weren't the type of coves back then to talk about love and romance."

The life had now deserted the academic chap entirely, and he had to sit down on the low wall. "It wasn't as though I ever wanted it to be a secret. I would have shouted my love to the rooftops if Star had accepted me. I did my best, but all she would say was that, in another life, she could have loved me deeply, but in this one it wasn't to be."

I felt like an intruder to be eavesdropping on the conversation, but walking away would have been even worse. I tried to melt into the background as my grandfather took up the baton.

"Wouldn't it be simpler if we all loved the right people? Wouldn't it be fairer if there was one person in the world for each of us and we fitted together like two pieces of a very simple jigsaw puzzle?"

This animated the Professor a touch. "Oh, but think how difficult it would be to find your other half!" This momentary pang of good cheer petered out, and his previous tone returned. "If there were only one person for each of us, I lost mine when I was still a boy."

"You needn't be so-" Grandfather began, but the Professor had more to say.

"That's the way I've always looked at it. I had my chance and it wasn't to be. Morwenna's death has hung over me ever since. She was my Star, and she's never left me. Whenever I think of that night, I think of your face as you came in to my room with the bad news. I can still remember that look of tortured anguish you wore, and it nearly destroys me." The sorrow had rushed from him like the water from a lock.

Walking closer, my grandfather placed a hand on his shoulder. "We should have said all this half a century ago. I feel I've lived my life in the shadow of my distress. It's not only Star's death. I carry the burden of my parents' shame after I refused to toe the family line, my wife's sudden demise and a hundred small failures in my career. I may have been celebrated in the press for my exploits in the police, but all I saw were the mistakes I made and the victims I couldn't save. You and I, Samson..." He had to pause then to find the strength he required. "You and I have collected guilt and disappointment, the way a banker

106

accumulates coins."

The Professor's smile blossomed, and I saw a flash of the Dickensian chap I'd found so charming three days earlier. "That's right, I'm positively flush with sadness."

"But we don't have to be." I think my grandfather had become intoxicated by the poetry of his words. He put his hand to his breast as though he were making some grand, patriotic speech. "For ten years after my wife died, I survived on pity and grief. The time has come to stop dwelling on the past; to never more harp on our losses and failings. The time has come to live again."

"You're absolutely right, old chum." The Professor stood back up and put his arm around Lord Edgington's shoulder. "But first, I'm ready for lunch."

The two of them strode off together, and I puffed along at their heels. I might not have been as moved by the moment as they clearly were, but I was most excited that we would find time in this investigation to eat.

CHAPTER NINETEEN

The scene was not quite so cheerful within the walled garden. Ariadne was there, but was trying not to look at me. The Professor's student Deborah maintained her nervous attitude, as though she felt spectacularly guilty over something. And Philomena and Elodie were once more united against my grandfather.

"Look at the litter that's blown in on the breeze!" They didn't actually say these words, but I could tell that's what they were thinking.

Grandfather wasn't put off by their contemptuous glares or gritted teeth. He was on a gentle cloud which had guided him towards the neatly laid-out table beneath a veranda covered in sweet-scented honeysuckle. Mabel, the unwilling maid, and Todd, the occasional chauffeur, were on hand to serve. Well, the sleepy young blonde spent most of her time making eyes at the strapping chap and paid little attention to any requests for service. She clearly wasn't one of those people who lived for their jobs.

Grandfather left a space at the head of the table where our host should have been sitting, but sat down nearby.

"Have you solved the murder yet?" Stuart asked with interest and immediately received a tut from his domineering mother.

"I have several theories to investigate." He was clearly not ready to divulge too much information. Anyone hoping for a neat resolution to the case over lunch would be disappointed.

During the subsequent overdramatic war of glares that inexorably followed, I took a moment to predict what Grandfather's theories might be. I gave them numbers to make them easier to remember.

1. Philomena "Mimi" Fontaine killed her former fiancé to protect a long-held secret, which might otherwise have put an end to her burgeoning political career.

2. The Professor's student, Deborah Fisher, was behind the Duke of Chandos's murder. The reason that she slayed a man she had only just met? I really can't tell you, but she did seem like a genuinely likable person and, in my experience, they are often the most likely to murder someone.

3. Professor Samson Filigree, to whom Grandfather had just been singularly far too nice, could have settled some historical score with his friend by plunging a knife through his heart. This was suggested by the fact that it was the Professor who had found the body, along with his aloof manner ever since, his inability to tell us what he was doing there in the first place and, as previously identified, his compulsive handling of several key pieces of evidence in the dead man's office.

4. And what about Ariadne Atwell, adopted daughter of the dead Duke and really quite adorable half-pixie, half-human wildling? Though I refused to believe she was involved, my mentor had taught me never to rule out possible suspects until they became impossible suspects and, even then, to keep them in mind.

5. Stuart Fontaine, only son and secretary of Lady Fontaine, took breakfast with my grandfather just minutes after the maid had seen the Duke asleep at his desk. Supposing he found a way to be in two places at once, perhaps he blamed the Duke for not marrying his mother and did away with the blighter. Though, from what I'd been told by my grandfather, that was her choice anyway. Still, he seemed like a nice chap, so I planned to keep a careful eye on him.

6. Elodie 'Lala' Rous; the last in the line of the Henham Rouses. She could have murdered the Duke in order to cast blame on my grandfather, her former paramour, but forgotten to plant any evidence. Furthermore... well, I didn't know much else about her as we'd never found the time for a chat. Note to self; I should probably instigate a conversation with her.

Of course, if number three were true and... no, hang on a moment, which was three? Perhaps I meant four? Never mind. If the Professor were responsible for the crime, he might well have been in league with the mystery woman he'd brought to the party. Or perhaps Mabel the maid was in on it. Wait, I've got it! Stuart could have been working with his mother and used my grandfather as an alibi to throw us off the scent. Or maybe he...

Actually, those were all the theories I could think of.

Halfpenny arrived with the first course and we ate our forced rhubarb and salt-marsh lamb terrines in silence. I know I might not always be complimentary about Cook's attempts at culinary experimentation, but the starter was out of this world. Using only local ingredients which she'd acquired that morning, she'd whipped up a Cumbrian feast. For the first meat dish, we moved on to Cumberland sausages on Grasmere Gingerbread toasts. They reminded me of poor Simon "Porky" Cumberland (may he rest in peace) but the dish was, again, delicious!

The next course was a famous Lakeland dish called Tatie Pot; a mutton casserole topped with potatoes, prepared by our dear Henrietta with a few extra key ingredients. Once more, it was delicious (despite, or perhaps because of, the whipped cream and beetroot).

I really only eat food to tide me over until dessert is served, and Cook did not disappoint on that front. There was a choice between Kendal Mint sorbet with damson preserve or piping hot treacle tart. Somewhat inevitably, I chose to eat them both. Oh joy, oh heaven! While it may not be the most original or profound comment to make; they were entirely, completely, absolutely, one hundred per cent delicious!

The problem with most of the murder investigations I've participated in isn't simply that we don't have time to eat, it's that I don't have time to talk about how much I love food. I had an extra helping of more or less everything to make up for all the exercise I'd been doing and, when I looked up from my plate, something strange had occurred. All that sumptuousness had loosened tongues and lifted spirits. My fellow diners had not only stopped their angry glaring, they were actually talking to one another.

"This reminds me of the picnic we had at the highest point of the valley." Surprisingly, it was Elodie who began this stint of nostalgic reminiscing.

"Only we never made it to the top because Reprobus was too lazy," Philomena added.

"Now, now," my grandfather put in to silence them in his earthquake of a voice. "I was not too lazy. I was merely tired that day." Even I was unconvinced by his explanation.

"You all keep giving hints to what my grandfather was like when he was my age, but none of you have told me any details." I looked around the table expectantly, and only little Ariadne seemed reluctant to participate.

"He was a trickster," Elodie offered.

"That's not true." Grandfather raised one hand as though it would protect him from their criticism. "I merely enjoyed a joke."

"A joke?" Philomena let out a disbelieving laugh. "You once convinced Bobbie that if he rubbed himself all over in garlic, by the next morning, it would make him more attractive to... It would make ladies..." She struggled to find a polite way to say this. "Well, you know what you told him. He smelt so bad that we couldn't go near him for a week."

It took me a moment to fathom what sort of claim would make a young man take up such a challenge. I got there eventually.

"Can anyone prove that it didn't work?" the old man retorted, while Philomena still looked embarrassed.

I spoke up to spare her blushes. "Grandfather wasn't always so scholarly then?"

"He always had his head in a book," Elodie continued, a smile forming on her lips for the first time since she'd arrived. "But I believe that was to hide the fact that he was normally planning some new prank."

"It was a long time ago." Grandfather sounded as though he would prefer to change the topic entirely.

"That's true, but I still have the scars." Elodie shook her head as she remembered.

"Do you mean that literally?" Deborah was more at ease now and allowed a half smile to shape her pale red lips.

"Oh yes. You see, Reprobate here thought it would be funny to put me in a rowing boat and push me out into the lake. I was quite in love with him, of course, and believed we were going on a romantic trip across the water. Then, as soon as he'd cast us off, he ran back to the shore."

"How was I to know that you couldn't swim, Lala?" Grandfather was the only one not laughing by this point.

"I was absolutely terrified and never forgave him."

"That's only half true," he insisted.

"You haven't explained the scars." Stuart spooned the last piece of treacle tart into his mouth and awaited the next part of her story.

"I didn't know what to do. So I jumped out of the boat, got caught up in the rope that was dangling off it and got dragged further out. For yards until it got deeper, my legs scraped along the floor of the lake."

"It's not a lake," Grandfather corrected her, just to be smug. "It's a mere."

"If Bobbie hadn't swum out to save me, I would have drowned."

"That certainly wasn't my intention." The old chap was taking this very seriously. He did not like to be laughed at.

The cheerful noise died down and, in a rather soulful voice, Philomena said, "I wish he were here with us now. How he would have enjoyed this."

There was a murmur of agreement, and then his adopted daughter spoke. "He used to tell me stories about you all." She finally looked up from the table. "They were always happy. Daddy was good at making me laugh. He wasn't like a normal father, but I loved him. And I know from his stories that he loved you all too."

Philomena stretched one arm out across the table and took the girl's hand. This sad note rather interrupted the carefree atmosphere the lunch had provided. I was loath to let the frivolity die away entirely though, and I addressed Elodie once more.

"So why are you still so angry with Grandfather if you forgave him for what happened on the lake?" It was a stupid, childish question which I should have held quietly in my head and never uttered. Far from maintaining the light-hearted mood, it hardened everything around me.

Elodie's smile hid away and, when she spoke, her voice had turned to ice. "I forgave him for almost drowning me, but I couldn't get over his cruelty years later."

Grandfather was normally the epitome of good manners, but he spoke over her to cut her off. "As I've already said, it was a long time ago. We're different people than we were fifty years ago."

"Fifty-seven," Lady Fontaine put in with delight.

But Elodie hadn't finished. "Your grandfather told me he loved me at the end of our penultimate summer here but, after Morwenna died, he simply changed his mind."

Grandfather instantly launched into his defence. "I was just a boy, then. I was far too young to make such decisions."

"You were old enough to join the police. You threw me away for a poor salary and a smart uniform."

"You were only fifteen, I was already a man." Grandfather was starting to contradict himself as he searched in vain for an excuse to explain his behaviour.

"I wasn't too young for you to promise that we would get married." Like a volcano about to erupt, her voice grew in strength and fury. "You destroyed me."

"I saved you from marrying the wrong person," he tried one last time. "I cannot mourn a reality that never came to be. Our lives would have been entirely different if we had wed. My children and grandchildren would never have existed and we simply wouldn't have been happy. I knew I was not the man for you."

She was balling up the tablecloth in her fists. "Well, the man who I was meant to marry never materialised because I spent so long waiting for you to change your mind. You may have your children and grandchildren, but I have nothing and no one. When my father dies, I will be totally alone."

Grandfather looked back at her, desperately searching for some answer to her claims – some elucidation that could put things right. When he realised that was impossible, he pushed his chair back and rose from the table.

"What are any of us doing here? A man is dead – your friend is dead – and we're sitting having a tea party." He glanced around our faces to find seven distinct expressions staring back at him. "Come along, Christopher. We have work still to do."

CHAPTER TWENTY

He stormed from the garden and through the nearest door into the main wing of Chandos Grove.

"You could have told me," I shouted down the corridor after him, once I was certain we were alone. "I don't expect you to be perfect. You can be human sometimes too."

He stopped where he was but would not look in my direction. "I've never claimed to be anywhere close to perfect. I just don't want to hurt more people than I already have." He expelled a noisy breath. "Elodie's right. I played with her feelings and she didn't deserve it. By bringing everyone together, I hoped to make up for past mistakes."

"Wait, that can't be true." I was still trying to understand my grandfather's erratic switches in mood. "We drove all the way to Henham Park to tempt Elodie out to see you. You knew that she wouldn't come up here without some persuading. You camped on her land and then sped off across the country in the hope she would follow you. If you regret playing with her feelings, why are you still doing it now?"

I could see him quite clearly in the huge, gilt-framed mirror on the wall beside him. I thought he might at least tell me that I'd got the wrong idea, but instead he shrugged and turned to leave.

He entered a gloomy lounge with an escritoire in one corner and some mouldy old paintings on the wall. Though presumably celebrating various deceased patriarchs of the Atwell family, they looked as though they all depicted the same rather glum chap in a red military uniform.

"I'm right, aren't I?" My voice shot ahead of me as I entered the dismal space. "You organised this whole thing from the start based on your idea of justice. I'd be inclined to think you had something to do with the Duke's death yourself but, if that was the case, you'd have landed on the perfect method to make sure no one suspected you."

"Oh, really, Chrissy. Try to resist the urge to be so dramatic."

He paid no attention as he hurried around the room, opening drawers and looking behind furniture. When he couldn't find whatever he was looking for, he rushed back out to the corridor and began to peek into various rooms.

"I'm worried about you, Grandfather."

"Ha ha! Good!" He turned to smile at me momentarily before cutting off the corridor and speeding up an open staircase. The further we explored, the dustier the spaces we encountered. The first floor of the wing was a different proposition entirely to the state rooms we'd been roaming through. There were bedrooms with furniture stacked almost to the ceiling. Dining chairs were balanced upon old tables as though they'd been discarded after a child's game. One room was so full, we couldn't force the door open.

While Grandfather appeared entirely dedicated to his task, I couldn't shake my feeling of dread over his inconsistent behaviour. "Would you please calm down and explain what's happening."

"I would have thought it was obvious." He opened another door just a crack, shook his head, and then closed it again. "Didn't you notice that, in the hut by the lake, all the papers related to Bobbie's memoirs? Well, there was a rather turgid selection of poems he'd written, but the less said about them the better."

"That's not what I meant. I want-"

"You want to know why I keep shouting and practically bursting into tears, like some mawkish continental type?" He didn't wait for confirmation and pressed on along the corridor. "I'll tell you why, Christopher. In our previous investigations, I had the advantage of people underestimating me." He put on an unusual voice then, and sounded rather like our decrepit school chaplain. *"Old Lord Edgington is a fossil. He'll never discover the killer. We needn't worry about him.* The ruse has worked quite admirably up until now, but this case is different."

He stopped speaking at that moment and nipped through another door. There was a loud, screeching miaow, and he reappeared a moment later. "Ummm, that's an airing cupboard." Apparently still committed to his task, he increased his pace. "Here in Chandos, I am among a group of people who know me well. It may sound unlikely, as I have spent so little time with them over the last six decades, but I am convinced that there are few people on this planet who see through me in the way that they can."

"So you're acting?" Even if I'd already had a sense of his manipulation, it was odd to hear it confirmed.

116

"Life is an act, my boy. I was clowning – playing the part of a grief-stricken soul whose senses have been robbed by the travails of a long, taxing existence. My friends know as well as I do that to solve such a wicked crime requires a calm and focused mind. I have diminished my capacities in their eyes and may now fulfil my task without fear of the killer complicating matters."

I let this sink in – it didn't get far. "But then how do-"

We'd arrived at the last portal on the long, creaking hallway and his face positively shone. "Here we are." He flung the door wide open and allowed me to enter ahead of him. I noticed a scrawled note saying "No cats allowed!" and knew that we'd come to the right place.

The room was marginally cleaner than the others on that floor, but it was not a great deal more elegant. There were three small holes in the curtains, which I had to assume the Duke had shot at. The once luxurious wallpaper was hanging off the wall in strips, and the Moroccan wool carpet was threadbare and patchy. Well… I don't know for certain it was Moroccan, but with its bright colours, eastern patterns and tireless workmanship it certainly wasn't British!

"Think of it like this, Chrissy," Grandfather began once more, as he found a filing cabinet to trawl through. "Murderers are, of a piece, desperate individuals. If our killer suspects that I am on to him, he might kill again to throw me off the scent. Who knows… you could be the next victim."

"Thank you. That's certainly very reassuring."

He didn't look up at me, but flicked through a pile of papers he'd extracted. "We needn't worry about that anymore. I am certain that there will be no more killings during our time in Chandos Grove, thanks to the sterling efforts I have made. I've always considered myself something of a thespian but I believe I've outdone myself this time."

"That's right. You are a fine actor with a very modest demeanour."

He paused his search for the three seconds it took him to recover from my barb. "In my book, modesty is tantamount to lying."

I decided I should probably lend him a hand and began to poke about the drab room. It was hard to understand why the Duke would have chosen that space to store his important papers. As well as being in one of the most remote corners of the property, it had little charm. The one interesting feature was a wall covered with truly ancient photographs. Considering that photography only became widely available in the middle of the nineteenth century, whoever had taken them must have been something of a pioneer.

"Is this Bobbie's mother?" I asked, as I inspected photograph after photograph of the same model, who was dressed in various elaborate outfits.

"That's right, Lady Chandos. She was known to be quite the beauty."

There were pictures of her dressed as Cleopatra, Joan of Arc and Boadicea, but it was the examples of her in contemporary dress where she appeared most natural. I imagine that the selection was from the 1850s at the earliest, as her dresses were the full-skirted, narrow-waisted type, common in Victorian England. Grandfather was right; she was stunningly pretty.

It's uncanny to look into the past at a woman who now lies in her grave and see that she was once a striking young lady. Her pale features and sunny hair stood out even in the black and white images, and I felt that her eyes must have been a rather enchanting shade of blue. There was one photo of her with her husband in a carefree embrace which was far from the staid, rigid photographs of my own ancestors back at Cranley. The photographer's devotion to capturing her in so many different states, and as so many characters, made me wonder whether Bobbie's father himself was the artist.

"I have another question for you, Grandfather."

"*Adelante*, my boy." I didn't know what that word meant, but went ahead all the same.

"You believe that the Duke's death is connected to Morwenna's."

"That's correct." Every time he interrupted, I felt less sure of what I wanted to say.

"Well… if that's the case, then why haven't we interviewed Elodie?"

Apparently having no joy with the first drawer, he opened the second. "Have you still not divined what I am looking for?"

There was no good answer to this. Whatever I said, I'd only succeed in poking the bear. I finally settled for a nice, neutral, "Mmmm."

"The will, Christopher. I'm searching for the last will and testament of Robert Atwell, the final ever Duke of Chandos…" He stopped perfectly still for a moment. "Well, unless Bobbie had a son that he never told anyone about."

118

Whenever I became embroiled in a conversation such as this one, there was a little voice in my head saying, *don't ask silly questions. Whatever you do, don't ask silly questions!* It was awfully helpful.

"What you are saying, therefore," I began, in a statement, "is that you think the Duke was killed for his inheritance."

He finally looked up at me. "What a silly statement, Christopher. I just told you that it's very unlikely that anyone but Ariadne will gain from his death. He has no direct heirs and, despite his reputation as a lothario, I have heard no reports of any children. We're looking for the will to rule it out as a possibility."

I wouldn't stand for that. "You said the exact same thing as me but in reverse."

He sighed and wore a beatific look. "If you say so, Christopher. Though it would be more helpful if you took the time to aid me in my search rather than plaguing me with unnecessary questions."

"It was a statement!" I answered back.

I have to say, I adored the old fellow. But he did have a way of making everything I said seem dim-witted so that it reflected better upon him.

"This is interesting," I said, to interrupt the silence that had fallen between us.

I was searching through a small desk beside a chaise longue. The papers upon it were mostly old bills and saucy letters to a woman in Essex who, from what I could tell, the Duke had never actually met. I could only think what my father (or, worse still, his haughty mother) would have thought of a member of the English nobility carrying out a romantic correspondence with an untitled woman from Essex!

"What have you found?" Grandfather helped focus my thoughts.

"Some letters to the Duke from Stuart Fontaine."

"That is interesting!" He positively hopped over to examine my discovery.

"It looks as though the Duke contacted Philomena to enquire about some details from their youth and, as her secretary, Stuart replied."

"Yes. I was certain she knew about his blessed book." Grandfather selected the first letter. "Dates, people's names, locations of the places we all visited. I'm surprised that Bobbie was so diligent."

"What if he was killed because of something in the book? This makes it more likely that Philomena or her son were involved, don't you think?"

There was at least half a smile on his face just then. "Yes, my boy. I absolutely agree that it does. Though I'm not sure that it's enough to warrant murder."

"You said it yourself. Lady Fontaine would do anything to protect her political career. Surely the fact that she knew about the memoir could suggest that she killed him to prevent any secrets from escaping."

He put his hand on my shoulder then. It was not so much a patronising gesture as a sign of grandfatherly concern. "Christopher, you must be careful with what you extract from our interviews. I don't necessarily believe everything I put to our suspects. Do I think that Mimi is a hard-headed operator with grand ambitions for her political life? Yes. Do I think that she would kill if someone came between her and a seat in parliament? Well… that remains to be seen."

"So, it is possible?"

"Yes, but the possible and the probable are not always happy bedfellows. Now, we must keep searching."

I looked on through the documents on the desk. There were plenty of receipts for sardines, which the Duke ordered in bulk deliveries of three hundred cans that arrived on the first day of every month. I still couldn't comprehend why he only ate sardines.

Grandfather had abandoned the cabinet and was once again peering behind the paintings and framed photographs which hung from the walls.

"Why would he have hidden anything in such a bizarre spot?" I enquired.

He looked at me again and I felt about as intelligent as a sleepy mouse. "Because Bobbie was paranoid."

"Yes, but, wouldn't he have wanted someone to find his will?"

"No, Christopher. Paranoid people do not want anyone to find their will as it could lead to them being murdered." I suppose he had a point. "Now, that looks promising."

He pointed to a framed photograph I hadn't spotted before. It featured the Duke's mother dressed as Queen Victoria, with a young Bobbie as the curly-haired, blue-eyed Prince Edward on her lap. Grandfather looked most pleased with himself as he stood upon the chaise longue to pull it down from the wall.

"Oh bother. Nothing!" His grand hope had turned out to be a damp squib when there were no documents concealed behind it or letters that fell at our feet.

He did not give up the search but continued to look in every corner of that room, even going so far as to flip back the tatty old carpet. I gave him the benefit of the doubt and waited a good five minutes before timing my next complaint to perfection. "How do we even know that the will is in the house? He could have left it with a solicitor or–"

"Here it is!" He had pulled back the desk from the wall and a neat, cream envelope, not so very different from the invitations I'd seen, fell to the floor with a satisfying thud. "That wasn't so very difficult now, was it?"

CHAPTER TWENTY-ONE

I was genuinely struggling to understand, not only how my Grandfather had managed to find our needle in the giant, mildewed haystack of Chandos Grove, but how the dickens his whole system of investigation made any sense.

"You say that order, method and a scientific mind are essential to solving a mystery," I put to him, "but we're dealing with a frenzied character here. The Duke might well have hidden his will up a chimney in the nursery, or under the sink in the kitchen. You had no possible way of knowing it would be in his upstairs office."

An almost excessively pregnant cat peeked out of the airing cupboard to hiss at us as we made the trip back downstairs. I walked a little faster as I found her rather intimidating.

"*Au contraire*, Christopher! *Au contraire!*"

"I do wish you'd stop speaking in foreign languages, Grandfather. It's difficult enough to understand you in English."

"It means that I believe the opposite to be true. You see, I don't think that my friend Bobbie-"

"Your friend Bobbie whom you've barely spoken to this century and whom you believe to be a murderer?"

"That's the fellow. I do not believe that Bobbie was mad. Paranoid? Certainly. Eccentric? Well, which of us isn't from time to time." He let out a most pronouncedly peculiar laugh to prove his point. "But he had as good a mind as yours or mine. Well, yours at least."

I stopped walking. "Grandfather. That was rude."

His strangely reedy laugh erupted once more. "I was teasing you, my boy. You know full well what I think of your abilities and they are improving by the day. Now, what was I saying?" He tapped the still closed envelope against the ball of his hand. "Bobbie! No, he was not mentally impaired in any way. If anything, I believe he exaggerated his behaviour for the simple fact he was a crotchety, lonely old man who could get away with what he wanted more easily if everyone thought he was a few sparks short of a full circuit."

"And what is the scientific basis for your conclusion?" I tried to sound like him when I said this.

"Well, my impertinent assistant, the reason I do not believe Bobbie was mad is the fact that he told us several times yesterday evening that he was, indeed, mad. He even had poor Ariadne believing it. And I've no doubt the cats would agree with her, if they could talk." He raised his eyebrows then, as though considering the possibility of interviewing the round ginger feline we had just spotted.

"And does his sanity play a major role in the case?"

"Of course it does." He pointed to the envelope again. "If we can't prove he was sane, this will could be contested."

As the seal was already broken, Grandfather thought it best to have a peek at the documents inside before reading them to the group. He didn't tell me what he'd discovered, but removed one sheet of paper, and put the rest back in the envelope.

"Why did you do that?" I was more than a touch surprised that he would interfere with a legal document.

"All will become clear in good time, my boy. Suffice it to say, I'm protecting the interests of one who needs protecting."

I would have asked him what on earth that meant, but knew I wouldn't get a clear answer.

I followed him back to the walled garden, where almost everyone was still at the table. Deborah had given our faithful hound some scraps of food – once more proving what a nice person she was and that she was certainly not to be trusted. Stuart, meanwhile, sat regarding the young lady admiringly. The old people were back to their stories, and the only suspect missing was Ariadne.

It was clear that the garden party had reached a new stage by the time we arrived. Our semi-professional bartender, part-time chauffeur and permanent hero, Todd, had mixed a bright, amber cocktail and Mabel the maid was, for once, doing her job and serving the other guests.

"Sidecar, milord?" the former offered, standing behind a small table that was laid out with all the necessary bottles, flasks, tools and various whatnots that I couldn't identify. "I believe it would be just to your taste."

"Very good, Todd." Grandfather was back in character and glanced about nervously as he spoke. "I'm glad to see you expanding your repertoire of drinks."

The flowing alcohol appeared to have done wonders for the

124

atmosphere; all Victorian propriety had been vanquished. As we arrived, Stuart pulled his chair over to Deborah for them to sit rather closely together. The delightful geologist appeared to have lost her nerves from earlier in the day and made an oddly satisfied, *hmmm,* to everything he said.

Grandfather sat down at the table with his three old friends.

"I remember you in red, my dear," the Professor told Philomena. "From the very first time I met you, I always picture you in red for some reason."

She looked up to the skies with a smile on her face. "It's true. Someone once told me it suited me and, to this day, I'm keen on it."

"I was never a scarlet woman." Elodie laughed. "Though I do remember borrowing a dress from you the day that Bobbie tried to go fishing."

As Elodie recounted a tale of one of the Duke's misadventures, Grandfather redonned the troubled mask he had worn before our brief departure.

"I have something to show you all," he stated, when the story had come to its natural conclusion (with Bobbie, soaking wet and covered in bruises, carrying a large, live trout through the house). Rather than explaining what he was about to do, Grandfather held the envelope up for all to see and opened it once more.

"It's the will," the Professor concluded. It was the kind of thing I might say, only he sounded far smarter.

"That is correct. Herein lies the settlement of Bobbie's fortune."

"What fortune?" Elodie enquired with a giggle in her voice. "The place is a pigsty, and he lived like a pauper."

"Precisely." Grandfather narrowed his gaze to focus on her alone. "Bobbie lived like a pauper and so his wealth went untapped. Though the Chandos family long since gave up operating factories for themselves, the estate maintains shares in countless industrial enterprises."

Her expression had changed, and she suddenly seemed less comfortable. "So he was killed for his money?"

"Anything is possible," Grandfather claimed, once again contradicting the point he'd made to me minutes earlier. "Prof, would you mind doing the honours?"

The cheerful chap took the proffered folio somewhat hesitantly.

He looked around the group to gauge the others' reactions. Apparently reassured, he cleared his throat before reading it aloud. "I, Robert David Atwell, Duke of Chandos, in the county of Cumberland, being of sound mind etcetera etcetera..." He came to a stop and skimmed down through the wordy document, which said very little. "Here we are... Leave all my worldly possessions to my children."

Grandfather was clearly frustrated by this. "Does he specify which children?"

"No, he doesn't give any more details." The Professor turned the page. "All he says is that, 'should said children not be located, all funds from the liquidation of the estate are to be divided up as the executor sees fit, with the proviso that neither Thomas nor Ginger Atwell are to receive a penny.'"

There was an intake of breath from darned near all of us then. Had we chanced upon the names of two previously unknown relatives for whom the Duke did not care? Had one of them sneaked onto the estate to settle a score? Surely this would be the key piece of information that would help us make sense of the whole case.

"Oh, come along, everybody," Grandfather snapped. "Use your brains. Tom and Ginger must be the cats!"

I couldn't help laughing at this, which drew a stern look from Philomena Fontaine.

"Who's the executor?" she asked with a scowl.

The Professor turned back to the first page. "A Mr Albert Pratsmouth from Manchester."

"So does that help to work out who killed him?" Deborah asked. The older generation immediately fixed their scornful gaze upon her, as though it was not her place to speak. I knew exactly how she felt. "That is why you're reading the will, isn't it?"

Grandfather was usually more forgiving than his peers and gave her an accepting smile. "Sadly not, my dear. I had hoped that this document would clear up any question of who would benefit from Bobbie's death. Instead, the clouds of mystery have descended further."

"Ariadne isn't mentioned in the will," I pointed out. "What does that mean for her?"

I looked around at my companions, but my question was met with a series of blank stares. The dull expressions matched the singularly uninspiring surroundings. Though it might once have been a grand Elizabethan garden, the only sign of colour in the place was the honeysuckle above our heads, and even that was turning a tired brown in the sun.

"I can't imagine that he officially adopted her," Philomena eventually replied. "Bobbie wasn't the type to worry about paperwork and formalities."

"And so?"

"And so she'll gain nothing. The will states that his children would inherit the estate. Not some poor orphaned girl who happened to live here. She's got as much right to contest this as the maid or the postman."

There was a murmur of sympathy and supposition then. Personally, I felt terrible for the wildling, whose absence was now something of a mercy.

Once enough time had passed to make his suggestion all the more potent, Grandfather spoke again. "Unless of course she *is* his daughter."

"You're not serious, are you?" Underneath Elodie's words, I heard a faint hint of disgust, which caught me by surprise. Until now, I'd considered this elegant, outspoken woman to be rather wonderful for the way she stood up to my grandfather. "She can't actually be his daughter. He just took her in because no one else would have her. He told me the very same thing himself."

"Of course I'm serious. Have none of you seen it?" He took his time before continuing. "Bobbie was as grey as a donkey when he died, but, when we were young, he was quite blonde. His mother was, too, and her eyes were quite the same shade as Ariadne's. I observed it the first time I saw her."

Philomena considered the facts. "My goodness. You're right."

"So would she inherit the estate?" My question was again met with silence.

Grandfather tapped the same two fingers over and over against the side of his face. "She might. Yes, she might well be the only benefactor. But she'd have to prove her parentage first. It wouldn't be enough to provide photographs and say they looked alike."

"The little guttersnipe," Elodie said in that same aggressive tone. "But at least we know who the killer is. The little brat's mother must have brought her up with the knowledge of who her father really was.

When she died, the girl came begging around here. She did away with Bobbie to get her hands on the estate. I've no doubt she has some way of proving her parentage up her sleeve, you mark my word."

"Oh yes, Lala?" Grandfather's gaze could have cut through blocks of solid lead. "She won't inherit anything until she comes of age. So why would she have murdered him now, several years in advance?"

"I have no idea." She turned away from us to glance at the untidy flowerbeds that were covered over with long grass and the odd weed. "Perhaps she was tired of eating sardines!"

She held her empty glass out, and Todd obediently skipped over to refill it from his cocktail shaker. Philomena glared at her son/skivvy and he snatched her glass to hold it out for Todd's attention. I was glad that I didn't have to work for my parents. It did not look pleasant.

"The problem with young people these days," Philomena began, on a somewhat tangential point, "is that they see no boundaries. When we were children, we lived in fear of our parents, but the war has changed all that. The Kaiser didn't just blow up half of mainland Europe, he put a ten-ton bomb under society itself."

Grandfather decided to ignore her complaints and return to the topic at hand. "If only we knew a legal expert who could answer questions of inheritance law for us." I couldn't understand the curiously exaggerated manner in which he delivered this lament, but then he turned to the Professor and it became clear.

"Legal expert!" he exclaimed. "I barely spent a decade studying law and I'm certainly no expert. Though I can tell you, it would be something of a challenge for the girl to prove she was Bobbie's daughter. At the very least it would take intensive investigation to gather evidence on her behalf and perhaps an upstanding member of society to back her claim." He smiled and turned the conversation back to Lord Edgington.

The two men nodded to one another before Grandfather conceded the point. "Very well, if I'm convinced that Ariadne had nothing to do with the crime, I will do what I can on her behalf."

"It's lucky she's not here now," I said, somewhat shortly. "If she heard what you'd been saying about her, she'd only run off again." I stood up, as I was tired of the whole sorry scene.

"Dear boy, no one's said the slightest thing against her," Grandfather attempted to reassure me. "There's no need to be sensitive."

"I did," Elodie interjected in the hostile tone to which I had become accustomed. "I called the deathly creature a guttersnipe and, if she were here now, I'd probably say worse."

It was hard to know whether it was the alcohol in her veins or the anger in her heart which made her so cruel, but it was interesting that she had come to the fore of the group. Philomena and her son were happy to study the impact of her words without saying anything themselves. The Professor and his student, meanwhile, appeared less confident. They looked like prisoners, forced to endure some personal psychological torture whenever the conversation reached a new peak.

Personally, I'd had enough of the lot of them. I took one of Cook's petit fours from a platter on the table – and then a couple more, as they were actually rather good – and ran from the garden with Delilah at my heels. Well, *ran* is a strong word. I walked at a steady pace at the very least, and I think they got the message.

CHAPTER TWENTY-TWO

Grandfather has often told me that, "Time is a detective's greatest resource and his most fearsome adversary." I'm aware, therefore, that I should have been racing about Chandos Grove in search of clues, or attempting to strike upon new motives for why the Duke was murdered, but I was not in the mood. Instead, my beloved canine companion and I explored the various gardens, hoping to discover where Ariadne had hidden.

I must admit that I found my emotions towards the girl really quite unnerving. I'd moved through a period of fear on first meeting, to sympathy when she discovered her adopted father had been murdered, to something approaching infatuation. I almost wondered whether Grandfather had known about the little cherub before we arrived and taken me up north to have my heart broken. I have no doubt he could have gone into great detail on the educational benefits of a torturous love affair.

It sometimes felt as though my grandfather was investigating the murder, and I was investigating him. I was desperate to solve our various mysteries, yet most of the information I'd gathered depended on the subtle prods and nudges that he gave me to interpret. He clearly thought that he was training me to follow in his footsteps, but what hope did I have of finding the murderer if I rarely understood what my mentor was talking about?

Delilah and I walked aimlessly but soon ended up at the lake. Not wanting to fall into another confusing conversation with the two policemen, I followed the shore in the other direction so that we came to the grove of trees which gave the estate its name. I collected as many smooth stones as I could find to skim across the water, while Delilah sniffed about for… whatever it is that dogs dream of finding.

She came to a stop when I did and watched with great curiosity as I spun the stones through the air. None of them skimmed the surface as I'd intended. The best I managed was a big splash before they sank most triumphantly before my eyes. I'd never realised that stones could communicate before, but these fellows were almost definitely saying, "Is that the best that you can do?"

"You're holding them all wrong," a voice explained, and I briefly considered that the stones were actually talking to me. "Up here, imbecile!"

Delilah and I turned to face the trees, where a skinny blonde girl was visible high above us at the fork of two thick branches.

"How did you get up there?" I asked.

Before she could serve an answer, she'd swung down to the ground on a thick, nautical rope. I very much doubted that I would have had the strength to climb to such a height. A brief, painful memory surged in my brain. It was of my gym teacher, Mr Bath, shouting at me to, "Get up that rope or every last boy in the changing rooms will whip you in the showers."

"Give me one." Standing quite close, Ariadne prised a stone from my fingers.

She waited until the warm breeze had stopped ruffling the water then pulled her arm back to release the round projectile. The stone skipped five, six, seven times, before gliding along the surface for a few seconds, then pausing for one moment longer. It was just long enough to say a cheerful, "Thank you! Goodbye!" to its thrower.

"It's not so difficult," she told me and grabbed my arm to show me how to do it.

She was rather rough in the way she manhandled me so that I was perpendicular to the lake's edge. And yet, I had never in my life felt quite so electrified. It was certainly the closest thing to a hug a young lady had ever given me. I don't come from the most tactile family. Even my cousins are more likely to offer a good firm handshake than a warm embrace. So, I imagine my blushing cheeks communicated quite clearly how Ariadne had made me feel.

"You pull your arm back, then release the stone with a snap of the wrist."

"It's all in the wrist," I quoted and, following her advice, I shot the next stone so far across the lake that it reached the other shore.

"Not bad." Her face was pencilled over with confusion. "But it's supposed to touch the water, not go flying over it."

I let out one of my standard nervous laughs. "Oh... I... Well, I obviously don't know my own strength. May I have another try?"

It took a few attempts, but I finally magicked the stones into jumping across the surface of the water. It might have been my imagination – well, it was definitely my imagination – but I like to think those cheeky little pebbles let out a gleeful weeeee as they skipped once, twice, three times and sort of sat there for half a second, before sinking to the floor of the lake. One of them seemed to say, "Excellent work, Christopher," just as my Grandfather had the habit of doing (approximately once per murder investigation).

"That was really good," Ariadne told me, and it felt even better than one of the old man's compliments.

Delilah woofed out her agreement. She thought our game was heaps of fun and watched each stone we threw as if to say, "I'll catch the next one... I'll catch the next one..."

"Thank you. I owe it all to my teacher."

Ariadne's cheeks reddened at the compliment, and she turned away to look for more stones. She was quite the expert and proceeded to give me a five-minute lecture on the topic. It turned out that the stones I'd been choosing were too heavy – a beginner's mistake if ever there was one.

I practised the new skill at her side as she spun her haul of stones away. She appeared deep in cogitation, and I was amazed how we had spent so long together without me saying the wrong thing or upsetting her in some way.

I felt really very at ease in fact, which is probably why I blurted out my next question without thinking. "So who do you think murdered the Duke?"

Her eyes immediately flicked to the ground, and I was afraid she would never speak to me again. She could quite easily have nipped back up the tree and hidden from me for the rest of our stay there.

"I'm so sorry," I said to make up for my gaucheness. "I just mean..." I couldn't finish that sentence as what I meant was exactly what I'd asked and there was really no nicer way of saying it.

"Everyone thinks *I* did it." She didn't look at me, even as this sad statement tripped from her tongue. "I know what you all think of me; I'm a freakful little orphan who betrayed the man who saved me from starvation."

"No, you're wrong. I would never think that. Neither would Grandfather." I wanted to reach out and comfort her, but one of my school's mottos is '*non tangere, quod non est vestrum*', which roughly translates to, 'Don't touch what isn't yours.' And besides, I was scared she might hit me.

"I didn't kill him. I hadn't seen him all morning when I met you in the garden, and that's why I was worried. They probably all think I was putting on an act, but I swear it's not true."

I couldn't hold it in anymore; the urge was too strong. I stretched my hand out and my fingers skimmed the pale white skin on her delicate arms. I'd been trying to make her feel better, but she barely noticed. I, meanwhile, felt like I'd been hit by lightning as electricity buzzed about my body. I considered jumping into the lake to cool myself down.

"None of them really knew Daddy," she continued, apparently oblivious to the spasms I was experiencing. "Not the way I did. They think he was the same man that they knew when they were children, but he'd changed."

I'd been afraid to say too much until then. I was worried my voice would come out as one long, pubescent squeal, but I found my courage and opened my mouth. "You can tell me about him. Or rather… I'd like to hear more if you'd like to tell me."

She smiled on the far side of her face. I could just make it out from the way her cheeks puffed up and her nose twitched.

"Daddy was incredible. He raised me even though he didn't have to." Her voice vacillated between the upper-class tones of her adopted father and the countryside accent of her infancy. "My ma worked in the bakery in the village and, somehow, word got to him that she was dying. He showed up at our little house one day on a pretty black gelding and did what he could to help. He paid for doctors and medicine, not that it did any good. I was scared of him at first; I was only little and I'd not spent much time with men before. You know, because of the war."

"Is that how your real father died?" It was another thoughtless question, but she didn't seem to mind.

"Aye. He died in 1914, the very first year of fighting, but I was only little so I barely remember him. I only remember Bobbie." She turned her chin up and peered into the perfectly blue sky to recall the man she loved. "The more he came to see me, the more he felt like part of my life. The other women in the village said he'd forget about us soon enough, but he never did. And when the nephritis finally killed my ma, he took me in."

I hadn't a clue what nephritis was, but it certainly didn't sound nice.

"Your Grampa and his friends all think that their Bobbie was some kind of outlaw. That he was a rakehell and a gadabout, off seducing women every night and most mornings too. But, if he was ever like that, he changed once I was here. He cared for me, not just tolerated my presence. He taught me all about the valley that he loved so much and all about the animals and plants that live up here with us. He took me hunting and fishing. He taught me to read and write; he taught me to skim stones too."

"That sounds wonderful. My father once took me to his bank in the city, but most of the time it's my mother who organises family outings."

She walked off slowly, following the curving shore. "The worst thing is that I've started to forget my ma. Sometimes I'll see an image in a book, or spot someone in town who looks like her, and I'll get a picture in my mind, but it never stays long. I don't want to lose Daddy the way I have her." She stopped and looked back towards the house.

"I can't imagine what that must be like." It was my turn to feel guilty. Though I had any amount of sympathy for her, my grandfather's training had inserted questions into my head that I couldn't resist. "Can I ask you something, Ariadne?"

She studied me for a moment. "You can do."

"Your father was writing a book. It's there in the hut, but I didn't have time to read much of it. Do you know what it's about?"

Her whole face brightened. "That was Daddy's hobby. He said it was going to make us rich one day, but I never thought he'd finish it. To be honest, I couldn't imagine who would want to read a book about all the women he'd been in love with. It's not exactly 'Oliver Twist'."

My eyes widened. "You've read Charles Dickens? I simply adore his books. I've read them all several times – even 'Bleak House', which is rather gloomy and probably too long."

"I prefer the Brontës," she said rather coldly, then followed it up with, "but Dickens isn't so bad." I made a mental note to read more of the Brontë sisters' work. "Daddy's book was nothing like them either. I never read any of it, but he used to tell me stories he wanted to include. In his twenties, after the fire, he tried to have a normal life here and he used to host parties for all the fashionable types from London. Poets and actors and lords and ladies would come up here to marvel at the wicked Duke of Chandos. He said he fell in love with a new woman each year, but they always broke his heart. None of them wanted to stay up here in the winter, and he refused to leave. You know, I think Lala was one of them."

This knocked me a step backwards. "Elodie Rous was the Duke's inamorata?"

"Aye. She still came up here in the summers when I was younger."

"And what happened? Why did she stop coming?"

She struggled over the answer, as though she were reluctant to spill her dead guardian's secrets. "They had a big argument a few years ago. She drove off at speed and never came back until today."

"Do you know what they argued about?"

"Yes, I think so." There was another pause, and then her eyes fell to the stones beneath our feet one last time. "It was about your grandfather."

CHAPTER TWENTY-THREE

We ran back to the house with Delilah speeding ahead of us in that excited way of hers. It was as though she knew what we were hoping to achieve and was determined to be a part of the action. Well, either that, or she thought it was dinnertime, but it was still lovely to see. It almost made me forget the fact that I was having to run again.

Pfff. Running!

The fete in the walled garden had become even more hedonistic in my absence. Grandfather was leading everyone in a song, for which Halfpenny had been summoned to accompany him on the tin whistle. Elodie had mounted a wall to lead everybody like a conductor at an orchestra, Mabel the maid was sitting with her feet up, still making eyes at Todd, and the Duke's two cats had appeared and were polishing off the remaining scraps of food.

Perhaps most surprising of all was that my usually excessively sober grandfather was clearly blotto. "Fine voices everybody, fine voices indeed. And for our next song, may I suggest the music hall staple, 'I'm *Henery* the Eighth, I Am'."

There was a rash of cheers and clapping and then we all fell quiet for Lord Edgington to sing the only verse he knew of the song, in a thick Cockney accent.

> "I'm 'enery, the eighth, I am,
> 'enery, the eighth, I am, I am.
> I got married to the widow next door,
> She's been married seven times before,
> And every one was an 'enery.
> She wouldn't have a Willy or a Sam.
> I'm her eighth old man, named 'enery,
> 'enery, the eighth, I am!"

Everyone joined in for the second time through, as the Professor danced about like Pan at some Bacchanalian feast. He had loosened his shirt and was waving his hands in the air with wild abandon. Stuart and Deborah were dancing together to a far slower piece of music, which only they could hear. In fact, the only person who did not seem moved by the frivolity of that sunny afternoon was Philomena Fontaine. She sat very upright at a small table some distance away. She had her hands interlinked before her and regarded the events like a dispassionate umpire.

When the song concluded, Grandfather noticed that Delilah, Ariadne and I had returned. He looked very sheepish as he shuffled over and, with a hiccup, said, "Oh, Christopher, there you are. We were just discussing where you must have gone." He glanced at the others who immediately attempted to straighten their clothes and appear more *upstanding*. In the case of the Professor, this would be difficult as he had just tripped over a table leg and was very much *down-lying* on the ground.

"Grandfather, I need your help for a moment. Would you mind accompanying me to the conservatory?"

"Three cheers for Bobbie Atwell!" the Professor yelled, as he staggered back up. "A duke among dukes!"

"Don't take your grandfather away from us," Elodie complained. "The old stick-in-the-mud was starting to have some fun."

Lord Edgington dismissed her complaint with a good-natured laugh. His eyes were swimming about in his head, and he appeared unsurprised that there were several of me standing in front of him.

"I will happily go with you, Christophers! You are some of my most treasured descendants, and I would follow you to the ends of the earth." He raised his hand unsteadily, and his whole body tipped backwards as though he were about to fall. "Now, if you'll just tell me where the conservatory is, I will meet you there forthwith."

I stepped closer to support him. "Maybe you should lie-down. You're looking a little tired."

"I'll lie down when I'm dead." The esteemed former detective (one-time scourge of London's criminal underground and current custodian of the largest estate in the whole of Surrey) belched out this reply.

"Ha! You shouldn't have had that last cocktail, Reppy!" Elodie let out a cruel cackle as I escorted the old man away.

"Really, Grandfather," I said, once we'd passed through the wooden gate on our way towards the open garden. "A man of your age should have learnt how to handle his alcohol."

He removed his arm from around my shoulder, straightened his back, and brushed off his silver-grey coat. "And a boy of your age should never underestimate his elders!"

Ariadne gazed up at him in astonishment. "So you're not drunk?"

My grandfather's acting was, if anything, improving as the day went on. We had fallen for his ruse once again.

"Of course I'm not *drunk*." He pronounced the word as though it were a terrible insult. "I've never been *drunk* in my life. And on the one occasion I was, I'm certain that someone put something in my drink."

"So why were you making such a fool of yourself?" I immediately regretted the choice of my words.

He released a breath from his nose like a dragon huffing out fire. "I was not, 'making a fool of myself'. I had assumed the necessary camouflage in order to observe our suspects without detection."

I couldn't quite see the logic of this stratagem, but was willing to give the fine old fellow the benefit of the doubt. "So, what have you learnt?"

"Well… It's hard to put into words, but I have my suspicions and will be acting on them accordingly."

I'd lost too many arguments over my grandfather's methods to challenge him again, so I moved us on to more important matters. "Well, I've learnt two very important things. First, the Duke's book was about all the women he'd been in love with. And, second, Ariadne has just informed me that Elodie was one of them." I turned to my golden-haired companion. Ariadne that is – not Delilah who had stayed behind in the garden to chase cats. "Tell him what you told me."

She looked shy again, but found her voice. "They were more than just friends. She used to visit him every summer. She didn't like me and would force Daddy to send me away whenever she was here. I wasn't allowed to eat with them and he was too soft to stand up to her, but I used to hide sometimes and watch them through the window in the conservatory."

Grandfather put one hand on her shoulder and provided an enthusiastic smile. "That's wonderful, you'll make a fine detective just like Christopher. Now, what was it that you saw?"

She looked at me before speaking. "The last time that she came here, they were talking about you. Daddy said that you were a good man, despite all that had occurred in your past, and Elodie flew into a rage. She said that she despised you and couldn't understand why Daddy didn't feel the same way."

"And I always thought the woman was mad about me," he replied, less than humbly. "However, the most salient fact is a far simpler one. The whole time we've been here, she's acted as though she hadn't seen Bobbie since our youth when, in truth, she was a regular visitor. I think it's time that Elodie and I had a conversation."

CHAPTER TWENTY-FOUR

The moment we stepped through the old wooden gate into the walled garden and re-joined the party, my grandfather took up his disguise once more.

"...I told him never to get too close to swans!" he bellowed out, as though we were deep in conversation. "But would he listen? No, of course not. He ended up with a broken arm and a chunk out of his leg."

There was no longer any music to hear, as Halfpenny had gone to attend to his duties, but Elodie was dragging the Professor about the garden in a waltz and Stuart and Deborah had not let go of one another.

"Boy," his mother hissed with all the spite and vitriol that bubbled beneath her surface. "Leave that girl alone and fetch me a book to read. This party is beginning to bore me and I'm tired of having to watch you with that hussy."

Those sober enough to notice froze where we stood. Her words were pure cruelty, but it was obvious she wouldn't back down. Stuart didn't know what to do. He peered between the shrivelled face of his prudish mother and the shocked features of his dance partner before finally capitulating.

"Yes, mother. Right away."

He let Deborah's hand drop, and she held it outstretched towards him as though believing he'd return. I was happy that Ariadne went to comfort Deborah, at least. The two of them began a slow foxtrot as silent tears formed on the young woman's cheeks.

Acting as though he hadn't noticed a thing, Grandfather left me behind at the gate to go over to his merry friends.

"May I have the next dance?" he enquired, and Elodie unentangled herself from the Professor.

The rotund chap landed on a metal bench beside a thicket of brambles. It was rather a shame that Driscoll was off enjoying his honeymoon, as he would have done wonders with that mess of a garden.

"I haven't danced this much since I was a boy," the Prof said before turning to the barman. "Todd, my good man? I don't suppose you could mix something for a sore head?"

Grandfather and Elodie were swaying cheek to cheek. Without his support, she looked as though she would have blown over in the breeze.

"Perhaps we could continue this somewhere more private," I heard him whisper. "I've always so loved the ballroom here at Chandos."

She didn't reply, but looked up at him with a fire burning brightly in her eyes. Taking this as his cue, he moved to escort her back to the house. He winked as he passed and discreetly signalled for me to follow.

I must say that I'd never imagined people in their seventies behaving so disgracefully. Drinking, dancing and dabbling in dalliances? Based on my own relatives, I'd assumed that there was a law which forbade anyone over the age of fifty from enjoying themselves.

I waited for Elodie and my grandfather to leave before following at a safe distance. As I left the garden, Lady Fontaine was sitting regally in her chair. I couldn't make sense of the sadistic expression on her face, but it was evident that she felt gratified by the way events had unfolded.

On the path to the house, Stuart passed me in a blur, with a dry-looking political treatise beneath his arm. The disappointed look he had worn had been replaced by one of quiet servitude. Poor chap! I wondered what it would take to get him to stand up to that ogreish woman. I couldn't imagine my mother calling anyone a hussy for as long as she lived.

As I knew exactly where my grandfather was leading our unwitting suspect, I didn't feel I had to run after them. In fact, I walked. To be honest, I greatly enjoyed the freedom. My knees barely raised from their normal height, I didn't get sweaty or out of breath, and I had plenty of time to enjoy my surroundings. I even spotted a rather chirpy bird in one of the hedgerows. I won't hazard a guess at what species it was, but I can confirm that he was small and brown.

By the time I got to the ballroom, the former paramours had taken up their pose, and my grandfather was leading them in a speedier dance than before. I hid behind a large chest just inside the room to watch.

"It's so wonderful to be here again," Elodie said in the woozy way people speak when they've had too much to drink. She sounded half ecstatic, half sad. "To be back here with all my beloved friends."

Grandfather twirled her under his arm and, rather than coming back to him, she stood apart for a moment and bowed low, before flicking an imaginary fan from her hand. What followed was a slow

Latin dance, unlike any I'd seen before. It was a sedate routine but would surely have set pulses racing back in the Victorian era.

"The Habanera!" Grandfather exclaimed with the amusement plain on his face. "I haven't danced one of these in decades."

Their footsteps were softened by the dust beneath their feet. Their only accompaniment was the drip, drip, drip, of water splashing down into a bucket from an exposed pipe in the ceiling. Though the Chandos Grove ballroom showed signs of faded glory, it couldn't hold a candle to Cranley Hall. There were cracks in several of the windows, an untraceable draught raced through the room and the grand piano was missing a leg.

Turning in unison, the dancers swayed together for Grandfather to perform a neat side-step and finish with his back to his partner's. "I feel seventeen again."

Elodie turned to observe him through glassy eyes. "It's amazing how there are some things we never forget." Moving to a side-by-side position, they joined hands in the air, then pulled back in a flowing dip. "There are some things which we still feel even after all these years."

"Did you never stop loving me?" my grandfather asked, and I had to stifle a gasp of surprise that he had the nerve to pose such a forthright question.

"How could I?" They froze in position, their hands still raised, their eyes almost level and their faces mere inches apart. "You were the first man I loved."

Grandfather held her gaze for several anxious seconds before he spoke again, and the spell was broken. "It's a shame I never felt the same way."

The energy and excitement drained from her face. "You did; of course you did!"

He pulled away and any pretence of romance and inebriation had disappeared. He was a policeman once more – calm, cold and detached. "No, Elodie. I tried to love you. I thought it a noble endeavour when I was eighteen. Mimi and Bobbie were engaged to be married and Prof only had eyes for Star; it seemed like the obvious thing to do. I was young and stupid and I believed in chivalry and magic and all sorts of foolish concepts that I forgot about the day that Morwenna died."

Her shock had subsided, and the anger that I had witnessed so often in her rushed to the surface. "You're a liar, Reprobus. Of course you loved me. If Morwenna hadn't died, we'd have been married. We'd have lived a happy life together. She ruined everything."

And yet, it was Lord Edgington himself who exploded with fury. "How dare you blame an innocent girl for dying and interfering with your childish plans?" He let out an astonished breath and shook his head. "I should probably thank you."

"What in heaven's name for?" She rubbed the back of one hand across her eyes, and her dark makeup became smeared.

"For so perfectly summing up everything that is wrong with you. I didn't break off our engagement because Morwenna died or I decided to join the police. I did it because of the cold-hearted creature you are."

Rather than seek out a considered response, she sent her open hand through the air and caught him on the cheek. One side of his face blossomed bright red and, when he touched it, a drop of blood came away on his finger where her nails had scratched him.

"I rest my case."

She attempted a second strike, but he was ready this time and caught her by the wrist. Whether it was love or hate, the strength of feeling between them was unmistakable. Their eyes were locked onto one another's and they might have remained that way for hours, but Grandfather had more to say.

"From the time you were a little girl, you treated people with cruelty and disrespect. You ordered us around as though we were your slaves."

"I loved you!" she replied, unable to comprehend the change in him.

"You loved my money. As the only girl and the youngest of three children, you never expected to inherit much from your family, so you set your sights on a bigger target."

"It's not true. From the very beginning, I looked up to you all, but you excluded me." Her shock had yet to subside and her mouth hung open between words. "You hated me simply because I was younger."

Grandfather's laugh roared out of him. "Oh, how wonderful to be able to pick and choose the memories which suit you best. I don't have that luxury. I remember every unkind word you said, every insult and demand you made. We got tired of including you because it became so unbearable to have you here."

I could see her desperation as she searched for an argument that could convince him of her good character. "You… You pushed me out into the lake. I could have died."

"Yes, and I've apologised a hundred times, which only served to conceal the truth. Ever since I was a boy, I believed in justice and you deserved what you got. Just before it happened, you'd been so vicious to poor Morwenna that she ran up into the fells and we couldn't find her for hours. You were so self-centred that you didn't notice the pain you caused; but I did, and I wanted to see you suffer."

There was a moment's silence, and her eyes latched onto nothing. "No, that's not right… If you'd only-"

He wouldn't let her say another word. "I'm tired of the long-dead past. I want you to tell me what happened today. You arrived here and, five minutes later, we found Bobbie dead."

Her head was shaking with tiny repeated movements, as though she were stuck reliving the same millisecond over and over again.

"So now I'm a murderer too?"

"Perhaps you are. Perhaps you killed him, wishing to see the havoc you could wreak on all of us."

"I was here with Mimi when he was killed!" She raised one hand to her head and pulled the tight bun loose in one violent motion so that her long grey hair fell about her shoulders. "Tell me what possible reason I could have to kill Bobbie?"

He stopped himself to prepare his response. "I will, but first, I have another question for you. When was the last time you saw him?"

She showed another moment's hesitation. It was only a fragment of a second, but it was enough for Grandfather to know what she was thinking. She'd been caught. She knew that Ariadne must have recognised her, which was why she'd been so cruel to her all day long. Either she could incriminate herself by denying the relationship she'd had with the Duke, or tell the truth and prove that she'd kept it from us.

"I've been to visit over the years. Unlike the rest of you, I didn't just cast him aside when he was at his lowest."

My grandfather nodded, happy with the path the conversation had taken. "As much as you'd like me to believe that you've spent your life waiting for me, it was Bobbie you really loved. You were so desperate to make me feel guilty for terminating our juvenile liaison that you came all the way here today."

145

Perhaps it was the alcohol, or my grandfather's psychological meddling, but Elodie could find no answer. She raised her fists to pound against his chest and, instead of screaming out more excuses, she burst into tears. Long, tortured cries filled the room before Lord Edgington wrestled her into a supportive embrace.

"Did you come here this morning to kill Bobbie before he could tell me of your relationship? Did you find him in his hut, then hurry back here once the deed was done?"

"No!" The word interrupted her own pathetic sobs. "I came here to apologise for giving up on him, not to put a dagger through his heart." Her voice broke once more, and I was no longer certain what I believed.

CHAPTER TWENTY-FIVE

I slipped from the room before Elodie returned to the dying embers of the Chandos Grove garden party. I didn't witness her departure, but had the definite impression that whatever power grandfather held over the woman had diminished in the confrontation, though it had not disappeared completely.

"What does any of it actually mean?" I asked once we were alone.

"It means she has a guilty conscience. It means she may well have a motive for wanting Bobbie dead and it means we've seen through the act she had maintained since she arrived." He let this information sit between us for a few seconds before asking, "What more could you want?"

"Well, the name of the killer, obviously." I crossed my arms and went for a turn around the ballroom.

"Patience, Christopher. We are closer than we were this morning. I'm sure of that."

"That's hardly reassuring. So is the end of the world!" I was in a contrary mood again.

Perhaps it was down to the fact my seventeenth birthday was only weeks away and I was growing up, but it turned out that being belligerent to my elders wasn't nearly as difficult as I'd imagined.

As I inspected the shabby ballroom, I remembered the scene at Cranley's sparkling spring ball several weeks earlier. I had to wonder whether our presence there at Chandos was my grandfather's way of dealing with the events of that cataclysmic night. Far from being an innocent trip to visit old friends, it seemed possible that he'd brought his clique back to the Lake District to prompt the very disaster we were now investigating.

This slightly macabre possibility triggered a chain of thoughts, which led me to declare, "You wanted everyone to come up here because you knew that it would lead to any number of calamities. Isn't that right?"

He looked at me askew, and I could tell that he was thinking, *gosh, how did he work that out?*

"I'm not going to disagree with you," he said, more than a little defensively. "But I never expected a murder. I came here to address the issues that we should have thrashed out when Morwenna died. I came here for justice."

"Justice?" The word rang a little hollow from my lips. "You still haven't found any evidence that she was murdered. And we read in the Duke's own hand that, to his final day, he denied causing her death. Did he really deserve the punishment you brought upon him?"

"Oh." I'd expected a rebuttal but received a look of surprise in its place. "You know, I've never considered it from that perspective before." The issue of his own responsibility washed over him, and he struggled to process the idea. He sat down on a chair with a large hole in it, and his eyes traced a pattern on the floor.

I couldn't imagine how a piece of furniture had ended up with half its stuffing emptied out across the room. After some careful consideration, I decided that, either Chandos Grove had a large problem with even larger mice, or it was another unwitting victim of the Duke's target practice.

"I'm not saying you're to blame for his death, I just keep wondering if it could have been avoided." I'd hoped my words would reassure him, but he sunk lower into his partial chair and would not look at me.

In the silence that followed, and because there was little else I could do just then, I looked about the room in search of bullet holes or large mouse droppings. I found neither, and my mind soon returned to the investigation.

Thoughts of guilt and motive circled my brain. The few pieces of physical evidence we'd discovered – the discarded tea set, the torn manuscript, the Duke's limp body floating in the lake and his will – appeared as clearly defined images with our suspects' names overlaid upon them.

"Grandfather?" I muttered when I thought I might have something worth muttering.

He turned to look at me at last. His eyes were tired, and the lines on his face seemed more pronounced. "Yes, Grandson?"

"If we could imagine for just one moment that the Duke was not culpable for Morwenna's murder, who do you think was behind it?" I imagined this to be an acceptable manner in which to broach the topic.

148

"No." He got to his feet in a sudden leap. "I refuse to discuss such hypothetical considerations."

Oddly, he was more willing to examine the part he'd played in the murder than reconsider the Duke's responsibility for the ancient crime.

I made one final attempt to persuade him. "If the fire wasn't an accident, as you yourself attest, we must at least consider who else could be to blame." He shook his head, but made no comment. "Is it possible to exclude any of your friends?"

He took a long breath and finally conceded. "No. Not entirely. The others claimed to be in their bedrooms, and there were no witnesses to confirm it. Perhaps the Professor is the least likely. I found him asleep in his room and there was no smell of smoke about him. But that's hardly proof."

"All right. Good." I spoke slowly, hoping to coax more information from him. "So, who would have benefitted from her death?"

He considered this point for a few seconds, before that familiar anger reared back up. "No one except Bobbie. He was the one who flirted with every girl, including Star. He was the one with the most to lose and he was the one who lied."

"You keep saying that, but what did he lie about?"

His reply came straight back to me. "He said he saw someone in the shadows as he went to rescue her, but then he changed his mind and denied it. He claimed that he'd been in the house, but his bed hadn't been slept in. His account of what went on was a pure concoction, and if the authorities had made even the shallowest of investigations, they would have turned up the truth."

"So perhaps the Duke's death had nothing to do with Morwenna. Perhaps he was killed out of jealousy or hatred. Perhaps Philomena murdered him because she didn't have the life she'd hoped for and coming back here reminded her of what she'd lost."

"Where's your evidence, boy?" he said, as though I was the one being emotional.

"It's just a theory, but at least I'm trying." My shrill words died away, and I forced myself to challenge him again. "I must say, Grandfather, you keep telling me that you know your friends so well, but I haven't heard you examine who is most likely to have murdered the ringleader of your little gang."

He took exception to this. "It's not that simple, Chrissy. There are too many forces at play to summarise their motives."

"Are there?" The ballroom walls rebounded every sound back to me. "Or is it because you were too involved in what happened? You constantly remind me about the importance of method and process, but it doesn't look like you've been following your own advice."

He rolled his eyes without conviction. "That's ridiculous."

"Prove me wrong. Take your time to examine why each of your friends would have wanted Bobbie dead."

He held in his response as he struggled over the answer. "Very well. But not here. You're right that I am not myself. I need to go somewhere I feel more at home."

CHAPTER TWENTY-SIX

The kitchen at Chandos Grove would have once employed a large staff of cooks and maids to keep the Atwell family fed. Of course, the need for such a range of employees was negated by the dead Duke's adoption of a tinned-sardine diet.

It was a bright, airy space and, with our own cook's touch, the place had come back to life. I felt as though we were in the kitchen of Cranley Hall. Henrietta sang an old hymn as she rolled out pastry, Halfpenny was buzzing about as ever, looking worried, and Todd was in the corner reading a book – of which, I have to say I was rather jealous. I had just got to the part in 'Pride and Prejudice' when Elizabeth Bennet discovers that– Well, perhaps I shouldn't give away the plot.

"Alice." My grandfather frowned when he saw our maid pop through the door. "I forbade you from setting foot in this kitchen. Now return to the comfortable cottage, amid the spectacular countryside, that I have put you in charge of for the weekend."

"Yes, milord, but–"

He raised one eyebrow, and she let out a giggle, then turned back the way she'd come. I had to assume that my broken heart was now mended. Her presence there had stirred little more than a pang of fond reminiscence for those immature days when I had assumed myself in love with her. Oh, the follies of youth!

Grandfather sat in one corner with a view of the room, sipping at the sugary tea that Halfpenny had served us. "More than just summarising why my old friends would have wanted Bobbie dead, I think it's important to point out the unanswered questions with which we are faced."

"Excellent idea," I agreed, and I was happy that he was approaching the investigation more rationally again.

"So…?" He angled his head to regard me. "Perhaps you could begin?"

I hadn't been expecting this. It was one thing to tell my grandfather that he wasn't doing his job properly and quite another to have to do it for him. "Well… I should say… The most important question is, who killed the Duke of Chandos?"

He looked at me keenly. "Yes, that's rather an obvious one. Anything else?"

"Oh, yes, definitely." I was warming up now. "To be able to answer that, I think we need to know why someone would want to kill the Duke of Chandos in the first place."

"That's more like it."

I was encouraged. "And another important point, of course, is, how exactly did someone kill the Duke of Chandos?"

He no longer looked so positive and pursed his lips. "Shall I put you out of your misery?"

"Oh, please do." I breathed a sigh of relief.

"The question is not just, why would someone want to kill him? The question is, why did someone kill him when they did?"

I attempted to identify the subtle difference between the two questions. "You mean at nine thirty in the morning?"

"No, Christopher, I mean today, this week, this year!" He shook his head. "Bobbie has been minding his own affairs up here for years and no one popped by to stop his pulse. So, why now?"

"Ahhhhh," I said, as though I'd finally grasped his meaning. I hadn't. "You mean you're starting to feel guilty about causing his death."

That ruffled his feathers. "No, not at all." He glanced down at his hands, and I knew this was not entirely true. "I meant you to consider what has changed recently that would have precipitated the man's murder?"

I didn't need to think long to answer him. "The book?"

"Yes, that is one possibility. And it would uphold my conviction that the two murders are connected. Whatever the reason, I have no doubt that what happened to Morwenna Fairbright all those years ago and Bobbie's murder here today are inextricably linked."

I considered the other uncertainties that the case had presented and added, "The body. We still don't know why the killer moved the body either."

His eyes travelled about the kitchen for a moment before resting on our hardworking cook. "Yes, though I do have my theories." He spoke absentmindedly, then came back to the present with a start. "Now, I believe you wished to know more about my childhood companions. With whom would you care to begin?"

I searched through the list in my head. "Elodie. I think you should tell me what she's capable of and whether she has any interest in

Bobbie's death."

He seemed surprised by this. "You were there in the ballroom with me. You heard what I said to her."

"Yes, but what you say to a suspect and what you really think aren't always the same thing."

He relaxed back into the wooden mesh chair and laughed. "That is very true, Christopher, and you're wise to remember it." He paused to collect his thoughts. "The truth is that, while everything I told Elodie just now was accurate, the words did not necessarily chime with my thoughts on the case. She was a cruel child. She was always desperate for attention and could treat those around her quite wickedly, but to build a murder enquiry on the back of such flimsy evidence would be exceedingly superficial detective work."

I let out a noise which I hoped made me sound both wise and contemplative. "Hmmm. But it still doesn't paint her in a good light. And considering that she kept her relationship with the Duke a secret for decades, I was wondering…" I hesitated then, as my theories were barely formed in my head and I was worried that my grandfather would dismiss them out of hand. "I was wondering whether she had a reason to kill Morwenna herself."

His forehead creased up like a cross section of sedimentary rock that I'd studied at school. "Oh yes?"

"Well, we know she wasn't so madly in love with you as we'd previously thought and had only made you believe that all these years to make you feel guilty for leaving her."

He seemed less than overjoyed to be reminded of the fact. "And your point is?"

"My point is, what if she was always in love with the Duke and burnt down the orangery to do away with one of his admirers?"

He crossed his arms and examined the probability of my statement. "But Bobbie was engaged to Philomena. Surely Elodie would have killed his fiancé before anyone else."

I huffed out a breath. "Yes, I suppose you're right. I was just so taken aback by her anger in the ballroom, and it made me think about the fire. You see, if Elodie had exaggerated her love for you in order to hide the fact that she was the one who killed Morwenna, she might have killed Bobbie-"

"So, in your version of events, Lala was pretending to be besotted with me, even when we were children?" It was another theory to which he took exception. "That's preposterous."

I might have chuckled at his vanity then. "Try not to take it too personally, Grandfather."

He narrowed his eyes in protest. "I don't mean it's preposterous that any woman would fail to become smitten with me. I'm suggesting that it would be a pretty poor ruse for Elodie to have chosen."

"What about Philomena then? We know she's ruthless. Do you think she could have killed her former suitor?"

He stood up, drained his teacup and decided to go for a stroll around the kitchen while I sat drinking a nice refreshing glass of apple juice.

"I'm afraid it is not quite so simple, Christopher. The question is not whether Philomena is the type of person who could murder someone. The issue we must resolve is whether she had the opportunity and motive to carry out the crime."

"Isn't that the same thing?" I asked without much conviction, as I knew just what his answer would be.

"No, of course it's not." He stopped in the middle of the kitchen and addressed his favourite domestic. "Cook, you have a younger sister, don't you?" His knowledge of his staff's personal lives always impressed me.

"That's right, milord. Hilda, her name is."

His tone lightened. "That's the one; Hilda. And did you always get on when you were children?"

"No, milord."

"Did you fight and argue?"

"That's right, milord. Hilda was a real monster when we were girls. She once covered my hand in treacle while I was sleeping so that, when I woke up, my little rag-doll was practically glued to me. It took our daddy an awful lot of scrubbing to get me clean."

"That's despicable behaviour," the old man stated, and I could see what he was hoping to achieve. "Your parents must have thought her quite the devil."

"That they did, milord. A real bad 'un she was."

"Ahhh, a bad 'un indeed." His voice plumbed the low notes of an opera singer's range as he pronounced that incongruous word. "And, if you don't mind me enquiring, did Hilda end up in prison? Was she convicted of some heinous crime?"

Henrietta took a step back, and her skinny face transformed in surprise. "Milord, of course she didn't. She's a primary school teacher in Wokingham. She's got three children of her own and a heart of gold. We might not have got on as youngsters, but we're the best of friends nowadays."

"Oh, that is a relief." Grandfather's acting was good enough to convince our cook, but not me. I had no doubt he knew all about Henrietta's sister and that nothing she said had come as a surprise. "Thank you for your time, and may I say how much I'm looking forward to this evening's dinner… whatever it may be."

"I hope you're going to like it, milordship." She nodded enthusiastically and got back to work.

"What a well-made point," I said to appease him. "Now, do you think Philomena, or perhaps even her son, could have murdered the Duke?"

"Yes, of course she could have. Politicians are akin to murderers in countless ways and ruthless is just the word for Mimi. But why would she have gone to such an effort? If she feared scandal from whatever old nonsense Bobbie might have included in his book, surely a murder enquiry would attract far more dishonour to her name. And, as for the son, not only does the same apply, he's terribly beholden to his mother. He can't take a breath without her permission."

It was hard to disagree with him. "The Professor then?"

"Samson?" For a moment he sounded surprised that I would make such a supposition. "I can't see it myself."

"His student? After all, we don't know what she was doing here in the first place. And she wasn't far away at the time of the murder. She could have hurried back from killing the Duke to sit with you and confound our timetable of events. We certainly can't rule her out." I resisted mentioning the equally damning fact that she was the nicest person in Chandos Grove.

"That is true. Though I'm willing to believe that she was simply an unwitting companion on an ill-fated holiday."

I didn't want to have to say the name, but, barring members of staff, there was only one person left on the list. "And Ariadne?"

He looked at me through the side of his vision. "Yes, what do we think about Ariadne?"

If I was being honest, I would have told him that she was the most beautiful young woman I'd ever met, with the complexion of a heavenly cloud and the sunflower-yellow hair of a comely angel. Instead, I opted for, "I think she seems nice. And... have you gathered any information on her?"

"Not a thing," he stated quite cheerfully and, as much as he was enjoying himself, I thought our ignorance nothing to be proud of.

"Oh." I said, as how else can one reply to such news? "In which case, we've ruled out every last suspect."

He delivered his response in a whisper. "Just for the moment, my boy. I'm certain that, if we keep pushing, one of them will slip. The solution will fall into our laps, you wait and see."

I'd assumed he would be able to call upon a wealth of evidence by this stage in the investigation. Either he wasn't willing to disclose it, or he was telling the truth and we were weeks away from identifying the killer.

I was about to run through the facts we knew on the Professor – another nice character I would normally have overlooked – when the man in question arrived to drop some evidence in our laps.

"Reprobus, there you are." He was red faced and looked out of breath, but at least he'd sobered up. "I've been looking all over the estate; I should have known you'd be wherever the food was."

Grandfather straightened up and appeared mildly cheered to see the man. "And what can I do for you this evening, old friend?"

He peered around the kitchen in case of spies. "Well... I don't mind telling you that the violence we saw at the hut this morning cut deep within me. I haven't been able to think of anything else since."

"Oh, yes?" Grandfather got to his feet to receive whatever news the man might have for us.

"That's why I went searching for something to help explain what happened to Bobbie. I was looking in the old wing when I came across the child's room and... well, it's a little different from most adolescent girl's bedrooms to say the least." He brought forward a scribbled picture of a body in a desk chair, with a knife placed through the heart and lurid red blood pouring from the wound. "I think you should probably come with me."

156

CHAPTER TWENTY-SEVEN

Ariadne's room was within the maze of corridors in the oldest part of the house. It was hidden away at the end of a twisting hallway which would once have housed Chandos's servant quarters. It was hard to fathom why she had chosen such a spot as her home, but it suited the wild creature that lived within her. The Professor had located Ariadne's den.

It was actually a small suite of rooms which looked quite out of place in the rest of the house. I could only assume that the Duke had decorated them in the manner which he imagined a small girl would appreciate. Every wall and thread of fabric was pink. From the curtains on the windows to the carpets and upholstery, it was like jumping into a vat of strawberry ice cream.

There was a large bookshelf on one wall, covered from floor to ceiling with porcelain dolls, all dressed in their finery. One hundred pairs of eyes stared at us as we entered and, I must say, I found it a little unnerving.

"It's very…" Grandfather struggled to find the words to describe the sheer intensity of the décor. "…feminine."

"At least I understand Ariadne's sartorial choices a little better now," I thought aloud.

"The drawing wasn't in here," the Professor replied. "Follow me."

We trailed behind him through an adjoining dressing room, which was inevitably filled with exquisitely ruffled robes and dresses. The next space we came to was a bathroom – pink, of course – and then the final area was different from the others. It was free from the adornments of the rest of the suite and was sparsely furnished with a small chest of drawers and a draughtsman's desk placed in front of a wide window.

The most interesting feature on display was the vast number of carefully drawn diagrams that were pinned to the walls. Ariadne's neat, methodical hand had captured small details from the world outside that window. Here was a tiny picture of a fox's paw, there a dark stone which might have contained some ancient fossil. There were pictures of fish from the lake, a deer's antlers and an intricate depiction of a wintry leaf. The neat way in which they were displayed reminded me of the cases of artefacts at the Natural History Museum.

"This was where I found it," the Professor explained, pointing to the desk in the corner. It held a selection of coloured pencils, a pad of unused paper and what I had to conclude was a rabbit's skull. "Surely it explains what went on here."

"It does nothing of the sort," Grandfather contested, much to my relief. "It merely shows that the poor child has lived a difficult life and takes solace in the minutiae of the natural world that so vividly surrounds the estate."

"Oh, come along, Reprobus." The Professor pointed at several of the more macabre artworks. "I know you like to think the best of the downtrodden and underprivileged, but the child is clearly obsessed with death. She killed her father and then came here to draw his disfigured corpse."

Grandfather let out a disbelieving snort, and the three of us fell quiet as we took in Ariadne's creations more carefully. I must admit that the first picture had shocked me, but the longer I spent there, the more I realised that this was not the pastime of some savage, but the refuge of a confused child. The pictures on the walls and the small pile of matching trophies on the desk were Ariadne's attempt to make sense of a world which gives and takes. A world where innocent creatures are eaten by predators or fall to their deaths, but where the sun rises each morning to allow us to start afresh. A world in which both her parents had died when she was a babe before a kind man gave her a second chance.

I was buoyed by the fact that my grandfather had arrived at a similar conclusion. "This is not as strange as it might look. I imagine that Bobbie gave her these rooms to have somewhere to feel safe when she first arrived here. And I have no doubt there are all sorts of interesting psychological and psychoanalytical explanations for the drawings. To me they suggest she has-"

"I know plenty about the workings of the mind, thank you." The Professor was not convinced, and there was a smack of cynicism in his voice. "But none of that explains the picture she drew of a man's dead body. The girl is mentally disturbed."

Grandfather would not give up on his belief. "Really, Prof, nothing is so black and white. Perhaps Ariadne chanced across the scene, and

158

that's why she was already so upset when she came looking for her father this morning. Or perhaps she used her imagination to try to understand how he was killed. Don't forget that she was with us when we inspected the body. She will have pieced together what happened. The picture is evidently her attempt to make sense of tragedy, much like her sketches of dead animals and her collection of bones."

The Professor had been inspecting the chest of drawers where I assumed Ariadne's art materials were stored. "Oh yes? Then how would you explain this?" He motioned for us to join him and I made the short journey with undiluted apprehension running through me.

I almost couldn't bring myself to peer into the drawer out of fear of what might be inside. For a moment, I imagined finding a severed head or perhaps just a hand. I was frankly rather relieved when it turned out that it was merely the murder weapon.

"Oh my gosh." Grandfather reacted a little woodenly. His words hardly captured the moment.

"It still doesn't prove anything," I said, and the old man raised one hand before speaking for himself.

"Did you plant this here, Samson?" His voice was firm and calm, but despair ruled his face.

The Professor had to steady himself against the wall to process the accusation. "No, of course I didn't. Why would you say such a thing?"

Lord Edgington took his time before replying – his eyes never leaving our suspect. "I believe you did. You drew us here and made sure we found the knife."

The Professor's round face clouded over with a look of disgust. "The others are right about you, Reprobus. You've lost your mind."

"No, no." Grandfather shook his hand erratically in front of the man's face. "I thought it was odd at the time. I heard you splashing about in the water after you found the body; there was the plop, plop, plop of the tea set too. You must have removed the knife, but why?"

"I've never heard such balderdash." The Prof acted as though he were shocked by the accusation, and went marching across the room. "I was trying to help you solve the murder of one of our oldest friends, but you're beyond help. You really are." He took three steps forward, as though he wished to deliver another rebuke, but could only produce a frustrated gurgle. With one last furious look, he bustled from the room.

"Well, that was unexpected," I said, before blowing my long fringe from one eye. "Does it mean that we've caught the killer?" I sounded awfully cheerful over the idea, but even before I'd finished the sentence, I heard a little voice in my head say, *when will you learn not to jump to such conclusions?*

It was immediately echoed by my grandfather. "When will you learn not to jump to such conclusions? The Professor's actions do not make him a killer, just as Ariadne's drawing does not make her a crazed lunatic."

"Oh, and you didn't 'jump to a conclusion' when you accused your friend of taking the dagger from the scene of the crime?"

He tutted and looked away. "Not at all. I accumulated the necessary evidence and came to..." I could tell he wanted to say, *a conclusion*, but he sought a synonym instead. "...the right answer. Samson has been acting nervously for most of the day – even drinking himself to distraction to cover his odd behaviour. We already recognised that he intentionally interfered with the crime scene by touching everything in sight. But the fact he so selflessly came looking for evidence, in such a remote part of the property, struck me as suspicious."

He listed off the evidence in a brusque, concise manner. "When we first saw the body, the right-hand side of the Prof's jacket hung a little lower than I would have expected, thus suggesting he was carrying something in the internal lining. It only makes sense that he cut a hole in his pocket and hid the knife therein."

I was still attempting to unravel this thorny knot of logic and, before I could say anything, he continued with his analysis. "While it might seem damning that the Professor would not only take a murder weapon from the scene of the crime but plant it to incriminate another suspect, I'm sure there's a perfectly innocent explanation."

I searched every last corner of my brain to understand what possible reason someone could have for committing such an act. "That's an incredibly charitable view you're taking. The obvious reason to place a murder weapon in someone else's bedroom is to frame that person for the murder you've committed."

Grandfather did not react to my hypothesis, but picked up a cloth from the top of the heavy wooden bureau to extract the knife. It was short-bladed as he'd predicted and had a pretty golden handle with small stones on it. I wondered if it had come from some distant exotic country – like India or Holland. With the evidence he needed in his possession, he left the room.

I only knew that he wanted me to follow him because he continued talking as he left. "Tell me this; if the Prof is the killer, why would he have waited until the body was in the water to remove the knife?"

"How do you know that he did? Perhaps he just splashed about to make you think that was the case."

"Oh, bravo, Christopher." He was most excited again and shuttled off along the hall. "You're getting terribly good at this game you know."

"It's not a game," I replied as I attempted to keep pace with him. For a moment, I rather wished he was one of those doddery old types who took an age to get anywhere.

He waved his free hand through the air. "Oh, very well. Inspection is not a game, though it is an awful lot of fun!" He looked a lot like my brother on Christmas morning just then – before he opened his presents, as opposed to after, when he was always disappointed with what he had received. "However, I ardently believe you are wrong to pick the Professor as our culprit. There's a far more significant..." He was about to say *conclusion* again. "...inference we can draw from his actions."

I opened my mouth to enquire what that might be, when a small, blonde creature emerged from the top of the stairs and stopped dead in her tracks. Ariadne studied us with those lively cobalt eyes of hers, which seemed to glow even in the dim hallway. She took in the blade which grandfather was holding between gloved fingertips, glanced along the corridor to assess where we'd come from, and immediately ran back downstairs.

CHAPTER TWENTY-EIGHT

"Well, go after her, boy. What are you waiting for?"

Still staring at the space where Ariadne had been standing, I knew he was right. My legs propelled me down that corridor before my brain had told me it wanted to go.

"You know what they say, Chrissy," the old man shouted after me. "Faint hearts never win fair ladies!" And then he started whistling a Gilbert and Sullivan melody as I turned off the corridor and went racing down the steps.

I hoped that I'd finally found something for which it is actually worth running.

I took the stairs in six big jumps and then had to stop to guess which way she had escaped. I heard a door slam to the right and turned to follow. Dashing back inside the ballroom, I made it to the adjoining salon, which was as dusty and grim as all the other staterooms in Chandos and made me long for the genteel surroundings of Cranley Hall. Through lounges and parlours I passed, catching the briefest glimpses of Ariadne, as though she were the white rabbit in 'Alice in Wonderland'.

She knew the house far better than I did and could cut in and out of passages before I had time to see which way she had gone. But my heart was far from faint; it was positively bold, and I managed to keep pace with her.

When we ran out of rooms, we came to a dead end at the far end of the old wing. I'd already been there once that day, when we'd gone to telephone the police, but the room now appeared to be deserted. This didn't make any sense, as it was the only place to which Ariadne could have escaped. I scanned about the dingy space and, sure enough, there she was atop a large wardrobe in the corner. It was all dark wood and carved flourishes, with an angel sitting prettily above it.

She had got changed for the evening and wore a white shift dress with lace embellishments. Her hair was hanging loose, and a beam of dying light settled upon her like a halo. I had to think for a moment to work out how to reach her.

"You're rather a good runner," I told her, as I panted out half a lung or two.

163

"You should lose weight," she replied, and I thought her both terribly mean and possibly accurate.

"That's not what you told me earlier." I laughed gracelessly. "I thought I looked like a sausage roll."

Her head brushed the ceiling, and so she crouched a little lower. "Sausage rolls are tasty, but they're bad for you. Sardines are much healthier. Daddy used to say they were the food of champions."

I didn't know what to say to this, but had finally encountered the path she must have taken to reach such heights. An old rocking chair had been pushed up against the window, beside which a cabinet gave access to the top of the wardrobe. I began my arduous trek up to her, fairly certain I would fall and split my head open. Being so far from civilisation, it would take any doctor hours to reach me, by which time I would surely be dead. But I climbed from the chair to the cabinet all the same.

Though it was a little rickety, I was surprised at my surefootedness and made it all the way up there without even a splinter. Of course, once I'd shuffled in next to her, I hadn't a clue what to say.

"I like sardines too." This opening salvo was less than Casanovan in its conception, and she did not reply. I tried a different tactic. "I have a confession to make, Ariadne. You see, we went into your bedroom, but only because we-"

"You saw the picture I drew of Daddy." She remained surprisingly calm. "I know. I watched the Professor go upstairs. He found the picture, went back to his room and returned a few minutes later, with something hidden in his jacket."

"Yes, that was the murder weapon. But, don't worry, we don't think you were involved."

She wouldn't or perhaps couldn't respond to this. But after everything that had happened that day, I didn't blame her. She must have thought my Grandfather was about to have her locked up; even my words weren't enough to soothe her fears. I tried again all the same.

"My grandfather says that he thinks you probably drew those pictures to make sense of all the death in your life. Losing your parents and now the Duke must have been terribly difficult. I can only imagine how that would feel."

She finally turned to gaze upon me with that rare intensity that was typically her. "Death isn't so scary. Everyone lives in fear of it, but

164

it's the only thing that we all have in common. Some babies are never born, but they all die."

I wondered for a moment whether Casanova ever tried to woo a lady with such talk, but didn't know how to change the topic, so replied with, "I had a pet rabbit once. I was awfully sad when she passed away, but I'm starting to get over the loss now."

She offered a sympathetic smile. "I'm sorry. When did she die?"

I had to think. "Oh, about seven years ago, but the memory is still painful. Poor Betsy Rabbit was my best friend."

She laughed at me. I probably deserved it. "You're not like the boys from the village. You're softer and sillier. Most of the Chandos lads like fighting and breaking things. I've never met a boy before who's read Charles Dickens or the Brontës. You're different."

She wriggled a little closer, and I stooped to see her better. It was ridiculously uncomfortable up there but, as grandfather had pointed out, *faint hearts never win fair ladies* – though they presumably lead to fewer back problems.

"My father says that it's not good to be different. He says conformity is the greatest ambition one could hope to achieve and we must strive not to stand out at all costs."

She ruffled her brow. "Your father sounds like a stuffy old man."

"He's definitely stuffy, though I don't think he's very old."

She laughed again, and her fingers walked themselves over to brush past my arm. It was as though her hand had a mind of its own that she could do nothing to control.

"Did you know that you're funny?"

I'm uncertain whether it was the height we were sitting at or the unusually high temperature, but I suddenly felt extremely hot and had to open the top button of my shirt. "No one's ever told me that before. I've been called funny looking plenty of times, but not funny."

"I think it's better to be different and funny than stuffy and dull."

I looked down at the thick wooden shelf we were sitting on and was worried that it wouldn't support my weight. "You don't hate me then? I thought I might have upset you again."

"Sardines are all right I suppose, but I love sausage rolls." She'd been moving closer the whole time we'd been speaking and, by now, her face was only inches from my own.

I thought I would do something embarrassing – like sneezing in her face or commenting on how she smelt – to ruin that wonderful moment. Despite the fact I was sweating like a wild boar and could no longer breathe at a normal volume, I managed not to do anything so stupid.

I closed my eyes and waited for her lips to touch mine, just as the door to the room opened and someone hurried inside. I couldn't make out who it was from where we were sitting, but we could hear quite clearly.

"Cambridge 634, please," the young lady said into the handset and I recognised the voice of Deborah Fisher. "Yes, it's me…" There was a pause whenever she had to listen for a response, but I couldn't hear what the person at the other end was saying. "It's dreadful, just dreadful. This is the last place I should ever have come…"

Hearing that note of panic in her voice, Grandfather's words came back to me and I felt I knew why the Professor had been acting so strangely all day. I had long since wondered what Deborah was doing there. It didn't make sense that her university supervisor had invited a total stranger to an intimate party. This – added to the fact that she was far too pretty and charming to dismiss as a suspect – told me exactly what I needed to "infer" from the Professor's actions.

And as this masterstroke of critical thinking came to me, she said something which only confirmed my darkest suspicions.

"I have to get away from here… I've made a terrible mistake."

166

CHAPTER TWENTY-NINE

I waited for Deborah to leave and then, somewhat indelicately, climbed back down from the wardrobe. As I got to the door, I remembered what I'd been doing moments before and called up to Ariadne.

"Terribly sorry about the kiss. Would love to try it again some time. Perhaps you're free after dinner?"

She scowled down at me, unimpressed by my wooing. I considered paying her a compliment or apologising again to make up for my faux pas, but Deborah was getting away. I let out a disappointed breath and shot from the room.

Except for the odd cross-country race – and one games class when my physical education teacher, Mr Bath, shouted at me ad nauseam to run around the playing field four and a half times until I fainted – the first sixteen years of my life had passed at a relatively sedate pace. Until my Grandfather's re-emergence from his living coma, I'd filled my days with peaceful pastimes such as bird-watching, reading classic literature and strolling about the grounds of my family home at Kilston Down. Sadly, those tranquil days were a distant memory as I rocketed across Chandos Grove for approximately the nineteenth time that day.

Deborah left the oldest part of the house, headed towards the Victorian wing with its heavily patterned wallpapers and dramatic landscapes covering every wall. I kept my distance so that she wouldn't spot me, but did not let her out of my sight for one moment. She was the second suspect I'd followed in the space of an hour. If that wasn't good training to become a detective, I couldn't imagine what was.

She stopped in a doorway and looked about before nodding to herself and wandering through. I made it to the door with no further problems and put my eye to the keyhole to see her in close conversation with the Professor.

"I was a fool to let you talk me into this," she said, her voice nearly breaking.

The Professor's response when it came sounded quite heartfelt. "I am so sorry, my dear. I couldn't have known things would turn out like this. I only wanted what was best for you. I'll call a taxi and you'll be away from here in-"

I would love to reveal what he said next but, sadly, someone interrupted their tête-à-tête. Even more regrettably, that person was me. I'd been leaning against the door, not realising that it opened inwards.

"Oh, I'm awfully sorry," I said as I got back to my feet and brushed off my neat summer ensemble of white shirt and cricket trousers. "I was looking for the bathroom." I glanced about at the games room as though I couldn't fathom where I'd found myself. It was elegantly decorated with a plaster relief ceiling and dark marble arches on the three doors which led into it. It was quite the smartest room I'd seen at Chandos, in fact.

"It must have been an exhaustive search if you were peeping in through the keyhole of every room," the Professor said, dropping his supposed student's hands to march over.

"You little sneak," Deborah added. Though there were signs of tears in her eyes, her panicked tone had left her. "You followed me here, didn't you? I thought I heard footsteps."

I wasn't used to having suspicion fall upon me. Being my grandfather's investigative assistant meant casting aspersions on everyone around us and feeling thoroughly superior to all the wicked-doers. I didn't like it now that the worm turned.

"Tell me what you're doing here, boy!" The Professor demanded in an aggressive tone which I wouldn't have imagined the soft chap employing.

"I…" I began, before remembering that I wasn't the one in the wrong. "I'll tell you what I'm doing here." I summoned the spirit of the great Superintendent Edgington as I said this and paced in front of them, just as he would have. "I'm here to lay out my suspicions of your involvement in the murder of Robert Atwell, the Duke of Chandos."

"Insanity!" the Professor spat. "And why, please tell, would either of us have killed my dear old friend?"

Admittedly, this was one area of the case which I was still a little unclear on. Luckily for me, it is a detective's prerogative to control the release of information, and so I ignored the question and delivered the version of events which seemed most likely.

"The two of you have been working together. One of you killed the Duke and the other got rid of the evidence and framed a dear sweet child who had nothing to do with the crime."

Deborah had to lean against the billiard table to steady herself. "For a moment, I thought this day couldn't get any worse."

"Well, brace yourself, madam. I've only just begun." This roaring riposte sounded a lot better in my head. "Deborah, you went to the Duke's hut, stabbed him in the heart and ran back to the garden to sit with Stuart and my Grandfather, only for your 'professor' here to drag the body out to the lake and conceal any evidence which placed you at the scene. Working alone, you wouldn't have had the time to do all this, but by making it look as though your accomplice had chanced upon the body, whilst you were with Lord Edgington, you distanced yourself from this terrible crime."

"Insanity," the Professor howled again, but this time he did not sound so confident.

"You cannot deny that you hid the murder weapon?"

He was about to do just that, but hesitated and I knew that I had him. "I... I still say that the foundling is involved."

I was not willing to put up with such an aspersion. "Ariadne is not a foundling, she's an orphan. An innocent soul who very much adored the man who saved her from the hardship and indignity of a public orphanage."

It was then that Deborah's tears really sprang from her. "I never wanted to come here in the first place. I don't know what I was thinking. I told my auntie on the telephone that I'd made a mistake in coming here!"

"Your auntie?" I really felt like an abysmal person to cause that sweet, gentle human being such pain. Of course, if she was the killer, that was just what she wanted me to feel, and so I pressed on without mercy.

"I'm not interested in your stories. Tell me why you came here!" I wasn't expecting an answer and turned to her accomplice instead. "Not only did you hide the murder weapon, you threw the tea set into the lake – thus ensuring I would get wet in retrieving it!" This probably wasn't the worst of his crimes, but it felt good to address the issue. "And to complete your deception, you touched several important pieces of evidence within the hut, presumably to obscure the prints Deborah had left behind before she fled the scene."

They were both ignoring me by now and the Professor had gone to comfort his accomplice. "Don't listen to him, Deborah. The foolish boy doesn't mean anything by it." He put his arm around her and she cried into his shoulder. This was my first hint that I'd got something very wrong.

"Really, Chrissy, you do insist on complicating matters." My grandfather was standing in the doorway, looking less than thrilled by my performance. "How did you arrive at such an outlandish conclusion?"

"Oh… Hello, Grandfather." What else could I say? "Lovely to see you."

He stepped into the room and began to hold forth. "That's quite the theory you've struck upon – the Professor and his assistant working in tandem to murder Bobbie. But why would Deborah have agreed to participate in such a plan?"

I looked between my inquisitor and my own inquisitees. "Well, I hadn't quite-"

"Unless, of course, you're suggesting she was working as a mercenary on the Professor's behalf." Something wasn't right with the way he laid this out for me. My grandfather never let me off the hook so easily. He was a man who believed in appropriate punishment for even the lightest of offences. "It's a clever theory but… Well, I think it's better if the Professor reveals why he and Deborah really came to Chandos Grove." He turned to gaze at the pair of them with a most pious expression. He looked like the alabaster tomb of some ancient bishop. "After you, my good fellow."

The Professor bowed solemnly and extricated himself from the distraught woman he'd been consoling. He took a few steps closer to the centre of the room, then changed his mind and returned to his young assistant.

"The truth is…" he began. "The truth is that Miss Fisher and I are very much in love and I brought her here to introduce her to some of my most treasured friends." He looked into Deborah's eyes then. Her expression remained hazy for a moment before she reached out her hands to him.

"That's right," she said. "If the Duke hadn't been murdered, we were planning to announce our engagement. That's why Christopher

170

overheard me on the telephone, lamenting our misfortune to my dear auntie."

I felt like a total scoundrel by this point and practically melted into a puddle right there on the carpet. How could I have suspected two good, kind-hearted people of such wickedness?

"There we are then," Grandfather said. "Everything is explained, just as I knew it would be." He looked at me as he spoke, and I realised that an apology was expected.

I cleared my throat and tried to get my voice under control. "I am so terribly sorry for the things I said." I addressed this to Deborah, but she wouldn't look at me. "Congratulations to you both for the love you've found. I'm sure it couldn't have happened to a nicer couple (despite the half-century age difference)." Don't worry, I didn't actually say these last six words, though I must admit the sentiment had occurred to me.

"I look forward to seeing the ring at dinner," Grandfather added. "Speaking of which, we must prepare ourselves for the feast. Christopher, off we go." He pointed to the door; and I was happy to turn and hurry out.

Still bearing an unusually innocent countenance, he pulled the door closed, and I had another apology to make. "I'm sorry, Grandfather. I honestly am. I would never have said anything if they hadn't been acting so suspiciously. You see, I couldn't understand why Deborah had come to Chandos Grove, and then I overheard her on the telephone saying she'd made a terrible mistake. So I followed her here to the games room only for the Professor to recommend that she beat a hasty retreat in a taxi and... well, I put two and two together and ended up with a carriage clock or a piece of stringy bacon."

He'd moved off down the corridor before I finished speaking, and I followed him to share one final thought. "Now that I know the two of them are courting, everything makes sense."

"No, it doesn't." His usual shrewd look was back on his face. "Far from it, in fact."

"You mean that you don't believe their story?"

"Not one single word of it. Not for the first time today, the Professor has fed us a pack of lies."

CHAPTER THIRTY

We retired to our rooms to get changed for dinner and I attempted to extract more information from my grandfather.

He was less than forthcoming. "I hoped you would have filled in the gaps by now. Think about their behaviour, I'm sure you'll work out what's happening before too long."

I had a good old think to try to understand what he was talking about, but it yielded limited results. "If you already know the truth, why didn't you put it to the pair of them just now?"

He was tying his cravat in front of a tall standing mirror, but paused to look at my reflection over his shoulder. "There are some things I know for certain, but we still have more to discover. And besides, it's essential that our suspects continue to think of me as a shadow of the detective I once was. After all the effort I've expended to create that impression, it would be senseless to undo it now."

Still looking at me in the mirror, he paused what he was doing. "Tell me exactly what Deborah said on the telephone."

I thought back to the nervous tone the young lady had used as I described the conversation that Ariadne and I had overheard.

He took a moment to consider the story and then delivered his first question. "'I've made a terrible mistake,' you are sure that those are the words she used?"

"Certain," I replied and, for once, I was. "There was a noise out in the corridor after that and she ended the call."

Grandfather bit his lip. "Would a killer refer to her crime as a *mistake*, I wonder? Perhaps Deborah stumbled on the body on the shore and, rather than reporting it immediately, ran away. That sounds like more of a mistake to me than stabbing a man to death."

"Unless…" I sometimes speak before I know what I want to say; this was one of those moments, but my brain eventually caught up with my mouth. "Unless there was some sort of altercation between Deborah and the Duke, which led to her fighting back and accidentally killing him."

"So where did the knife come from?" He was awfully quick at finding the chink in my argument. "And, why would a girl with no apparent connection to Bobbie go to the hut with him?"

He went back to tying his silky cravat. It was the first time in weeks that I'd seen him in anything but grey morning attire. Though he was evidently loath to abandon his own unique style, custom dictated we don black tie for the evening meal. I have to admit that I was distracted from the details of the case and asked a question that had been weighing on my mind.

"Grandfather, don't you ever get... hot?"

In four neat moves, he tied the knot and his gaze returned to me. "I beg your pardon?"

"Wearing your morning suit all day long? I've been in summer clothes and I've felt like a roast pig. I can't imagine how you must have cooked in a woollen suit."

He shook his head and sighed. "My dear boy, temperature is merely a state of mind. If you tell yourself you are cool, then that is how you will feel."

I somewhat doubted the scientific rationale behind this statement, but I didn't dare argue with him. "Well, if you're not going to let me into any of your secrets, perhaps you'll reveal what the next stage of the investigation might be."

He turned to face me. "Very well, but first you must tell me how I look."

I walked over to pick a small cotton thread from his lapel and he straightened my bowtie. With his long silver hair swept back from his face and his beard freshly trimmed that morning, he looked quite pristine.

"You look wonderful, Lord Edgington," I said in the obsequious voice of our footman. "The colour suits you."

"You don't look too bad yourself. We're sure to make a grand entrance, though I've always considered black to be a rather obvious choice for formal attire. As you have no doubt detected by now, grey will always be my first choice. And in case there's any doubt on the matter, I'd like you to ensure that I'm buried in it."

The mention of his passing filled me with sadness. It must have shown on my face as he followed up this observation by saying, "Not that I plan on shuffling off for quite some time, mind you."

"That is a relief."

He smiled and motioned to the door. "Now, as for my plans, they are *to wait* and *see*."

"But you said you would tell me-"

"You misunderstood me, Christopher. Those *are* my plans. I plan to wait and see what unfolds this evening before deciding on our next move. Or more precisely, to observe the interactions among our suspects over dinner. We have shaken the apple tree several times today; the moment has arrived to see what will fall out."

He put his arm around my shoulder, as much for my support as his own. Feeling cheered by the positivity he'd projected – and the fact he hadn't called me a dunce for implying that Deborah was a savage killer – I accompanied him downstairs. It was beginning to seem that no obstacle was too great for the pair of us – until I saw Ariadne and remembered how I'd so thoughtlessly abandoned her. She refused to look at me for the third time that day, and I pondered why love had to be quite so complicated.

Halfpenny, Todd and even Mabel had pulled out all the stops to get the dining room looking just right. I'm certain that they'd fetched a stepladder to dust every corner of that now-elegant salon. The room shone, just as Chandos Grove itself would have during the youthful visits my grandfather had paid to the estate.

The table glittered with silver from the six-armed candelabras to the chargers beneath our plates. Candles flickered wherever my eyes landed, though the last beams of light still penetrated the windows as the sun went down over the mountains. I'm sure the room could have caught fire and we wouldn't have noticed the difference.

I took my place beside Ariadne, who immediately turned to talk to Stuart and tittered as though everything he said was hilarious and fascinating. I knew she was only doing it to upset me, and it worked. I wanted her to laugh at me, not him!

"The police say the coroner has removed the Duke's body, milord," Halfpenny revealed a little overeagerly as Grandfather took his place. "They also asked me to inform you that there were no fingerprints on the kettle other than Lord Chandos's, no weapon in the lake and that they had a lovely cup of Earl Grey."

"Very good, Halfpenny. Keep me up to date with any *significant* developments."

It was rare for Lord Edgington not to sit at the head of the table, but he had clearly left the space free in deference to our absent host. Philomena Fontaine had no such objections and immediately occupied the vacant seat.

"So you do know how to dress for an occasion," she said, as proud and prim as ever.

Her eyes scanned the table, and I felt an odd burning sensation as they passed over me. It was quite excruciating in fact, as though her gaze had been sharpened to cause maximum discomfort. Even her own son was not spared a disapproving look and he seemed to shrink from her just as much as the rest of us.

"It's just so wonderful to be here with you, Mimi." Grandfather was the only person with the courage to meet her gaze dead on. "I've always said, there's nothing like old friends."

"And we're nothing like old friends!" that cold stare suggested, though the woman herself remained silent.

The Professor and his beloved were the next to appear. They made something of a show of the unusual engagement ring on Deborah's finger. I can't say for certain, but it looked rather like a rubber washer from a tap. We weren't the only ones to notice their proximity to one another. Stuart looked most disheartened and barely had time to impress Ariadne with another dry story about meeting the Prime Minister of Great Britain. Yawn!

There was a murmur of speculation as we realised that Elodie still hadn't turned up ten minutes after we'd all sat down. As I watched the others' nervous expressions, a thought entered my head. My grandfather had once told me that the first time a killer strikes is the most difficult, but that it becomes progressively easier with each new victim. This idea panicked me and I found myself jumping to my feet to yell, "Grandfather, we must leave at once. I have a terrible feeling that Elodie Rous has been-"

"Don't be ridiculous, boy," he said, just in time. "Here she comes now."

I peeked outside to catch a glimpse of her. The sky had turned a stormy grey and, when she stepped through the French window, she was accompanied by an invasive gust of wind. I wasn't the only one who was impressed by her entrance. Every man there breathed in deeply as the lady glided across the room to us in a deep green dress with a necklace of emeralds and pearls. Halfpenny almost fainted.

"You look quite the picture," Philomena told her friend, with more than a touch of bitterness. I noticed that she refrained from describing the sort of picture to which she was referring.

As my fears of a second murder subsided and we settled down to eat, I examined the various factions and feuds that were on display in the small group. Stuart had taken against the Professor and was glaring at him throughout the meal – which, in case you were wondering, consisted of quail consommé, a plate of oysters, three different meat dishes, citrus ice and a raspberry syllabub for dessert. The Professor himself spent that time fawning over Deborah, who glanced around like a deer in the forest when anyone addressed her.

Elodie attempted to be as sparkling in her conversation as she was in her choice of outfit. Ariadne made the occasional glum comment but largely stared at her plate – perhaps disappointed there were no canned elements to Cook's veritable feast. And, now that I think of it, the only person who didn't speak was my grandfather. True to the old man's plan, he observed the unfolding events.

He was a hawk on a wire, a kestrel hovering over us. His precise vision was trained to seek out the slightest movement, his ears were channelled to catch any unexpected sound and I'm certain that he was listening to every last conversation at once.

If he was there as a witness, it was Philomena's role to judge. "What a disappointment you all are!" she declared when she could take it no longer. "For fifty-seven years I have held up our friendship as a yardstick; a mark by which to measure all others. My time here at Chandos was the crucible in which my thoughts, personality and behaviour were born and yet, here you all are, with nothing to show for yourselves. A retired police officer, an underachieving professor, a woman in her seventies still dressing like a debutante and our uninspiring offspring and hangers on."

"Please, Mimi," my grandfather put in with a mischievous laugh, "don't feel you have to restrain yourself."

Her eyes locked onto his, and she rapped out an angry response. "I'm not the sort of person to hide what I really think, Reprobus. I would hope you knew that better than anyone. I've lived my life with one clear goal in mind. I have sought only one outcome and here I am, married to the Home Secretary of our great nation, with the promise of my own constituency finally within my grasp. I have worked for half a century to speak in parliament and my ambition will soon be realised. I have a raison d'être. What do you have?"

I tried to be like my grandfather and sought out every reaction to her cold, cruel speech. I was extremely interested to see that the person who was most affected by her words was her closest friend.

"Come along, Philomena," Elodie began, still smiling despite the hostility. "There's really no reason to be so critical. We've all had moments of failure and success."

I realised then that this moment had been coming all day. Ever since the Duke had been murdered, Philomena's amiable façade had been slipping away to reveal the monstrous entity underneath. It came as no surprise that, when she spoke again, her invective had only increased.

"Oh, have you?" I wouldn't like to have been Elodie as that titanium woman peered down the table at her. "Please, enlighten me as to what you've achieved."

"Mother!" Stuart chastised her, but the heartless character who had birthed him wouldn't even look in his direction.

"I've…" this was as much as Elodie could produce. Seeing that poor lady's suffering made me want to throw my glass of water over the gorgon who had so upset her.

Luckily, the Professor reacted first and managed to lighten the mood. "Speaking personally, I've used my life to read a great number of jolly interesting books."

This drew a laugh from Grandfather who joined in with the ragging. "I've arrested a host of ghastly individuals, no doubt avoiding the murders of any number of innocent people."

Rather enjoying the resistance to that wicked old woman's bad mood, I dared participate. "And don't forget your moustache, Grandfather. You have cultivated a truly splendid display of facial hair. Several of my friends at school commented when they saw it."

"Of course!" He slapped his knee beneath the table. "Why didn't I think of that. I'd like to retract my previous answer and put forward my prodigious moustache as my greatest achievement."

The tense atmosphere which Philomena had foisted upon us was forgotten.

"I've…" Elodie tried once more, before finally pushing through her nerves. "I've enjoyed myself a terrible lot and have no regrets to show for it!" With that, she raised her wineglass and tipped back her head to swallow down every last drop. When she next looked at us, her eyes shimmered in the candlelight and the smile on her lips would not fade.

There was quite the riot of joy breaking out, and I considered raising a toast of my own when Philomena spoke up once more.

"You're a disgrace. Every last one of you lives as though your position in our society has no value. You live as though there are no standards to be upheld or morals to impart to those less worthy than ourselves. Well, let me tell you this, the war didn't change everything. Society still requires moral leadership and without it we will all come to ruin. Heed my words, or we'll soon end up like-"

Before she could finish her apocalyptic entreaty, a window noisily blew open. The wind roared at us, and every last candle in the room was extinguished. The storm clouds had extinguished the last of the evening light by now, and it was impossible to make out what was happening, even a few feet in front of us.

Another dreadful thought invaded my mind, and I shouted out a warning before it was too late. "Everyone stay right where you are, the killer could have staged this very moment in order to-"

A scream rang out. A scream so high and terrifying that it cut through me like an executioner's blade.

CHAPTER THIRTY-ONE

"What happened?" Grandfather said as Todd rushed forward to relight the candles and Halfpenny secured the window.

"Is everybody all right?" Elodie enquired.

I looked around the group and, to my genuine shock, they were all still alive.

"Who screamed?" I asked, and we whipped our heads about the place like we were performing a very unusual dance indeed.

A small voice finally spoke to explain what had occurred. "I'm sorry, it was me." Deborah raised her hand in confession. "I didn't mean to scare anyone, but the sudden darkness and Christopher's words put such ideas in my head that, when Samson reached out to comfort me, I thought it was the killer."

It was my turn to apologise, but I decided against it. My Grandfather always told me I said sorry too often and, to be perfectly honest, I didn't feel like doing so.

I was struggling to process the idea that Philomena was still breathing when she let out one of her unimpressed moans in Deborah's direction. "What a susceptible creature you are. Make sure you never go into politics or we'll eat you alive."

Our heartbeats returned to their normal pace and the cheerful mood we had worked so hard to foster returned. Even Ariadne looked spirited by the dramatic scene and participated in the conversation for the rest of the meal. For the second time that day – thanks, I can only assume, to the wine – the old friends spoke to one another like... well... old friends.

No one was murdered for the rest of the night – or even attacked for that matter – and, seeing how little impact it had made on anyone, Philomena did her best to contain her disapproval.

At the end of the meal, the Professor called for Todd to fill his glass with wine and then raised it skywards. The candles lent a dual shadow to everything they shone their light upon, so that his arm appeared to branch out on the ceiling above us.

"I feel that, even though Bobbie is not here, he is still here with us." He patted his heart with his free hand and cast his eyes down. "If today has taught us nothing else, it is clear we have our differences. And yet, the wondrous summers we spent here formed us, just as Philomena described. They turned Reprobus into a sleuth, Mimi into a politician and me into a ditherer!"

There was a short burst of laughter at this and Grandfather shouted a hearty "Hear, hear!"

"We all have souvenirs that we have kept with us since those days. We all have our memories of Bobbie… and Star. And whatever happens between us, whatever we have or haven't achieved, those treasured mementos will never fade. Reprobate over here thinks that Bobbie was a murderer. And I always knew he was a knave. Mimi decided she wouldn't marry him, whereas Elodie always hoped that she could."

Grandfather frowned at this, perhaps wondering how another member of their clique had known more about Elodie's intentions than he had.

"But I only have one more thing to say on the matter." The Professor leant forward to take a teaspoon from its saucer and gave the long-stemmed crystal glass a satisfying ping. "Our friend was many things but, love him or hate him, his absence leaves a hole that no one else can fill. So… Here's to Bobbie!"

Slowly at first and then picking up speed, we echoed the words and raised our glasses one by one. Philomena was the last hold-out, but even she reluctantly participated. "To Bobbie. May he have all the sardines and kittens that a dead man desires."

There were a few laughs at this, and Ariadne shot up from her seat to run around the other side of the table to where the Professor was sitting. Before he could see what was coming, she threw her arms around his neck and grasped him in a tight embrace.

I have to say, it was rather endearing. Though he'd recently tried to frame her for murder, his tribute to her father had apparently set things right. When she pulled away, there was a half moment before she ran from the room when I could see the sheer gratitude on her face. The Professor was right; the Duke was many things to many people, but to Ariadne, he was a hero.

Philomena finished the last of her wine and, to put a stop to all that unnecessary emotion, she spoke again. "The time has come for the ladies to retire. You may be far too modern for such a practice, but it's one custom I insist we uphold."

"Oh, mother," Stuart pronounced with affection as we rose. "There are some changes in this world for the better. Surely you can see that?"

It was another moment for her son to gaze fondly upon her whilst she completely ignored him. It made me think of my father. I knew exactly how much my mother loved me as she told me approximately once an hour, but Father was more of a double-locked library than an open book, and his feelings were a mystery.

"Cognac will be served in the Italian lounge," Halfpenny informed us, as Mabel led the ladies off to another section of the house. A year earlier, I would have been sent to bed at such a moment. I was happy that my grandfather deemed me old enough to participate in the after-dinner libations. Of course, I hoped there might be some fruit cordial for me, as I certainly didn't fancy the brandy.

The Italian lounge wasn't as grand as it sounded, but it was clean and comfortable. Cranley Hall's staff had done themselves proud with their work that afternoon, and I had a definite sense that Alice had been roped in to the preparations. The cosy room, complete with wood panels and nineteenth century portraiture, contained just the right number of large leather armchairs for the three men (and me).

"What a curious day," Stuart began. "It certainly isn't what I would have expected from a visit to one of Mother's old friends."

"We're probably not like most of the people with whom she associates." Grandfather injected no humour into the statement and peered into his brandy glass as though he held the world in his hands.

"I'm not like most people with whom anyone associates," the Professor announced most proudly, before a thought occurred to him. "You must tell me, dear chap, why in heaven's name do you put up with the old battleaxe when she treats you like a whipping boy?"

The young man looked as wistful as my grandfather just then. "Oh, I suppose that's what one does in a family, isn't it? We live up to our parents' expectations. Mother told me I would go into politics and so that's what I will do. She told my father the same thing, and he might yet become the Prime Minister, so it seems that she knows what's best for me."

"I never did what was expected. I chose my own path," Lord

183

Edgington said, and we all turned to look at him. His chair was in front of the fire, and the light seemed to lick at him like the flames of hell. "Throughout my life, people have told me what I should do or say or be, and I've ignored them and done the opposite. It is both my greatest achievement and my deepest shame."

That distant tone remained, and he wore an expression of great pain. "It's really only my wife, Katharine, who knew how to influence me. Love makes lap dogs out of bulldogs and I was the fiercest mongrel around until she arrived. Of course, I made a lot of enemies along the way. Defying one's family comes at a price, so I do not blame you for taking the simpler route, my boy."

Stuart nodded his acceptance, but even he had reservations, "I'm not saying I wouldn't have liked to branch out on my own..." I thought this would be the greatest criticism he would utter of his mother's chosen path for him, but once the words were out, more soon followed. "I don't mind being her secretary and I can put up with the long hours, it's the social element I find most taxing. You see, I'm thirty-five years old and I still haven't met a woman that my mother approves of."

The two older gentlemen made a breathy laugh at this and the Professor addressed the issue. "That's a mother's prerogative, old bean. No woman is ever good enough in their eyes. But there comes a time when you simply have to say *poo-poo* and take love and life in both hands. I know that better than anyone as it's a step I failed to take... until now, I mean."

Grandfather made an irritable click with his tongue and spoke more brusquely. "For goodness' sake, Prof. Put the poor fellow out of his misery. We both know that you and Deborah are in no way affianced. Tell Stuart the truth so that he doesn't have to cry into his pillow tonight."

The Professor adopted the same scandalised look he'd worn when I'd put a similar accusation to him that afternoon. "Really, Reprobus. I'd hoped we'd got beyond all that. I've expressed my feelings on the matter and I'd like to think you could be happy for me."

As the normally amiable fellow looked off sullenly through the window, Grandfather mouthed some words to console the heartbroken young man in our midst. I'm no great lipreader, but I think he said something along the lines of, "Don't worry about him. Deborah is clearly besotted with you. The Professor has boxed himself into a corner and won't admit the truth. Banana, lettuce and ice cream sandwich." I don't think I quite caught the sense of the final sentence somehow.

Changing the topic to move on from this awkward moment, Grandfather continued aloud. "What I'd like to know is why Bobbie wrote to Philomena this year."

Stuart thought for a moment to make sense of this. "About his book, you mean?"

"That's the one. We found the replies you sent to Bobbie in a room upstairs."

Perhaps encouraged by the old man's earlier hopeful message, Stuart took a sip of brandy and relaxed into the large, comfortable chair. "It was all pretty standard. He wrote to confirm some dates back in the 1860s when you were here for the summer. I get lots of requests for information about my parents from journalists and the like. Luckily my mother has always kept detailed diaries from the time, so it's no great hardship for me. To be perfectly honest, I thought little of it, until my mother announced we'd be coming here."

"Did he tell you anything about the book?" Grandfather raised one eyebrow to show his curiosity.

"Only that he wanted to leave a record behind of his life and the history of Chandos Grove. It sounded rather dry."

This jogged the Professor back to life. "Ha! You clearly didn't know Bobbie if you think his autobiography would be anything less than scintillating. I heard that he once hosted the Monets here, along with Pissarro and Whistler. There were even rumours of an affair with Lady Adolphus Vane-Tempest." He looked around as though we should all recognise the name. "You know; one of Prince Edward's mistresses."

We all said, "Ohhh!" but I hadn't a clue.

Grandfather continued with his questions. "Did you tell your mother about the book?"

Stuart paused, as though as to reassure himself that he really should reveal such information. "Well, yes. She told me a little about her life here and thought it was marvellous to hear from the Duke after so many years. I responded each time he wrote and eventually the requests came to an end. We were most surprised to receive the invitation last week. I wondered if perhaps he'd finished the book and

185

was looking to celebrate." He turned this statement into a question and looked about in search of an answer.

I remembered the few sentences I'd read in the hut by the lake and, as I hadn't said anything for some time, decided to respond. "It didn't look that way to me. If anything, I think that he hoped this weekend would provide the ending he required."

Grandfather winced at this. "That's not the most delicate phrasing, Chrissy. But I'd been wondering the very same thing." He raised his thumb to stroke his long beard as he formulated his next sentence. "Was Bobbie hoping for some revelation? Beyond my own promise that the truth would become apparent, of course. Or had he planned to explain something that none of us had known before?"

The four of us considered this in silence, but it was the Professor who finally responded. "I must say, old chap, Bobbie spent his whole life denying that he had anything to do with Star's death. Isn't it possible that you're mistaken and he wasn't to blame?"

Grandfather turned his full gaze upon him. "Anything is possible, but that does not mean I am wrong." It seemed that this was the biggest concession he would make on the matter.

The Professor continued his point. "Deborah and I were discussing whether-"

"Enough, man!" My Grandfather's hackles were already raised. "It was a convenient lie at the time, but no one believes that the two of you are engaged. Just give up the pretence and stop making a fool of yourself."

The Professor didn't respond at first. He sucked in a sharp breath, tipped his head back to finish his cognac, and rose from his chair. "We've evidently spent enough time reminiscing." He wiped his mouth with the back of his hand in a deliberately uncouth manner. "I'll be leaving in the morning. Consider this my farewell."

Grandfather couldn't bring himself to look at his friend. His eyes studied the golden liquid in his snifter as the Professor walked away. The jocular chap stood in the doorway as though he had more to say, but Lord Edgington hurled his glass over his shoulder to smash in the fireplace.

"Good riddance, Prof." His words came out in a wolfish growl. "If I see you again in this life, it will be too soon."

186

"Grandfather," I began, "how can you-"

He raised his hand to silence me, as the door slammed shut behind the Professor.

"I think I'll call it a night too." Stuart spoke with all the patience he had learnt from tending to his own crotchety elder. "It's been an... interesting day, and I'm glad to have met you all."

Grandfather nodded, but would not say another word until we were alone.

CHAPTER THIRTY-TWO

"Must you be so rude?"

He didn't reply immediately. Instead, he listened to the sound of Stuart's footsteps plodding down the corridor until he was certain that no one could hear us.

"Ha!" this single raised note led to several further copies. Grandfather was nearly crying with laughter. "I should never have joined the police; I was born for the London stage."

"You were acting?" I was actually quite angry with him for tricking me again. "It's not funny. Manipulating everyone like that is terribly cruel. And, if you insist on doing it, you could at least warn me first."

"Oh, your face, Christopher. It was worth it just to see the look of horror. Sensational." He dried his eyes with the handkerchief from his top pocket and I waited for him to become more sensible. "I couldn't help myself. Perhaps it's being back up here and reverting to my childish ways."

"Or perhaps you really have lost your mind," I said quite pointedly, as another burst of laughter broke the air between us.

"Yes, you may be right." He spoke gravely, as though considering the possibility, but then shook his head. "Who can say?"

I thought it wise to indulge him no longer. "And what, please tell me, does any of your *clowning* achieve?"

"I've planted seeds of doubt and disaster in our suspects. Every single one of them has something to hide. It's not just the killer whom we need to provoke, all of my friends will play their part tomorrow."

"Why? What's happening tomorrow?"

His cheerful expression deserted him, and his face looked gaunt in the shadows of the fire. "First thing in the morning, we will unmask the killer."

"So you already know who it is?"

He mouthed a few words experimentally before voicing an answer. "I'm not certain just yet. But I will be."

I looked at the wooden clock on the mantelpiece. It had stopped many years ago, so that didn't help me, but I calculated the hour to be ten o'clock at the very earliest.

189

"What do you think will happen between now and then that will tell you what we need to know?"

He got to his feet before answering. "I'm going to read a book. It's very long, and I have no doubt there will be an awful lot of waffling and self-aggrandisement, but I'm sure that Bobbie's memoirs will provide the final clues we require."

He was at the door already, and so I reluctantly gulped down my lemon cordial and joined him. "Couldn't you at least give me a clue, Grandfather?"

He stepped outside into the corridor where the only light came from a buzzing electric chandelier several rooms away. "No, I cannot."

"Just a hint then? I'm always the last to find out who the killer is. It's frankly quite irksome that you don't trust me with more information as our cases unfold."

He sighed and slowed his pace a fraction. "It's not a question of trust, boy. I trust you more than almost any other person in England." He said this in a way that made me question whether he had a more cherished confidante in another country. "It's a matter of you learning to form the right conclusions for yourself."

An appealing thought occurred to me then. "You haven't a clue who the killer is, have you? Admit it; you're hoping this book will give you all the answers."

"Tut tut, Christopher," he said these words rather than sounded them. "How little you must think of me."

"Then prove it! Tell me who the killer is before you read the book, or I'll know you were cheating."

We turned off the corridor to walk through the conservatory. The air outside was still warm, but the dark clouds had consumed the sky and I could feel the first raindrops beginning to fall.

"No, Christopher, I'm not going to give the game away just like that. A good teacher doesn't do the work on his pupils' behalf. I will draw your attention to a few relevant points and you must do the rest."

"You don't know who the killer is!" I sang to an infantile melody, just as my fellow pupils mock one another at school.

He was clearly irritated, but replied nonetheless. "Very well then. I will seal the name of the culprit in an envelope, and you can open it once the police have made the arrest. Would that prove satisfactory?"

"That sounds perfect," I said with a smile. "Now, tell me all the clues. If they are anything like the mystery puzzles I've read in Father's paper, they'll be awfully simple. *Who killed Milly Summerstead the florist? Was it, A) Jeremy Brown, the local bobby, B) Dr Vincent, the verger or C) Derek Alderton, the shoe salesman? A man with a brown hat and a size thirteen boot was seen at five o'clock at the north-western end of the Old Kent Road. He was holding a bunch of petunias and a baton.*"

He did not appear amused by my comparison. "No, it's nothing like that… though, now you've made me curious as to who killed Milly Summerstead."

I thought for a moment. "Oh… ummmm… Let's say it was C) Derek Alderton, as he put bigger boots on to throw the police off his trail."

"Yes," he replied very seriously. "A classic piece of diversion." He nodded as though he approved of the fictional Derek Alderton's modus operandi.

"Thank you," I said for no reason at all. "Now what about the case of Bobbie Atwell, the Duke of Chandos?"

"I'm not going to rehash the details of the murder. I'd prefer to direct your attention to the key questions that remain." We'd made it through the gardens by this stage and were headed towards the pebbly shore. "First, and the key doubt I have returned to throughout the day, why would the killer have moved the body? Second, as the maid saw Bobbie alive at nine-thirty, what time was he actually killed? And my last, but equally significant point – which you must consider if you wish to arrive at the name of the killer – is what, if anything, does the Duke's murder have to do with Morwenna Fairbright's death fifty-seven years ago?"

"'If anything'?" I quoted back to him.

"Exactly!"

"But you've spent the day telling me how the two cases are definitely linked!" I must have sounded a touch vexed.

"Yes, but are they?" he asked, as we reached the Duke's hut.

I felt like stamping on my hat but, as I wasn't wearing one, I kicked the stones in frustration instead. They were harder than I'd expected, and I hurt my toe.

We opened the door to find the two officers snoring on either side of the desk. It gave me the opportunity to imagine the scene from that morning when Mabel the maid had come to deliver the snoring Duke's can of sardines. This visual re-enactment did little to tell me who the murderer was, so I stepped inside.

"Evenin', guvnor," Phil said, jerking his head up as we approached.

"Keep it down, Phil," Jim added. "I was havin' a lovely dream about cream o' mushroom soup." He put his head back down, but his colleague soon prodded him awake and the two of them stood to salute their superior officer.

"Anything to report, men?"

"Yes, guv," Jim replied, then looked to Phil to do the talking.

"That's right, guv. We haven't found anything of note, 'cept the maid's fingerprints on a can of sardines and the door. Oh, and that big chap…"

Jim took a scrap of paper from his pocket. "Professor Samson Filigree."

"That's the fella. We found his prints too. Oh and the little lass's."

"The wildling," Jim explained.

"That's right, the baker's lass. We found traces of her about the place, though she wouldn't let Jim take her prints."

Grandfather looked confused. "So how do you know who they belong to if she wouldn't provide a sample of her fingerprints?"

They scratched their heads in unison, before Jim solved the riddle. "It's cos she's got the smallest fingers, see. We reckoned they must be hers."

Former Superintendent Edgington shrugged his shoulders and accepted the information. "Very good, gentlemen. I'll relieve you for the night. No one will be able to tamper with the evidence while I'm here."

This information made Jim's day. "Wonderful stuff. The Mrs told me there's cream o' mushroom soup if I get home this evening. I've been looking forward to it all day."

"Nighty night," Phil said, and the two men wandered out, discussing their favourite types of soup as they went.

Grandfather shook his head with cheerful resignation. "I've known quite a few officers like those two. Unimaginative and docile, but with hearts as pure as lambswool. They can always be relied upon to put in the long hours and make a good cup of tea."

"How nice," I said, as how else is one supposed to reply to such a remark?

My grandfather pulled his long tailcoat off and hung it on the back of the Duke's chair. He took a moment to find a plain piece of paper and a fresh envelope in a drawer, then scribbled something down without me seeing.

"There," he said, folding the paper away and propping the envelope up against a photograph of Ariadne and the Duke. "You know, you needn't stay with me. I'm going to spend the whole night reading. You might just as well get some sleep in a comfortable bed."

"That's all right." I considered offering to read one half of the book, but I was sure I would miss any relevant information. "Actually, wait here, I'll be right back."

"I had no intention of going anywhere," he said, as though I'd suggested otherwise. I reflected for the thousandth time that my grandfather's brain really doesn't work the same as most people's.

I strolled back to the house, up to my bedroom, and collected my book. I was tempted to visit Ariadne, but couldn't quite remember if she was talking to me and didn't want Grandfather worrying that I'd got lost.

Of course, when I got back to the hut, he was so trapped within the Duke's memoirs that he didn't look up as I sat down in front of him. If I'd been in a bad mood, this would have upset me most terribly. The younger, less mature Christopher would have thought, *there's a killer on the loose and he wasn't the slightest bit worried about me!* But I was too old for such petty complaints and kept it to myself.

I got comfy in the big leather chair, opened up 'Pride and Prejudice' and tried to concentrate on the Bennet sisters' trials and tribulations. Perhaps I should have been examining the evidence of who killed the Duke of Chandos, but I had other things on my mind. After the week I'd had, my head felt like it had been hacked open with a small axe. I had lost my one true love to another man, only to find another one true love who could only bear to be in the same room as me intermittently.

Matters of the heart were clearly more difficult to resolve than murder investigations. As I read, I wondered how my parents had ever managed to fall in love. Perhaps my father possessed a guidebook that could explain the finer points of courtship. I doubted it would say anything about women who want to eat young gentlemen like sausage rolls, though, or whether a prospective partner who counts sketching dead animals and climbing on furniture among her hobbies is a suitable match.

To be perfectly honest, I didn't know the first thing about women. But then, how was I supposed to navigate the mysterious waters of love when I hadn't finished reading 'Pride and Prejudice'?

"You are overthinking things, as you always do," Grandfather explained, reading my very thoughts.

"How did you…"

"Life is far from being a Jane Austen novel, Chrissy. Just like crime, there is no one single system for falling in love. Every romance – and every criminal – is different." He looked at me pensively, as though he'd provided me with the most poetic sentiment that humankind were capable of delivering.

"Thank you, Grandfather." I tried to sound casual and carefree. "But if you were to think of any useful advice on the matter of… love etc., I would receive it just as gratefully as if it were related to one of our investigations."

He nodded quietly then gazed down at the large tome before him. So that wasn't much help. For a moment, as he pored over the book, he looked like one of those ancient monks, sworn to silence as he studied his illuminated scripture. Now that I think about it, Grandfather would have made a competent friar – though he would never have let them cut his hair.

He read his book, and I read mine. I journeyed on through Netherfield and Pemberley, was charmed by Mr Bingley, felt slightly appalled by how rude Mr Darcy could be, and quickly fell in love with all but one of the Bennet sisters – Lydia is far too silly. But the further I read into Jane Austen's masterpiece, the less sure I was of the path I should take in my own love affair.

Was the lesson of the book that I should be cold and aloof to win my true love's heart? Or perhaps I should be a cad like Mr Wickham and have my wicked way with every girl. It really was too difficult to decide. I returned to the hope that my father would inform me of the best strategy on my eighteenth birthday.

Another side-effect of staying up late to read in a warm hut with

194

just my silent grandfather for company was that I grew quite tired. I could tell that I was about to fall asleep as elements of our investigation kept invading that serene regency tale. A dead body turned up just as Lizzie and Jane were discussing Mr Bingley's intentions and, soon enough, Mrs Bennet herself – with carving knife in hand and blood-drenched empire-line dresses all around – turned out to be the killer.

At that point, the dream became even stranger. I don't remember exactly what occurred, but I'm fairly certain that my grandfather was dressed as an Indian Maharaja and arrived at my wedding to Georgiana Darcy on the back of an elephant.

Suffice it to say, I woke up the following morning more confused than the night before. Oh, and the hut was on fire.

CHAPTER THIRTY-THREE

It was the sound of the flames that had woken me. More than just a crackle at the far end of the hut, they positively roared as the wall itself and all the trinkets on the shelves were consumed by fire. The smoke had reached us and I immediately started choking, but at least I was awake. Lord Edgington had passed out on the table and I had to hope it was from the boring text he'd had to read, rather than smoke inhalation.

"Grandfather, wake up!" I screamed, pushing my chair back and covering my mouth with the crook of my elbow in an attempt to breathe more easily. "Fire, Grandfather. Fire!" I'd always been told that this was the thing to shout in an emergency, but it did no good.

He had something of a smile on his lips, and I almost felt guilty for waking him – though surely burning to death would be more of an inconvenience. As he wouldn't stir, I edged around the side of the gigantic desk, the heat rising with every step. It was like walking into an open oven and I thought about all the poor loaves of bread I'd eaten in my life who'd endured such a fate. Still, there was no time to worry about inanimate foodstuffs when my grandfather was in danger.

I shook him by the shoulder, but he showed no sign of life. It was clear that drastic measures were in order. I turned his chair around and tried putting his weight over my shoulders, but I couldn't stand back up. He was an awfully tall fellow and deceptively weighty for such a slender chap, so I let him collapse onto the desk instead.

I thought another solution would be to put out the flames myself and so I seized his coat from the back of the chair and used it to beat at the fire. This was a terrible plan and merely led to the blaze spreading around the hut a little more evenly. The coat was soon aflame too, and so I threw that into the corner where the majority of the fire was concentrated.

I manoeuvred my grandfather's limp form to its original position to prevent him from rolling onto the floor. And that's when the solution came to me. Back in the leather swivel chair, I could load him up with the Duke's manuscript and simply wheel him from the room.

Whoever had the genius idea of putting wheels on chairs should be given a knighthood. It makes it so much easier to save aged family members from certain death. In fact, as there was still space remaining on his lap, I decided to rescue a few more choice items from the hut.

My mother is something of a connoisseur of antique objets d'art. She has always taught me not to rush into deciding what would make a good purchase, and so I examined the artefacts carefully. There was a nice painting of some hounds jumping a fence with the hunt in the background, a Staffordshire pottery figurine of a woman in a large hat, a series of plates depicting pastoral scenes, which I must admit were a little tricky to remove from the wall, and a small, framed portrait of a beautiful young girl that was rather hidden away in the corner of the room.

Grandfather showed no objection to bearing all that weight, and we positively sailed to the exit without a care. The only problem arose when the chair wouldn't fit through the doorframe. With the conflagration getting closer by the second, there was nothing else to do but tip my grandfather through the door and then jump through myself to pull him to safety.

I was terribly disappointed that the set of plates cracked on the pebbles in front of the hut. I was fairly certain they were from the seventeenth-century and would have fetched a good price at auction. I'm glad to say that the other items, including my grandfather, survived the fall. I pulled him to the edge of the lake – as I assumed that was a safe place to be in the event of a fire.

There were noises coming from the main house, raised voices and screams of fear. I thought I might have spotted a cloaked figure standing in the copse on the other side of the lake as well, though my mind was on other things and when I looked a second time, it had disappeared from sight.

Though Grandfather was unsinged, he did not appear to be breathing. Not knowing any other manner to save the poor chap, I copied the technique which I had seen the Professor apply in that very same spot the morning before. I'm not sure whether I got the rhythm right, but I flapped Grandfather's hands back and forth like a mad thing and pushed down on his chest to expel the smoke from his lungs. I felt like rather a fool and was glad there was no one around to see me molesting an unconscious lord.

After fifteen or so compressions, I heard a faint spluttering and my

198

dear old grandfather lunged onto his side to cough out his lungs. I'd never heard such welcome retching in my life and whooped with joy. This spontaneous reaction evidently caught Todd's attention, and he raced over with a bucket already in hand to put out the fire.

"Are you all right?" the efficient fellow enquired, and his master waved him away to get started on his next heroic deed.

"You saved me, Christopher," Grandfather declared once he could breathe again.

My cheeks were bright red just then, and it wasn't from the fire. "Oh, I don't know about that. I merely transported you away from danger and made sure you didn't burn to death. I doubt-"

"Wait a moment." His eyes darted about in a panic. "Where's my coat?"

I turned a deeper shade of crimson. "I'm… I'm afraid it fell victim to the fire."

He looked most put out as he pushed himself up to sitting. "Damn shame. That was my favourite dinner jacket."

I was struggling to understand his priorities at that moment. "Well… perhaps we could have a memorial for all its years of service."

He shook his head, dusted off his cuffs, and got to his feet as though nothing had happened. "Well, at least you saved the Duke's memoirs." He finally managed a smile.

"And you, Grandfather," I reminded him, in a faintly didactic tone.

"Yes, my boy. And I am very grateful." He paused, as though deciding whether it was the right moment to say his catchphrase, before finally giving in. "Excellent work, Christopher."

I felt like jumping for joy, but restrained myself and asked, "So you really do know who the killer is?"

"Of course, I do. I already knew last night. But, unless you thought to save the envelope, you'll never be certain whether I'm telling the truth." A mischievous expression consumed his whole being. It was not just his mouth and eyes which gloried in that moment; his cheeks grew rounder, his shoulders hunched in towards one another and his chin stuck out with glee.

I was less ebullient. "Bother."

He straightened back up and walked purposely away from me. "It doesn't pay to grouse over spilt milk, my boy. We have work to do."

"Are we going to call the police to tell them what you've discovered?"

He came to a stop beside our frantic chauffeur and grabbed one of the buckets. "Eventually. But we're going to put this fire out first."

Halfpenny, Cook, Stuart and even the less than agile Professor all soon appeared, and we formed a chain to send water from the lake to the still raging inferno that had eaten up half of the Duke's office. Made of nothing but wood, and filled with his papers, it was a real tinderbox and went up like… well… tinder. When Todd was too exhausted from the heat, we reshuffled the line and Stuart took his shift at the front. I was worried that, on my turn, I'd end up singeing my eyebrows or burning my fingers. Luckily, he was a good worker and saw us through to the end.

By the time the fire was out, the sun had come up. We sat at the water's edge, exhausted, but proud of our work. There wasn't a great deal left of the hut and we could see right into its charred core as the wall closest to us had burnt away entirely. Most of the roof was gone too, but I could still see the crossed oars fixed above the far door and the electric kettle in the corner where the Duke had made his last ever cup of tea.

"Do you think it was an electrical issue?" the Professor suggested.

Grandfather looked dubious. "No, I think someone did it on purpose." The old man studied his friend for a few seconds, before turning his attention to his staff. "That was a most impressive effort you all made. You went far beyond my expectations."

"I think we might have earned a holiday, Milord," Cook joked and the old fellow took it in good spirits.

We sat there in silence for a few minutes and I considered the circumstances which could have led to a second fire on the property. As my wise forebear had concluded, it was surely too much of a coincidence to be an accident and reinforced his belief that the fire that had killed Morwenna was started intentionally. It seemed inevitable that the scene in front of us would cool and rot away, leaving little more than the frame of the orangery which scarred the Chandos lawn.

The others began to chat amongst themselves, and Grandfather turned to whisper to me, "The only question I have now is whether the killer hoped to destroy Bobbie's book or we were his main target."

CHAPTER THIRTY-FOUR

By the time the others had returned to the house for a change of clothes and some breakfast, the sun was high above the mountains and Grandfather and I sat alone on one of the upturned boats.

"I really am very proud of you, boy," he said in a sombre tone. He wasn't looking at me. He'd found the small portrait I'd retrieved from the hut, and his eyes traced over its fine brushstrokes, as though he were repainting it in his mind. "You saved Morwenna from the fire."

It took me a moment to understand what he meant. "Is that her?"

He nodded, and I found myself copying his careful examination. Morwenna was looking straight at us from the afterlife, a smile on her lips and her auburn hair full of light. For a moment, I felt that I knew her just a fraction better. It was easy to understand why a girl with such joy inside her could still be so important long after her death.

"Bobbie was always painting when we were children. He was really quite good." He shook his head wearily. "I suppose that's why I took it up this year; old rivalries never die."

His sadness, which normally only ever came out in flashes, had reared to the surface. I stood closer to my grandfather to comfort him, but didn't know what to say.

Seconds passed before he repeated his quiet exclamation. "You saved Morwenna from the fire."

To save me from saying something inappropriate, Constables Jim and Phil arrived at that moment. They had brought along another officer. He had sergeant's stripes on his shoulders and was a little taller than Jim and a little shorter than Phil. When they stood in a line together, they looked like a set of stairs.

"Ah, deek at that effort, eh?" the sergeant said, folding his arms across his chest in disillusion as he took in the damage that the night had wrought. He spoke in the same local dialect that the constables had used. I think I could make out a preposition, but the rest of the words were beyond me.

Grandfather went to stand beside him. "Yes, it's a terrible state of affairs."

"Some donnat's made a right maff of it. It's in a gay ole scrow."

Lord Edgington breathed out expressively. "True, true. But at least no one was hurt. And the important thing is that I have all the information I need to identify the Duke's killer. Would you like me to tell you now?"

The white-haired sergeant was suddenly lost for words and looked to his men for help.

Jim stepped forward to explain the situation. "Well, guvnor. You see, the thing is…" He waited for Phil to take up the task.

"Yes, milordship, the thing is, Sergeant Massey came all this way, special like, to see you in action. We told him we had a celebrity here, so he drove up the mountain cos we thought you were going to put on a show for us."

"If it's not too much trouble," Jim added.

"A show?" Grandfather sounded perplexed.

"That's right, guvnor. You know the sort of thing, laying out the evidence and telling us how you got to the truth, without revealing exactly who the killer is until the very last moment. That sort of thing."

Grandfather whistled softly. I could tell he wasn't nearly as reluctant as he wanted us to believe. "Oh, very well then. I'll send Todd to round up everyone in the house and bring them here."

"Cushty barie," the senior officer said with two thumbs up.

"I wouldn't get too excited just yet, Sergeant Massey. We'll have to convince the suspects to leave their breakfast behind and I can't imagine they'll be too eager for that."

Still working to salvage what he could from the fire, Todd heard his instructions and shot off towards the house. Grandfather sat down on the boat, only to jump straight back up again.

"What a brilliant idea," he said, grabbing the old green vessel and flipping it over with surprising ease.

I thought I might know what he had in mind, so I helped drag a few more boats to the shore and we checked the hulls for cracks. I had to imagine that they'd once been used by the Atwell family on sunny days such as this one. Boating lakes were quite the thing in Victorian times and the Chandos Grove estate came with one ready-made.

"Grandfather, can you tell me what you discovered last night?" I asked as I pushed the first boat into the water.

"There were a number of important points, but first and foremost I discovered that it was not one single chapter that the killer removed from the book but the whole period of our youth." I failed to see the relevance, but he was clearly impressed by this fact. "You see, I'd assumed somehow that it would have been Elodie's, Star's or Philomena's chapter missing, but it was all three. It rather proves my theory, don't you agree?"

"Oh, absolutely," I lied.

By the time we'd found oars for the boats, and checked that they still floated, the rest of our party had started to arrive.

The Professor came over to talk to us in a noticeably furtive manner. "I wanted to apologise for last night, old chap." He addressed the comment to his friend but glanced about at the scene. "We both said things we didn't mean and, I'm sure I'm in some way to blame for that."

Grandfather was rarely interested in apologies and addressed a more significant issue. "Does that mean you're ready to admit your lies?"

The Professor huffed and fidgeted but still would not comply. "I've said what I have to on that matter. I just thought it would be a good idea to clear the air."

"There are no hard feelings on my part, Prof. But you must understand that the truth will soon be revealed." I caught something in his words that I couldn't quite identify. Some beseeching note, which made me wonder about the Professor's involvement in the twin mysteries we'd been investigating.

Philomena and Elodie were the next to arrive and seemed quite charmed by the idea of a leisurely boat trip.

"I trust it's not a trap this time?" Elodie joked, and I could tell that some of the anger she'd held onto had finally ebbed away.

"And I trust you've learnt how to swim in the intervening years?" Grandfather had a twinkle in his eyes as he helped her into the boat which Todd had already boarded.

"What happened to Bobbie's hut?" Philomena enquired. She was apparently the only one to find it strange that we were heading out on the lake after surviving a minor disaster.

"It was just an electrical fire. Nothing to worry about." Grandfather was the master of the nonchalant wave. "You know how these modern appliances are. An electric kettle may sound like a wonderful invention in principle, but in practice, one faulty wire transforms it into a ticking bomb."

Even Stuart, who had seen the force of the fire first hand, was unconcerned and jumped into the quaint red rowing boat for his mother to join him. "This does look like fun. I was something of a rower at Oxford. I never made the team, but I could give most of the fellas there a run for their money."

Deborah and Ariadne, who appeared to be on the path to friendship, were the last to join us. Looking more than a little apprehensive, Deborah got into the boat with her fake fiancé and Ariadne made it clear that I would be with her.

"I'll be rowing," she said, and I thought it best not to argue.

"Grandfather, are you sure this is a good idea?" I asked, before I climbed inside. It wasn't just the water I was afraid of – though swimming, remember, is not my strong suit. "Won't it be difficult to catch the killer if he decides to row off?"

"I have my reasons, Chrissy." He thought for a moment, then reassured me with a gentle tap on my shoulder. "And besides, should our culprit attempt to get away, the police are on hand. We have nothing to fear."

I looked at the three men who had each taken a boat of their own. They were having trouble working out which end was the bow and which the stern. It did not fill me with confidence over their ability to apprehend a devious murderer.

Grandfather let out three high-pitched whistles, and we waited for a moment before Delilah came bounding through the garden gate and all the way over to us. She jumped on board his vessel as though she'd known all along that we'd be going boating that morning.

"Off we go then." Lord Edgington's voice boomed across the water and up the slopes of Chandos Valley. His words were met with a cheer from the other rowers, and he pushed his boat out into the water and climbed aboard.

I must say, I was surprised when, instead of launching into a speech, the ex-officer lay back in his boat to relax and allowed the momentum he'd built up to carry him across the glass-like surface. The others chattered happily, and even tight-laced Philomena seemed most relaxed by the excursion.

"We should have done this as soon as we arrived," the slightly terrifying society dame said with great peace in her voice. "If only Bobbie were here to see us all."

"I remember doing the very same thing our first year here," Elodie added, and the two women smiled across at one another.

I got the impression that Stuart was showing off just how fast and strong he was. He kept circling Deborah's boat and the poor Professor got in quite a muddle with the oars.

"I think you have to use both at the same time, Samson," she explained. "Otherwise, we'll go around in circles all day."

"Thank you, my heart." He already sounded out of breath. "As with so many things in this life, I know the theory, but the practice is another matter altogether."

Despite the lake being large by most – if not Lake District – standards, we stayed together in a messy grouping as we made our way from the shore. It was a still day. The sun had burnt the clouds away, spots of light glittered on the surface of the water like floating diamonds, and I was again reminded me of an impressionist painting I'd once seen.

"I don't suppose we'll ever know what happened to Bobbie now," Elodie said in an airy, mournful voice.

"Oh, I wouldn't say that." Grandfather sat up to get his boat moving again and glided alongside his former fiancée. "One of us is a killer. We can't just wander back home as though nothing has happened."

I was watching for Philomena's reaction; it did not disappoint. Her owlish eyes peered across the water to fix on my grandfather. "You know who's responsible, don't you?"

"Yes, indeed."

As though it was a flat, smooth stone that Ariadne had skimmed, her vision jumped back to the shore from where we'd departed, and I could tell that she regretted her decision to join us.

"So this is a trap after all." Her voice was as dry as old leaves before a bonfire.

"I wouldn't say that." Grandfather's contentment was pronounced, even for him. "I merely thought you would enjoy one last adventure together before we disband for good."

With this announcement, the atmosphere changed. It might sound odd to suggest that – out in the open, with all those hectares of blue sky above us – there would be a tangible mood to identify, but, I swear, something in the air changed. In a moment, it felt as though the temperature had dropped by five degrees.

The two constables and their sergeant had discovered how boats work just in time for the start of Grandfather's speech.

"The fact is, any one of us could have murdered dear old Bobbie… myself included."

"Oh, how exciting," Stuart said, somewhat tactlessly for a man I had found to be the soul of propriety until then. "I do so love it when a master detective holds a secret over everyone."

"May I please go first?" Elodie waved her hand through the air to get my grandfather's attention.

He rowed away from her with a disconcerted air about him. "What do you mean, 'go first'?"

She showed no embarrassment over the matter. "If any one of us could be the killer, tell me what evidence you found to suggest I'm the guilty party."

Grandfather looked up at the sky as though he were checking for rain. "I believe we've been through all that. You were vile to Ariadne for one thing, presumably because you were afraid she'd disclose your secret. The secret that you and Bobbie had continued an intermittent affair since you were in your twenties. By all reports, you wished to marry him, but he wouldn't leave Chandos behind. As I'm sure you soon discovered, this is a lovely place to spend the summer, but not suited to someone of your character come the cooler months."

As though as to prove his point, Elodie gave Todd a hungry smile as the strapping young chap continued his rhythmic movement with the oars. Happy to make us all wait, she eventually turned back to my grandfather. "So why would that make me want to kill him?"

Lord Edgington was himself quite adept with his navigation and charted a large circle around the group. "You tell me. Why did you lie about it?"

Elodie bit her lip coquettishly. "You know why… I wanted you to feel bad about leaving me all those years ago. I thought if you'd known about me and Bobbie, it wouldn't have had nearly so much impact." She looked about at the other boats. "The truth is that I may not have a husband or children of my own, but I've had a simply wonderful life. I have dined with princes, been chased by Prime Ministers and woken up everywhere from palaces to park benches. I have no regrets over any of it."

"Good for you, old bean," the Professor said with a cheer.

"And you knew about all of it, Prof?" Grandfather timed his strokes to arrive alongside him as he delivered this line.

"I might have done."

"In fact, the one thing I couldn't make sense of as I carried out my investigation was how you could all know so much about one another given that we've barely crossed paths in all these years."

Every last member of their group looked dazed just then, as though he had uncovered some terrible secret. He spun the boat around in a sudden, dramatic movement so that he could address the lot of them at once. "Now, tell me the truth. Why have you all been lying?"

CHAPTER THIRTY-FIVE

There was a truly torturous silence just then, and I wondered who would be the first to break. I don't know if intense staring is a technique that they teach in the Metropolitan Police academy, but my grandfather's gaze was more forceful a weapon than any pistol or club.

It was the Professor who eventually melted under the pressure. "We didn't want to upset you!" he wailed out and Elodie hissed for him to be quiet.

"What on earth do you mean?"

The three policemen, who had kept their distance until now, came closer to hear.

Philomena was happy to provide an explanation. "It's nothing personal, Reprobus. We just continued to meet up from time to time without inviting you."

"What on earth do you mean?" He said once more for luck. His voice had risen a semitone, and his eyes were too big for his head.

"Well, you were such a misery, always gibbering on about Morwenna and justice, that we decided it would be preferable if we didn't see you anymore. If it makes you feel any better, Bobbie didn't come either."

Grandfather tried to suppress the response, but it finally burst out of him. "Thank you, Mimi, but that doesn't make me feel better in the slightest."

"I still like you, Grandfather. Even if no one else does," I said, in the hope it might comfort him. I don't think it did the trick as he continued to pour out his rage.

"I've spent my whole life imagining that you were my loyal and treasured friends only to discover-"

"I'll go next," Ariadne interrupted him, and I was awfully glad she did. She hadn't made a peep until then, but had been listening attentively throughout. "I don't like this game, but I'd rather you get it over with. Tell me why you think I could have killed Daddy."

Grandfather's anger subsided, and his face crumpled up with compassion. "I don't think that you killed him, Ariadne. I never have."

"You can still tell me why it might look that way. I want to know."

Lord Edgington turned to me for confirmation; but the decision had already been made.

"The will, my child. When I gave it to the Professor to read, I retained a second envelope with your name on. The note inside spoke of a letter which was to be handed to you in the event of Bobbie's death. But that letter wasn't in the envelope when I opened it and I believe it must be in your possession."

Her gaze fell to the waterline on Stuart's boat, which had come to a stop alongside my own. He had given up on impressing Deborah and looked just as gripped as the rest of us.

When Ariadne didn't respond, Grandfather continued. "I believe that Bobbie wrote the letter to affirm his biological paternity. I know you grew up believing that the Chandos Village baker was your father, but anyone who has seen photos of Bobbie as a child would know that wasn't true. You look just like him."

There were tears in Ariadne's eyes when she spoke. "Yes, I have it. I found it a year ago when I was exploring the house. It didn't change how I felt about him. If anything, I loved him more. I would never have killed him to get his money."

"Of course you wouldn't." It was my Grandfather's turn to hesitate. "But there were other factors I was forced to consider. You were the one who led me to the body in the first place, and you also revealed Elodie's relationship with your father. You must forgive my suspicious nature, but this did make me wonder if you were trying to distance yourself from the crime."

She tried to speak again, but no words would come. I put my hand out to comfort her, and she fell backwards into my lap. I wrapped both my arms around her and wouldn't let go. I felt such tenderness in that moment, such compassion, that I thought I might just know what love means after all. We would stay like that until it was time to row back again, and I would remain with her for just as long as she needed me.

"Let's move things along, shall we?" Philomena was the only one there who appeared unmoved by what we'd witnessed. She looked at my grandfather with her usual prodding stare. "Feel free to list my many sins." She smirked at this, as though any such transgressions could only be found in the mind of a pedant.

"By all means, dear Mimi." Loosening his shoulders, Grandfather propelled his boat back into the centre of the cluster. "We've all known

210

your motive from the start. In fact, I think you've gloried in your role as the likely culprit."

She scoffed at this, but turned one finger in circles for him to continue.

"That's right. You were the one who saw her life so clearly when we were young, but it all went wrong. You claimed yesterday that Bobbie ended your engagement, and I couldn't understand why you would have bent the truth. We all knew what happened after the fire in the orangery. The papers talked of little else for weeks. It was your parents who made you abandon him, though I doubt it took much persuading. In all my years rubbing shoulders with aristocrats and otherwise, I've rarely met another person who cared so deeply about status and scandal as you do. So why did you lie?"

She found her voice once more. "You and your rhetorical questions, Reprobus. You know full well why I changed the facts, and yet you insist on this mummery. I heard such wonderful things about the legendary Superintendent Edgington, but you're still playing games, just like when you were a boy."

The old man wasn't intimidated and continued with his well-rehearsed routine. "You lied because you would rather I thought you heartbroken over a man who deserted you, than jealous of a life that should have been yours."

I couldn't see the logic to this, as they both sounded fairly damning in the context of a murder investigation. Luckily, my grandfather was there to explain the difference.

"The first case may be pathetic. It might even have driven a lesser woman to kill, but you aren't the sentimental type, my dearest Mimi. We all know you should have been the lady of this beautiful estate. And I can quite imagine you sticking a golden dagger through Bobbie's heart to punish him for what he denied you."

"Except of course that I didn't kill him!" The sentence was one unbroken cry and, for the first time that weekend, I saw that she was capable of genuine emotion. It was not the hollow look of concern that she had feigned so often or the cynical disdain that normally flowed from her, but pure, inimitable fear.

Grandfather gave her a moment to recover before revealing the truth. "That's right, you didn't. I'm sure there have been times in your life when you wish that you could have, but there are more important things to Lady Philomena Fontaine than revenge. The slightest whiff of scandal had already derailed your life once, you wouldn't dare get caught up in another murder."

I think we all registered these last two words he had delivered. They sent a ripple across the surface of the lake and the faces of his audience. But there were more revelations to come.

"Lady Fontaine is many things. She is a sophisticated character assassin, a backroom operator, a scandalmonger and a politician in every sense of the word, but she had no hand in Bobbie's death."

I admit, while I didn't have a clear sense of anything that had been going on for the last day or so, if I'd been forced to pick a culprit, I would most certainly have gone for Philomena. That lady scared me.

As the tension that had built between the two elders faded away, a tentative smile formed on Stuart's lips. "What about me then?"

"Oh, do shut up, Stuart," his mother spat. "Nobody cares."

Like a kicked puppy, he sprung back from her. I was sorely tempted to row closer to them and give his mother a poke in the ribs and poor Stuart a friendly pat on the back. I didn't of course. For one thing, I hadn't the first idea how to row a boat.

Grandfather opted for a gentler response. "Well, you're Philomena's son for one thing. That was enough to keep your name on my list of suspects for quite some time – even if you were there with me just minutes after the Duke was last seen alive."

Stuart nodded and looked back at his mother, who was still reeling from her time in the limelight. He pouted his lips slightly, and I could see that he wanted to forgive her. I suppose that sons love their mothers no matter how cruel they can be.

The hush that had descended wouldn't hold. The possible falcon was above us in the bright sky again and, as it let out its discordant cry, a murmur of speculation ignited. I suppose that everyone had done the simple sums and eliminated each of the relevant suspects, thus leaving just two possible names. Well, three including Mabel the maid. After all, she didn't have an alibi and was the last person to see the Duke alive. But, as she wasn't in a boat on the lake just then, it seemed safe to assume she wasn't the killer.

More slowly this time, Grandfather cut his oars through the water and turned to face Deborah and the Professor.

212

CHAPTER THIRTY-SIX

"My good friend Professor Samson Filigree not only discovered Bobbie's dead body, floating face down on the lake, he removed the murder weapon and tampered with evidence at the scene of the crime." Grandfather came to a sudden halt and stared at the accused. "Or perhaps that's what you wanted me to think."

We'd already been through these accusations with the Professor, and so it was Deborah I watched. She had the same panicked look that she'd displayed for most of the previous day but, this time, her fear went deeper. She clawed at her companion, as if begging him to row away.

Like the Phantom of the Opera, gliding through his underground lake, there was a glint of evil on my distinguished ancestor's face as he delivered his next line of attack. "It is quite the most convoluted alibi I could imagine a killer constructing, but what if you took the knife in order to make me think you had just arrived on the scene and were covering up for someone else?"

"You've lost the plot again, Reprobus." The Professor gently moved the boat around to put himself between Deborah and the retired policeman. "Why would I have killed Bobbie?"

"For the very reason I've said since the beginning. For our little Star. The girl you loved; perhaps the only girl you've ever loved."

The Professor was incensed, his stout cheeks turning red as he tightened every muscle in his body to reply. "Will you stop this! How many times do I have to tell you? Deborah is my-"

"Yes, Deborah is your fiancée and you are very much in love." Grandfather, meanwhile, maintained his signature calm. "I know; we all know. And that's why you brought her with you."

"That's right."

"And why you tried to hide her involvement when she killed our friend."

"Yes... no!" His change of response was almost immediate. A gasp went up from the other boats as we strove to understand whether this was a genuine confession or the result of my grandfather's manipulation. "No, I didn't move the murder weapon. I didn't throw the tea set in the water, and I didn't mean to touch anything in the hut.

You've got it all wrong."

Deborah had turned into a stone garden ornament of a pretty blonde fairy or a heron and couldn't move an inch. It suddenly occurred to me that we had never taken the time to interview her as a suspect. I had to wonder if this was an oversight on my grandfather's part or he knew just what he was doing. Obviously, I should never have doubted him.

His questions were coming faster now. "Remind me, Prof, what kind of rocks do we get in these parts?"

He glanced over his shoulder for help. "I told you, I'm no geologist. That's Deborah's field of expertise."

"So then, why is she working as your research assistant? Your focus is philosophy these days, isn't that right?"

Despite being a supremely learned man, the Professor was not prepared for this inquisition and struggled to compose a convincing response. "Well... that's the one thing we lied about. She's not really my assistant. We made it up so that we could disclose the nature of our relationship after you'd got to know her. I met Deborah at the university, where she really does work as a geology research assistant. I saw her contribute to a talk at the Sedgwick Club and I was smitten."

Grandfather looked across at me, as though to say, "That's the first lie I've caught him in; there are more to come." With a few quick thrusts of the oars he had drawn his boat parallel to theirs so that Deborah could no longer hide from him.

"Tell me," he said out loud. "Are you not at all worried about marrying a much older man?"

She wanted to find the right response, but stuttered over the words. "I've never... No. Of course not."

"And what exactly is the age difference between the two of you?"

There was no hiding the fact that she was entirely uncertain of the answer and had to give her companion a quick look before muttering, "Fifty-six years."

The Professor let out a groan, but Grandfather ignored him. "So that would make you... nineteen?"

"No... I'm twenty-seven. I meant to say that age is not something to which we give much importance." She was getting more flustered with each question. "I don't like this pressure. I don't like being interrogated."

He didn't let up. "And what about your parents? What do they think

214

of you marrying a man who's old enough to be your grandfather?"

"I never knew my parents." A dry rasp had entered her voice.

Lord Edgington pounced on her answer. "Until this weekend when you met your father?"

It was clear to everyone watching what her silence meant. Grandfather had plugged the holes in her porous tale.

"How did you know?" the Professor said to confirm the theory. "Who told you?"

Grandfather relinquished the oars and leaned back to enjoy himself once more. "Nobody told me. It was clear from the very first time I saw her. Just as I knew the same thing when I met Ariadne and Mabel the maid. Bobbie's reputation wasn't inspired by rumour and hearsay. It was based on the fact he was an incorrigible rogue and could charm even the smartest of women. There were bound to be illegitimate offspring about the place. It was the only thing that could explain him hiring a maid who refuses to do any work and taking in an orphan who just happens to look the same as he did as a child."

Ariadne opened her eyes as these revelations sank in. It was hard to tell if she was pleased by the news, but all of a sudden, she wasn't alone in the world. She had two sisters (at the very least).

Grandfather turned his attention to Deborah, who remained oddly lifeless. "When I found the early photographs of Bobbie's mother upstairs, it only confirmed what I believed. You're practically her double, my dear. Your grandmother was a rare beauty and not the kind of person I can easily forget. And so, I came to suspect that you'd killed your father in the hope of inheriting Chandos Grove. After all, you couldn't have known there were any other heirs around."

"I'm sorry if I'm a little slow," Elodie interrupted. "But how does any of this tie in with the missing dagger and the tea set in the lake?"

"It all ties in with Deborah," Grandfather replied, still too vaguely to be useful. "I can only assume that the Professor spotted her at Cambridge and remembered Lady Chandos's stunning blonde locks, aquiline nose and pale blue eyes just as well as I do. He knew he'd found the rightful successor to the estate."

Elodie remained confused. "No, sorry. I'm still none the wiser. You haven't explained why any sot would go anywhere near a murder weapon."

Grandfather smiled a gentle smile before explaining. He regarded his old friends, and I could see the warmth he still felt for each of them. "The Prof was more than unlucky to stumble across the body on his morning walk. He saw the two teacups on the desk and the spots of blood in the office and he knew something was wrong."

Grandfather moved the boat a few strokes backwards to look at the Professor, who remained close lipped. "When the Prof found Bobbie's corpse outside the hut, his first thought was that *he* was to blame. He may not have held the knife, but by bringing Deborah to Chandos, by encouraging her to introduce herself to her father and stake her claim to the estate, he set about a chain of events that would lead to murder.

"He thought fast; he removed the teapot and second cup in case of fingerprints. He must have heard us approaching at that point and hurried to conceal the knife. It was a rash, foolish act, but typical of my warm-hearted friend. He couldn't bear the thought of a young girl being punished for the anger she felt towards her long-absent father, and so he did what he could to protect her."

I'd been trapped within the story, and the silence that followed it was jarring. Deborah was yet to break from her rigid pose. Her eyes were fixed on the horizon as though, by not moving, she might freeze time forever and never face the consequences of the terrible summer's day she had lived through.

The Professor had appeared paralysed throughout the conversation. It was time for him to put things right, and he finally summoned the courage to tell the truth.

"I feel like such an imbecile. I've lied and betrayed my friends, but I couldn't see another way out. Everything I did buried me deeper in the hole that I had dug."

There were sad faces all around, as our understanding of events became a little clearer. Never one to go along with popular sentiment, Grandfather let out an abrupt laugh. "Gosh, don't be so hard on yourself, man. You're not the first of my friends to fob me off with a tall tale. It can't be easy spending time with the 'legendary Superintendent Edgington'." He directed these last few words at Philomena, who was still perplexed by the details of exactly what had occurred to her onetime love.

"Are you saying that Deborah murdered Bobbie or not? You seem awfully cheerful about the whole situation, Reprobus."

"No, of course she didn't. She'd come to meet her father for the first time. What would have driven her to kill him as soon as they were alone together? There would have been nothing to suspect if Samson hadn't bumbled across the body and interfered with everything."

The Professor coughed in disbelief. "I know I'm a fool, but Deborah had told me she wanted to talk to her father yesterday morning and the next thing I knew, he was dead. I should have told you what I'd done, but I was the one who brought her here. For most of yesterday, I believed his murder was my fault."

Grandfather had lost his insistent tone. "So was I right about everything else? When I considered whether you were the killers, I had to assume you were after Bobbie's fortune, but did you really just bring Deborah here to meet her father?"

Though clearly affected by the emotional storm he'd passed through, the Professor could now speak the truth. "I thought that introducing her to Bobbie was the right thing to do. When we met at the geology society talk, it was as though Lady Chandos had returned from the dead. Deborah told me about her childhood and the fact she'd never known her real parents, and all the pieces fitted into place. When I received the invitation from Bobbie, I knew that I should bring her."

The numb silence which followed placed an exclamation mark on the curious tale. To be perfectly honest, I couldn't make head nor tail of what had happened. From what I could tell, nobody had murdered the Duke after all.

The Professor addressed my grandfather, his eyes pleading for an explanation. "If you knew all this, why did you put us through such misery?"

"My apologies, dear friend." The old chap sounded quite sincere at least. "I meant no harm, but I needed to be certain. And you can't say I didn't give you enough chances to tell the truth. I knew you were lying but, as I've told my grandson from the beginning, that didn't make you killers."

"Well, wait one minute," Stuart interrupted, his hands coming to a rest and his oars falling still. "If Deborah didn't do it, who on earth killed the Duke?"

217

CHAPTER THIRTY-SEVEN

Grandfather beamed across at his audience, luxuriating in the moment. His boat had drifted away from the rest of us and he held it steady in the water. The three police officers had moved even closer and were enraptured by the renowned detective's performance. The only sound they made was an occasional gasp at each new revelation.

Grandfather looked at me then. "Christopher, would you like to explain what really happened?"

"Um, no thank you." I didn't need to think long about my answer. "I haven't a clue who the killer is, and I'm not going to pretend otherwise."

"You wouldn't like to guess?" He stretched the words out and raised one eyebrow.

"Ummmm… Mabel the maid?"

"No." He laughed once more. "But that's all right, my boy. You've been invaluable throughout the investigation. You're still learning and can't be expected to spot every killer we come across (the number of which is surprisingly high!)." He didn't say these last seven words, though he probably should have.

He took a deep breath and started in on the final chapter of the saga of Chandos Grove. "Everything I have told you until now has focused on the events of this weekend. I've done my best to consider who Bobbie was when he died. He was a father to Ariadne, a chaser of cats and a sardine connoisseur. We all had our connections to him, but they weren't enough to explain his violent demise.

"The truth is that two murders occurred on this estate. The first was Morwenna Fairbright's, fifty-seven years ago, and the second was Bobbie's own, yesterday morning. But without the first, it is very unlikely the second would ever have occurred. Christopher told me yesterday that it was acceptable for me to be human. As Alexander Pope taught us, 'to err is human', to which I would respond, that to be human is to err."

"Grandfather, you're waffling."

He cast an unimpressed glance at me, and I decided not to say anything else.

"My point is that all those years ago, I made a grave mistake. I broke one of the first rules of police work and condemned a man based on my emotion at the time rather than hard evidence. The injustice I witnessed convinced me to become a police officer, but it also forced my friends away and drove a wedge through our group. I refused to relinquish the belief that Bobbie was a killer because I viewed Morwenna's death as the beginning of my story. It was this event which made me, so, if I was wrong, who would I be?"

Perhaps this wasn't a rhetorical question, but no one responded. I'd already taken a vow of silence, so he wasn't going to trick me into saying something stupid. I noticed that he was doing what he did whenever he had something taxing to consider; he was pacing up and down. As we were not on dry land, he performed this feat using the oars of his boat. He propelled himself a few yards along the lake in one direction and then back the other way.

"As I confirmed when I read his memoir this morning. Bobbie was not a killer," he said, propelling himself along in one direction. "The first page of his book bears the immortal line from John Keats, "Bright star, would I were steadfast as thou art", and the more I read of his narrative last night, the clearer it was that the book and his whole life were a tribute to the girl he had loved for so long. Our *Bright Star.* Our little Morwenna who died in the orangery fire."

He turned the boat and went back the other way. "His account of those years was torn out by the killer, but the effect of that tragedy is felt on every page. Unlike the rest of us, Bobbie had known Star from the time they were babies. As the daughter of the Chandos Grove gamekeeper, she had been allowed to play in the grounds and the two grew up as equals. When his parents arranged his marriage to a member of the Fontaine family, there was nothing he could do about it, but that didn't stop him from loving Morwenna."

He fell quiet for a moment and allowed his own emotions to float to the surface. When he finally spoke, I think there was even the gleam of a tear in one eye. "Though a significant section of his memoirs is missing, it is possible to piece together the events of Morwenna's last night on Earth. They met in the orangery as they often did. She had fallen asleep, and Bobbie returned to the house before the fire started. He attempted to extinguish the blaze, but the wind was strong and it was beyond his control. It consumed the glass structure in minutes and by the time he got to the woman he loved, she was already dead."

I held Ariadne a little tighter as we listened to the sad tale. My Grandfather's eyes scanned the mountains as though searching for his lost friends.

"The only other detail I could find was his conviction that he'd seen someone standing in the shadows by the garden walls on the night of the fire. He said this person was kissed by the flames as he or she watched his dreams burn to the ground, and it took me some time to work out what he meant."

All of his urgency from a few minutes earlier had faded. He spoke in slow, dolorous sentences as though he were addressing a congregation at a funeral. "In the book, he explains that he lied about his love for Morwenna because he thought it would incriminate him. He invented a story and stuck with it for all these years. But he planned to reveal everything this weekend. He was tired of lying and ready to reveal the truth."

All of a sudden, he looked back up at us, and his speech came out in bullets. "If the two murders were connected, I was back to the same few suspects. Mimi, Lala and the Prof. I always thought Elodie too self-centred to care about anyone enough to murder them and I've yet to be proved wrong."

Elodie raised her hand as though toasting him. "Your words mean so much, my dear friend."

Grandfather wouldn't be distracted. "You didn't like Morwenna, but you had no reason just then to hate her and it was only later that your relationship with Bobbie began. In fact, of all of us, you may be the only one to whom he told the truth."

"Yes, I knew about his time with Morwenna. He never stopped loving her; it was one of the things which drove us apart. Even fifty years later, he insisted on rehashing the same sob stories. Every time I visited, I hoped that the charming rascal we'd known in our youth would be here to greet me. But he never was."

"So, only two names left," Grandfather said, his chin rising at the possibility. "Philomena was the obvious choice. We all know what she lost when she couldn't marry into the Chandos line. Perhaps she discovered the truth about Bobbie and Star and wanted to get rid of the competition."

"You said that I wasn't a killer," Philomena was quick to point out.

"No, I said you didn't kill Bobbie. There's a difference. But, while I couldn't dismiss your involvement out of hand, I decided that revenge was far too simple a motive for such a complicated woman and I moved on once more."

There was a pause as he stopped his pacing and turned the boat to chart another circle around the group. The three policemen chattered amongst themselves as though commenting on a play at the theatre. Again, I didn't understand every word they said; but they appeared to have enjoyed what they'd seen.

"My dear Samson, a scholar among scholars, had loved Morwenna ever since they first met. She was the kind one amongst us – the one with the biggest heart – and perhaps the Prof couldn't stand to see her with such an unfeeling scoundrel as Bobbie."

He allowed the silence to settle once more. A trout came to the surface beside our boat and then hid below again. A single cloud made its way into view and, somewhere along the valley, a deer released a drawn-out warning call. This was the game that Grandfather was playing; making us sweat, making us wait; making us wonder what mastery of thought he had produced to get to the final answer.

When his voice came back to us, it was gentler than before. "I am human and I'd made another mistake. I'd treated the murders as two separate mysteries when I was actually dealing with one single puzzle. But there was little chance of proving what happened to Morwenna all that time ago and so I re-examined Bobbie's death.

"We knew that he was alive at a half-past nine yesterday morning. Mabel saw him slumped, snoring over his papers when she delivered his can of sardines. Fifteen minutes later, the Prof went for his walk as Stuart and I took breakfast in the garden. As I sat there, I saw Philomena near the orangery. She'd been sitting on a bench in silence, partially obscured by the bushes ever since I'd arrived. She didn't see me, but I knew just where she was and I believe I know what she was thinking."

Elodie laughed at this. "You knew I was lying all along, you terrible man." She had a wicked smile then. "It was foolish of me, but I was sure that Bobbie's brat would tell you about my visits, and so I made up an alibi and forced Mimi to go along with it."

"I knew that the pair of you were lying, but I didn't know why. Fortunately though, there was no way you could have accessed the hut without passing through the garden after I heard your car pull up outside. Again, it is not the first time one of my friends has lied to me and I don't hold it against you." The pair smiled at one another again in that tolerant manner they'd adopted.

Grandfather returned to his summary. "Back in the garden, Deborah joined me a few minutes after Stuart had arrived. She was in no hurry and did not appear to be out of breath, so it did not appear as though she'd run to get there. Ariadne came looking for her father and we set off to Bobbie's hut."

"Grandfather," I said, despite myself. "You've just ruled out every last possibility. Are you saying that Bobbie wasn't murdered?"

"No, my boy," he replied, increasing the pace of his words once more. "I'm saying that Bobbie wasn't killed at the time we all assumed. I'm saying that he was already dead when Mabel went into his hut. She delivered the can but didn't go up to the desk. He was slumped forward, and she remembered seeing two teacups on the table in front of him."

"So the killer had already been and gone?" the Professor deduced. "The snoring was just a figment of the girl's imagination?"

"Not at all." That grin – that wonderful grin – straightened out my grandfather's moustache. "The killer was still in the hut, but had heard the less than light-footed maid stomping across the pebbles. He pushed his quarry forwards to conceal the wound and hid beneath the table to provide the audible evidence of Bobbie's slumber."

"But that still doesn't explain why we found the Duke's body in the lake." Another thought occurred to me. "Unless the Professor moved it?"

"Not quite. The Prof had no need to move the body, even if he believed that Deborah was to blame for the murder. And, yet it does explain why it happened. The murderer moved the lifeless corpse of the Duke of Chandos simply to suggest he hadn't died in his office. For us to believe that he'd been murdered sometime later, it was essential to confuse the timeline of events."

"For his own alibi?" Philomena suggested – she was clearly far cleverer than I was.

"Precisely."

I waited a moment and, as no one had offered an explanation, I put my hand up. "Sorry, Grandfather. Would you mind going through that one more time? I didn't quite follow everything."

He nodded and did as requested. "Of course, my boy, of course. But you needn't raise your hand, we're not in school now." I felt even sillier then. "The maid left. The killer saw his opportunity and dragged the body outside, then returned to the house in order to be seen at the moment that we thought that Bobbie was being murdered. If it had happened any later, the Professor would have seen the culprit getting away. After all, it takes time to have a spot of tea, confront an enemy, be stabbed to death and end up face down in the lake."

I scanned the faces of those present to understand what this now meant. Ariadne, Deborah and Stuart had all arrived moments after the killing.

"Furthermore, the killer had information to which we were not privy. He knew that the weapon had been removed by a third party and did what he could to deflect attention on to the Professor."

"So… it was…" I attempted, but I still couldn't pick one suspect.

"It was Ariadne all along," Stuart said, the shock plain on his face. My beloved instantly sat up, as though a shock of electricity had passed through her.

The only sound that followed was a crisp gasp from our witnesses until Grandfather replied. "No, Stuart. That's a fine attempt, but it wasn't Ariadne. It was you."

CHAPTER THIRTY-EIGHT

You could have heard a pin drop. Well, not on the water. That would have been too quiet, but if it had landed within the boat, you might just have... sorry, I'll get back to the story now.

"You were the one who went to great lengths to show us how much you suffer as your mother's put-upon secretary. In truth, of course, you worship her. You knew about Bobbie's book before any of us and calculated that it could put an end to her nascent political career. So you rose early yesterday morning to seek him out and went along to the hut to discuss your interest in the book. I imagine he discussed its focus, and you realised just how damaging its publication would be. Even if Bobbie hadn't identified your mother as Morwenna's killer, all the evidence was there.

"Bobbie and I were so consumed with our own misapprehensions of that night that we refused to consider who was really to blame. He bought into the belief that the whole thing was an accident and I was driven by the notion that he had got away with murder. But it was your mother who should have gone to gaol. Did she confess what she'd done or did you work it out for yourself?"

Mother and son stared at one another across their rowing boat as reality set in for them.

"Tell me, Stuart," Grandfather muttered. "Do you know the riddle of the prisoners in the black and white hats?"

Stuart couldn't reply. His guilt had disfigured his features and stolen his voice.

"There are three men in a line, each one wears one of two black or three white hats. They can only see the men in front of them, cannot remove the hats and must guess what colour their own is. The man at the front knows the correct answer and shouts it out. What colour is his hat?"

"White!" I attempted, as I love a good riddle.

Grandfather looked a bit put out. "How did you know that?"

"Oh, ummm. Law of probabilities, isn't it? There are more white hats than black."

He closed his eyes and shook his head. "No, Christopher. That is not the reason. The man at the front knows his hat is white as the other men have said nothing. If the man at the back sees two black hats, he knows that he has a white hat. He doesn't speak, so the others know that the he can see at least one white hat. If the man in the middle sees a black hat, he knows that his is white. When he doesn't speak, the answer is clear."

"I'm sorry," Philomena put in with all her usual superiority, despite the recent revelations. "Is there a point to any of this?"

His gaze drilling into her, he answered straight back. "The point is that I knew who killed Morwenna for the same reason. As soon as I realised that Stuart was to blame, it only made sense that he killed Bobbie to cover for your crime."

"That's cheating!" I said.

"Perhaps, but it doesn't matter because I was right. It may have been a simple motive for a complex woman, but Philomena killed Morwenna out of nothing but jealousy. Bobbie was going to marry her, but that wasn't enough; she wanted him for herself alone."

I noticed that the officers had been repositioning their boats to stop Stuart from getting away, and they now had him trapped.

"Don't expect me to apologise." When Philomena spoke, her arrogance was still there in her voice. "I saw them together – my future husband and that working-class trollop. I saw what they were doing, and I hated her with every fibre of my being. For the first and last time in my life, when Bobbie left the orangery, I lost control. I threw the lamp and stayed in the garden to watch the building burn. I wanted her to suffer, just as I had."

"You were the figure who Bobbie spotted there in his grief. It wasn't the flames gripping you. It was your red cape that he saw. Were you reliving that moment yesterday morning when he was killed? When your son followed in your footsteps to become a murderer?"

Stuart broke his silence, and his voice came out in a martyred wail. "It was the least I could do for her. She's worked her whole life to have her time in parliament. I wasn't going to let her potential slip away because of some disgusting old man's salacious musings."

"You killed for me, Stuart?" These were the first tender words I'd heard from Philomena that weekend. With her voice almost breaking, she reached out to touch his cheek. I suddenly found my own family to be very normal indeed.

"I've never held to the idea that behaviour is down to hereditary factors. But in this case, it may be true," Grandfather continued, unmoved by the compassion on display. "You both used me as an alibi. Philomena, you knew I would look for someone to blame when Morwenna died and your son made sure to be right there in front of me at the time that Bobbie was supposedly murdered."

Stuart glanced once at his mother and then around the circle of shocked faces who were all desperate to understand what had led him to kill. "I didn't go there to murder him. I went to persuade him not to publish the book, but he wouldn't listen. He was so smug, so terribly self-important, and I saw red. This was the man who should have been my father. I would have grown up in Chandos with Britain's industrial might at my disposal if it hadn't been for his petty love affair that ruined everything."

"How convenient to blame your victim for your cruelty!" Grandfather had reached the peak of his fury. "But it was your mother's actions that caused all of this, not Bobbie's."

His mother was still holding him as he spoke, still stroking his face with the gentle touch of a child with a new kitten.

He reached one hand out in front of him. "There was an old dagger on a stand on the desk and… It was just so easy. I was amazed how simple it was to kill a man."

He looked across at Deborah then, and I wondered if his feelings weren't entirely staged for our benefit after all. "When I heard the maid coming, I was sure she would realise something was wrong. My snoring was so over the top – so theatrical – but I could see her from under the desk and she barely looked at the Duke. She banged the sardines down by the door and turned back to the house."

His hands were shaking as he spoke and he looked at a point in the middle distance. "The door slammed shut, and it spurred me into life. I wiped my fingerprints off anything I knew I'd touched, which wasn't too much as Bobbie had opened all the doors and made the tea. I was afraid the maid would change her story when you interviewed her and so I moved the body. I walked through the grove to get back into the house and sat down to breakfast as fast as I could. It all happened in a few minutes and then I was chatting with you in the garden as though nothing had happened."

My Grandfather stood up in his boat, and I thought for one moment that he might walk across the water back to the shore. "There are no excuses for what you did – no mitigating circumstances. I have gone through my life without physically assaulting another person. I have stared into the eyes of the despicable individual who murdered several members of my own family, and yet I resisted the urge to seek revenge. So forgive me if I can summon no sympathy for a woman who was ruled by jealousy and a man who killed for little more than his mother's good opinion."

"Despicable is the word." The Professor's voice came out in a furious rumble.

Ariadne turned away from the treacherous pair, and I held her as she whimpered. Even Deborah and I, who were surely the outsiders in the group, couldn't hide our feelings entirely.

It was Philomena who eventually broke the deadlock. She turned to my grandfather and addressed him in an absurdly polite voice. "Reprobus, I have always considered you the most sanctimonious hypocrite, and your display here today has done nothing to change that. To the rest of you, I have enjoyed our friendship, but think nothing of the revulsion you no doubt feel towards me." She lowered her hands to her son's neatly ironed shirt and took hold of it. "Stuart, I have tried to instil within you the same determination that has driven me. What you did for me yesterday is the greatest compliment I could wish for, and I am proud of you."

"Mother," he began, as diamond-shaped tears appeared in the corner of his eyes. "Of course, I-"

He didn't have the time to finish the sentence as, with all her strength, his mother rolled them over the side of the boat and into the water. My grandfather was prepared for this and foolishly dived in after them, screaming, "Todd, with me!" as he went. Delilah was the first to join him, of course, but could do little more than paddle around their boat ineffectively as our chauffeur disappeared into the depths.

The three officers looked back and forth at one another, trying to work out if it was their responsibility to do the same.

"We should get the dog," Phil concluded, and they paddled round to rescue Delilah.

It was oddly quiet as we looked for some sign of where the others had gone. A few irregular bubbles came up in patches here and there, but time ticked by and there was nothing to say they would make it back up again. My head was filled with the sight of my grandfather, trapped in the weeds at the bottom of the lake, fighting for breath as Philomena held him down.

Todd was the first to re-emerge. There was a nervous second, which seemed to last an hour, and then Grandfather joined him. Both panted for breath before shooting beneath the water once more. This time, a discussion fired up about what we were witnessing.

"They must have sighted them," the Professor conjectured.

Elodie was on her knees in the boat, peering down into the water. "Or perhaps they're still looking and simply needed more air."

"They don't deserve to die here," Ariadne said, her whole body shaking as though she had plunged into the water and probed its icy deeps. "Stuart and his mother – they deserve long drawn-out punishments. This is too quick."

A great splash went up on the other side of the lake from where we'd all been looking and four sodden heads broke the surface. Todd held Stuart, who was fighting against his rescuer, and perhaps still hoped to swim to freedom. Supported by my grandfather, Philomena Fontaine wasn't moving.

With Elodie and the Professor's help, they got her onto one of the free boats while Todd pulled Stuart to the shore. His clothes dripping with water, Grandfather pulled himself onto the boat to see to Philomena.

"Is she breathing?" Deborah asked, before bravely stepping across to aid in resuscitation.

Perhaps it was the movement of the boat in the water, or Philomena's unceasing attachment to life, but she suddenly jerked over onto her side and spat the water from her lungs. A cheer went up, and I found myself genuinely relieved that she was alive. The policemen joined in with the clapping, and a moment later, Philomena was sitting up, able to breathe.

"I'm so glad you're all right," Grandfather told her in a soft, almost respectful tone. "I do so hate it when people go unpunished for their crimes."

She shook her head and coughed out another mouthful of brackish water. "Damn you, Edgington." She threw one hand into the air in anger. "In fact, damn you all."

CHAPTER THIRTY-NINE

Once we'd got the formalities with the police out of the way and everyone had dried off, it no longer made a great deal of sense to stay in Chandos Grove any longer. Grandfather told me to pack my things, which was easy, as I'd never found the time to unpack.

"Are we going home?" I asked, rather disappointed to have our holiday cut short, just because we'd solved a murder.

"No, of course not." He was rushing back and forth in his dusty bedroom, which didn't look quite so gothic and old fashioned with the windows open and bright morning light flooding in. "There is still so much of Britain to explore, so many adventures to be had and mistakes to-"

"Yes, yes. Mistakes to be made, I know all that. But what will we do after that?"

He stopped to look at me with a frown. "Well… then we will go home."

My response came out in a sombre whisper. "Ahh, I see."

He plumped down onto the bed and stroked his beard. "Is there something the matter, Christopher?" I didn't answer. "Would it happen to have something to do with young Ariadne?"

"I don't know what you mean." I have always been a terrible actor.

"If you think you're going to miss her, go and spend the last of your time here together. Or tell her how you feel, if that's what's important to you. But don't lurk around up here like a glum ghoul waiting to be exorcised."

"Do you really think I-" I didn't need any more persuading and had left the room by the time I'd got halfway through the sentence.

The only problem, of course, was that Ariadne had the run of the estate and there were a million and a half places she might have escaped to after the drama on the lake. I tried the suite where she slept, but there was no sign of her. I couldn't find her in the gardens either, but then – third time lucky – I scanned the high paths of the valley and spotted her back on the rock to which she had led us the previous morning.

I suppose it was all the exercise I'd been doing that weekend, but it didn't feel too difficult to mount the slope this time. When I reached her, she was sitting with her legs crossed and an envelope in her hand.

"Was that from your father?" I asked, and she nodded and handed it to me.

I felt odd taking possession of such a precious object. It was the only thing that could prove her parentage and grant her the estate. When I looked inside, I realised she'd kept the letter somewhere safe and all that it contained was a photograph of the two of them together. Ariadne was in her sailor costume, which she'd worn on our first night at Chandos, and the Duke was dressed as an eighteenth century general, with a red frock coat and a hat with billowing feathers protruding from it like a cockerel's comb. They were both smiling intently.

It was not the easiest start to the conversation I wished to have, but I wasn't going to give up now. "I hear that Deborah has agreed to stay and look after you."

"Yes, she seems very nice." There was no joy in her voice, and I didn't know how to respond.

In the end, I plumped for, "We're leaving soon."

"I suppose that makes sense."

"I'll miss you." This seemed like a friendly yet nonchalant thing to say.

"I'll probably forget about you in a couple of days" Sadly, this wasn't the response I was hoping for, but then she turned away and wouldn't look at me again, so I had to conclude she was fibbing.

"That's a shame." I took a deep breath and looked at the dappled landscape all around us. With the sun high in the sky to illuminate every angle, I'd never seen so many colours. Back home in Surrey, most things were one shade of green or another, but the palette of that northern valley knew no limits.

I forced myself to go on. "You see, I was wondering whether you'd like to stay in touch... maybe... if you don't think it's a bad idea. You know, letters and that sort of thing." This sounded terribly old fashioned and so I quickly added, "And perhaps the odd telephone call once in a while."

She gave no hint as to what she thought of the suggestion, but at least she turned to look at me. I'd known rabbits whose expressions were easier to read than hers.

232

"And then I wondered if you wouldn't perhaps want to visit me in the south at some point in the future, one day, when you have time."

Her eyes didn't leave mine, but that pretty smile of hers was nowhere to be seen. When she spoke, it was so quiet that I had to wait a few seconds to be sure it wasn't merely the whispering of that warm summer breeze on the bracken around the rock.

"Yes. I'd like that."

Though the words were as soft as goose down, they almost knocked me over. Instead of jumping into the air and saying, *thank you, that's wonderful, perhaps we should get married,* my voice reared out of me to enquire, "Would you?" in a slightly shocked manner as though I were dreadfully surprised.

She laughed then, and it made me feel a darn sight more cheerful.

"Christopher?" my grandfather poked his head into the garden to bellow in our direction. He was somehow conscious of exactly where I would be at any given moment. Delilah was running with great excitement between the garden and lake, and I knew that it was time for us to depart.

Not knowing how else I should leave Ariadne, I stuck out my hand, and she shook it. I had rather been hoping for a sentimental embrace and perhaps even a kiss on the cheek, but beggars can't be choosers and I was positively penniless in that department. Even though it was just about as formal as a boy's first romance could be, the feel of her fingers locked within mine sent a quiver through my body. I immediately went running back down the hill to hide how red my cheeks had become.

"It was nice meeting you," I shouted over my shoulder, and I knew that I would hold that moment in my head for months.

The cars were packed and ready and it was time to leave, but not before the last few guests at Chandos Grove came to say goodbye.

"I do feel guilty about framing an innocent child for murder, you know?" the Professor attempted to reassure us. "I genuinely thought that she was guilty when I found the drawing. I couldn't bear the idea of Deborah being blamed for it, so I left the knife in her room."

Grandfather seemed surprisingly laissez-faire about the whole situation. "Don't worry about it, Prof. We've all found ourselves in such a spot. I'm sure you had good intentions."

I looked at him side on, but didn't dare ask if he'd really done anything so nasty himself.

The Professor still looked embarrassed by his behaviour and clearly wanted to put things right. "I'll make sure that the girl gets her fair inheritance to make up for it. All pro bono of course."

Lovely, smiley Deborah (who I was very relieved was not a killer) stepped forward to hug us goodbye. "I'm going to stay at Chandos to get to know Ariadne. I've never had a sister before and I'm rather excited."

Mabel the maid was hanging off the Rolls Royce, looking heartbroken over our multi-purpose chauffeur's imminent departure.

Grandfather nodded his head in the girl's direction. "I'd say you have at least two sisters, in fact. And unless you want to share any possible inheritance with half of the north of England, I wouldn't go looking for any more."

He spun on the ball of his feet and boarded the glossy grey Aston Martin. Todd had evidently found the time to polish the cars between his duties mixing cocktails and saving lives.

"Come along, Christopher," the old man tapped the passenger seat enthusiastically, and Delilah jumped from the back before I could climb in.

"Goodbye all," I shouted, hoping that Ariadne might hear as the car pulled away.

CHAPTER FORTY

I must say I was rather sad as we waved farewell to my new friends. Our trip to Chandos Grove had been a wonderful, terrible experience, and I was certain that I would miss that wild estate for as long as I lived – just as my grandfather had.

"Grandfather?" I began, once the engine was humming, and we'd started our slow journey along that rumbling track. "Would it be all right if I ask you a few things?"

He didn't look at me as he steered around a pothole. "Fire away, my boy. Please, fire away."

It was hard to know where to start, so I went with a nice open question. "How did you know who the killers were?"

He let out a brief chortle and, slowing the car down, he answered my first point. "It was a number of things really. A lot of what we conclude in an investigation comes from a process of elimination. Our answers form in negative, only for the shape and colour of each to become clearer as the case develops.

"Stuart is a prime example. I knew he was one of the few people who absolutely couldn't have murdered Bobbie, and that made him stand out to me. The Professor hadn't spotted anyone leaving the hut, and so, assuming he wasn't the killer, something didn't make sense. Our time frame was unreliable. By working through the suspects, I came to see that, as his mother couldn't have done it, Stuart was the only likely culprit."

I needed an extra twenty seconds once he'd finished speaking to make sure I'd understood this, but I eventually answered him. "You didn't know where Ariadne was."

"But I knew she wasn't the killer."

"Ummm… no, you didn't."

"But it turned out that she wasn't."

"But you didn't know that at the time!" I was more than a touch vexed.

"This is getting us nowhere," he declared, as though I were the one being unreasonable. "Stuart marked himself out as the murderer in a number of ways. For one thing, he entertained the idea of a relationship with Deborah – despite knowing his mother would never accept such a match – in order to appear more sympathetic and draw attention to the Professor's meddling. From there, his motives became apparent."

"All right," I said, feeling semi-confident I understood this. "And you said it was important to consider why the Duke was killed now instead of years ago or last week or tomorrow."

"Correct. After all, what would have happened yesterday morning if Bobbie hadn't been killed?"

I had to think for a moment, but I soon remembered the argument that the Professor had stewarded between my grandfather and the Duke the night before he was killed. "You were supposed to go through the evidence of who killed Morwenna. The Duke hoped to prove himself innocent."

"Exactly, my boy!" He seemed quite happy with me then. "Stuart couldn't let that happen as he was afraid it would show the world who his mother really was. He had to kill Bobbie when he did, there was no other option."

I was ready with my next point. "Then what about Philomena herself? How did you finally see that she was responsible for the fire?"

"You mean the hat riddle didn't tell you everything you needed to know?" He was clearly a little disappointed by this.

"Ummm... not really."

"It was all through elimination. If Stuart killed Bobbie, then it made sense that Philomena had killed Star. It's just like a mathematical formula."

I decided not to remind him that he'd read my last school mathematics report and it wasn't particularly good.

"Remember," he continued. "Bobbie saw a figure in the darkness on the night Morwenna died, hidden among the ivy which grew along the garden wall. In his memoirs, he wrote that he thought it was the ghost of Star herself, picked out by red flames. But that was his sorrow playing tricks on him. It was Mimi who always wore a red riding cape when we went for walks. She'd burnt down the orangery but stayed to watch what happened.

"When I saw her there yesterday morning, staring at the charred remains, I thought it was sadness she was feeling, but I think it was most likely pride. She was out there again last night when the hut

236

burnt down. I saw her among the trees."

I recalled the figure in the darkness and decided he was probably right. It was a woman I had seen, a woman in a long red cloak. It hadn't occurred to me to question who had started the fire. "So she tried to kill us too?"

"I believe so. Perhaps the book was her main target, but we would have both died if you hadn't-"

"Grandfather, stop the car!" I hated to interrupt him just as he was about to compliment me, but I'd caught a flash of gold running through the trees that bordered the road. A moment later, Ariadne appeared from the woods.

The Aston Martin came to a crunching halt, sending gravel and earth flying beneath the wheels. I hopped from the car without opening the door, then casually strolled over to her. Only joking, I ran as fast as my legs would carry me and, when I reached her she grabbed me by the arms and pulled me right up to her.

"You may kiss me, if you like," I quoted, when she wouldn't say anything.

Her lips hovered half an inch from my own. I could feel her breath on my skin as she made me wait. Three seconds became an infinite, endless eternity, but then it was finally happening. Our faces pressed together – our mouths firmly closed, of course – and I was no longer an unkissed sixteen-year-old boy. I was a man of the world.

When we pulled apart again, she looked happier than she had all weekend and she chattered like a baby sparrow. "I'll write to you. And I'll ring you too. In fact, we should plan your next visit. Or I'll come down to you. Yes, that would be very nice."

"I'm sorry it was this weekend that we met," I began. "I mean, after everything that happened with…" I couldn't find the words to finish that sentence, so I didn't try.

"You mustn't think like that. There were two possible circumstances this weekend. In one, my father was murdered and, in the other, my father was murdered, but I also met you. I think it's obvious which one I prefer."

Todd, Cook and Halfpenny were clapping from the other cars, while Alice told them not to be nosy, but I didn't feel embarrassed. I held Ariadne's hands and squeezed them tightly. When I let go again,

I knew it really was time to leave.

I backed away from her and got into the car without looking. Grandfather started the engine, and Ariadne and I waved until we couldn't see each other any longer. When she was gone, and I was alone with my grandfather, there appeared to be a small but crucial part of my internal biology missing. My heart stung like nothing I'd experienced before.

"Excellent work, Christopher."

I couldn't control the smile on my face and so I went back to our previous conversation. "I still have one more question actually."

"About the investigation, you mean?"

"In a way, yes." I would finally address the issue that had been foremost in my mind since we arrived at Chandos Grove. "Why did the Duke eat all those sardines?"

Grandfather thought for a moment. "I haven't a clue. Perhaps he felt he needed more iron in his diet."

"So it had nothing to do with his murder? I was sure they were going to be important."

"No, Christopher, sometimes a sardine isn't even a red herring. It's just a sardine." He winked at me, before turning onto the smooth surface of the public road. "So, where are we off to next?"

"You tell me," I said, reaching into the back seat to pull out the selection of maps so that Delilah jumped onto my lap again. "England is our large, flat oyster."

The End (For Now...)

Get another
L♥RD EDGINGT♥N ADVENTURE
absolutely **free**…

Download your free novella at
www.benedictbrown.net

"LORD EDGINGTON INVESTIGATES. . ."

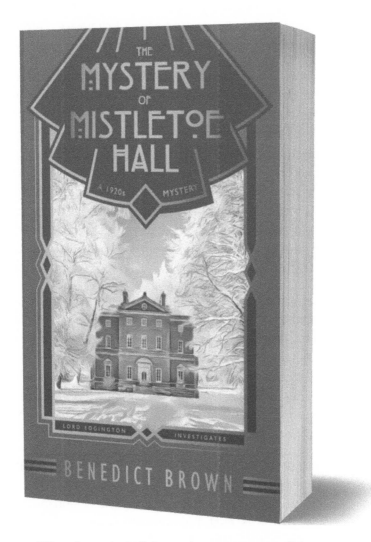

The fourth full-length mystery will be available in **November** at amazon.

Sign up to the readers' club on my website to know when it goes on sale.

ABOUT THIS BOOK

I think it would be fair to say that this book either took two months or thirty-eight years to create. The sights and scenery that we get to enjoy on Lord Edgington's circuitous route across Britain are a highlights reel of so many holidays I have taken throughout my life.

When I was a kid, the Brown family would seek out the rainiest places in Britain and chart a course for a walking holiday under grey skies. We took trips to Yorkshire, Northumberland, The Peak District, The Cotswolds and, the one I remember most, The Lake District. I was probably only seven when I went there but I still recall the colours of the place so vividly – it helped that it was spectacularly sunny the whole time we were there! The Lake District was Britain's first National Park, is a UNESCO heritage site, and it really is a stunning place to visit. It's filled with mountainous landscapes, countless sheep and lots of lakes (well, meres and tarns at least). Search for "Lake District Cinematic Drone" on YouTube to see some incredible footage of the scenery.

As I haven't been there in three decades and couldn't travel before writing the book, I spent a long time researching the area and watching videos to get a feel for the majestic setting. I looked into stately homes in the area too and Chandos Grove is something of a hybrid between Holker Hall – complete with Elizabethan and Victorian influences and its history of a terrible fire – and Satis House from Dickens' "Great Expectations". I hope I've managed to promote this incredible region through my book and just wish I could have visited again before writing it.

Perhaps not so dramatic, but still one of my favourite places in England, the countryside of Suffolk is lush and flat. My family and I go to Latitude Festival every year and we've fallen in love with Henham Park where it takes place. At the festival, my mother spends most of her day at the stage on the lake (where Chrissy fails to catch a fish) and though Henham Hall – where Elodie lives – no longer exists, it's a beautiful park with woodland, lake swimming and a large plateau where the main music stage is located. Cambridge, Great Yarmouth and Sherwood Forest are other nice stops on the journey.

In terms of the story, I wanted to learn more about Lord Edgington's past and it's always a big surprise to see where each book takes him. Before writing, I knew that there would be a historical mystery to be solved and a new killer to deal with, but not much more than that. I'm really pleased with the way the two plots have developed and wound around one another. I had originally planned to reveal how Lord Edgington met his wife, but the book was already getting long and so I'll keep that plotline for one of the books next year.

I'm also happy to see Christopher developing. The difficulty with characters in a mystery series is that you can't have too much change from one book to the next in case people read them out of order. I have the added problem with Christopher that he's rather sweet as he is. I know some of my readers don't want him to grow up too soon, so I hope I've found a good balance.

If you loved the story and have the time, please write a review on Amazon. Most books get one review per thousand readers so I would be infinitely appreciative if you could help me out.

THE MOST INTERESTING THINGS I DISCOVERED WHEN RESEARCHING THIS BOOK...

I always come across a lot of fascinating historical facts as I research my books and here are a selection of the ones I discovered this time around.

I chose the name Chandos for the dukes in the book as it is a defunct title in Britain. The last Duke of Chandos died in 1789 without any male heirs and so the title disappeared. In the past I've invented titles for places that are very unlikely to have them. For example, Lord Edgington's son is the Earl of Croydon. This is not a title which has ever existed and Croydon – my nearest big town when I was a child – is a famously unglamorous place (which I love!)

I have, however, used a real family name for Henham Park near Southwold, but in this case it is the house which no longer exists. The real-life estate is still in the Rous family, but the Georgian mansion mentioned in the novel was knocked down by the fourth Earl of Stradbroke in 1953. More's the pity!

When Chrissy and his grandfather go to Suffolk to visit Elodie Rous, he talks about the place names of that region. His supposition is correct and many towns still hold their ancient Saxon names. Henham, for example, would have been the hamlet or homestead (ham) of a chieftain called Hen. Suffolk itself was named for the people who lived there – Suffolk means *south folk* and there is Norfolk to the north. The region was an Anglo-Saxon stronghold, and we recently visited Sutton Hoo where King Rædwald of East Anglia's burial ship was found in the 1930s containing a wealth of treasures which are now in the British Museum. It was my mother's dream to visit there (her words) so I really had to take her along. A film about it called 'The Dig' was released last year.

Sticking with my mother, it was also her dream (she has a lot of them) to go to Great Yarmouth further up the coast. Charles Dickens

244

writes in his novel David Copperfield that "it was well known… that Yarmouth was, upon the whole, the finest place in the universe" and he paints a very quaint picture of the town. Much like Chrissy in the book, my mum was a little disappointed by the creep of modernity that has turned the picturesque seaside resort into a giant funfair, but I liked it!

Probably the most extensive area of research for me throughout these books is the changing role of women after the First World War. In the first book, I talked about Clara being one of the first women to be admitted to a full university degree at Cambridge and in this one we have the imperious Lady Fontaine. I was fascinated to read about the real first female members of parliament of the 1920s. The very first was Constance Markievicz, an Irish revolutionary who never took up her seat in Westminster, but was Ireland's only female cabinet minister until 1979. She was the daughter of the Arctic explorer and adventurer Sir Henry Gore-Booth, and died having given up her considerable wealth. She was sentenced to death for her part in the Easter Uprising (but later pardoned) and was a hands-on soldier in the Irish Citizen's Army, and also designed their uniform and anthem. A colourful character indeed.

Far closer to Philomena in the book though is the better-known Nancy Astor. Astor was an American who married into the Waldorf family and, like our Mimi, pushed her husband into politics before beating a path herself through Westminster. She was a formidable character – with some completely unacceptable anti-Semitic and racist views – who served in the House of Commons between 1919 and 1945. Though a traditional conservative, she had friends from across the political spectrum, including George Bernard Shaw. She is perhaps most famous today for butting heads with Winston Churchill and is commonly attributed with saying to him, "Oh, if you were my husband, I'd put poison in your tea." To which he replied, "Madame, if I were your husband, I'd drink it with pleasure."

Another formidable lady I came across is Virginia Oldoini, the Italian Countess of Castiglione. I came across her by chance, but she is fascinating. She became notorious in France for being one of Napoleon the third's many mistresses. One encyclopaedia entry lists her as a "mistress, spy, and photographic model" and it was this last role that caught my imagination. A famous beauty, she was known for making grand entrances in incredible dresses in the French court and she attempted to recreate these key moments of her life through photography. She spent most of her fortune (and several decades) capturing seven hundred photos, most of which are held in the Metropolitan Museum of Art in New York. If you look online at the photos, it's fascinating to see this incredible woman's image dating back to 1856.

I had no idea when C.P.R. was conceived but I soon discovered that the most common type of artificial resuscitation in the 1920s was the Dr H. R. Silvester method. As described in my book, it involved kneeling behind the patient and pushing their hands onto their chest, then pulling their arms up into the air to aid respiration. It dated back to the 1850s and was used in cases of drowning and still birth. There were other methods by the 1920s but this seems to be the most successful one.

I always have fun looking up food to include in my books and one thing that surprised me this time around was just how abundant Victorian menus were. Three-course meals were not common in rich houses, and you were more likely to get three dishes for every course. There's a definite Victorian influence in the books due to Lord Edgington's age and I think he would have been happy to relive the meals from his childhood.

Some of the dishes are my own creation of course. I spent some time looking at the most popular Cumbrian dishes and working out what was available back then (Sticky Toffee Pudding, for example, does not appear to have existed much before the 1970s). Forced Rhubarb, damsons, lamb and Kendal Mint Cake are all key Lake District exports and so I mixed them together and came up with a delicious-sounding meal.

Kendal Mint Cake is a sugary treat that Sir Edmund Hillary and his Sherpa companion ate when they became the first explorers to climb Everest. Tenzing Norgay apparently left some behind to appease his gods. Perhaps because of this, mint cake is popular to this day with walkers and climbers.

Treacle Tart dates back to the nineteenth century and basically consists of pastry and golden syrup, baked in the oven – yum yum! It is also

Cockney rhyming slang for "sweetheart" and, apparently, Harry Potter's favourite dessert at Hogwarts.

It's really not a Benedict Brown novel without a song in it and there were two this time to make up for the terrible dearth of lyricism in "A Body at a Boarding School". "Lovely Mary Donnelly" was written by the Irish poet and diarist William Allingham (1824–89) who was a contemporary of Alfred Lord Tennyson and Dante Rossetti. "I'm Henery the Eighth, I Am", meanwhile is pure fun. It was written in 1910 by Fred Murray and R. P. Weston and was associated with the music hall performer Harry Champion. It, improbably, became the fastest selling song in history in 1965 at the height of the British invasion when Herman's Hermits sang it on American television programmes like The Ed Sullivan Show.And last, but not least, I thought this book needed a dance scene. Along with crime fiction, my family also love dance. My mum goes to London whenever she can to the Sadler's Wells dance theatre. When we were kids, she convinced my brother Daniel and me to attend classes – I may or may not have a GCSE in contemporary dance. When Marion and I got married, we started ballroom classes, and our little Amelie never stops dancing – she went with her grandmother to see Carmina Burana at the theatre last week and spent her whole time throwing herself about like it was a rock concert.

I don't get the impression that Lord Edgington would have known how to Tango and so I found a more sedate precursor that was popular in the nineteenth century. The Habanera, or contradanza, came from Cuba via Spanish sailors, and swept the globe. From what I can tell it's somewhere between the Tango and the more formal dances of Regency England – think, Elizabeth Bennet goes Latin.

Thanks again for reading. I wonder what fascinating historical facets the next book will turn up! Suggestions for what you'd like to see worked into my stories are always welcome. Please forgive me if you've ever tried to send me an e-mail through the contact form on my website. It hasn't been working for a long time and so I probably missed a lot of messages. It's working now though, so please get in touch if there's something you wanted to share or ask.

ACKNOWLEDGEMENTS

I'm going to start off with a sorry to the whole of Cumbria and its inhabitants in case I've made any major mistakes with the dialect, landscape or cuisine of your region. I've given it my best go, but it's a bit trickier than normal to research when I'm a thousand miles away and essentially prohibited from travelling home. I hope I have put across my absolute love and appreciation for one of the most beautiful places I've ever visited.

Thank you as always to my wife and daughter for being inspirationally wonderful, to my family for reading my books and my crack team of experts – the Hoggs, the Martins, Esther Lamin and Lori Willis (**fiction**), Paul Bickley (**policing**), Karen Baugh Menuhin (**marketing**) and Mar Pérez (**forensic pathology**) for knowing lots of stuff when I don't. Thanks to my fellow writers who are always there for me, especially Pete, Suzanne and Lucy.

Thank you many times over to all the readers in my ARC team who have combed the book for errors. I wouldn't be able to produce these books so quickly or successfully without you so please stick with me, Izzy and Lord Edgington to see what happens next…

Rebecca Brooks, Ferne Miller, Craig Jones, Melinda Kimlinger, Deborah McNeill, Emma James, Mindy Denkin, Namoi Lamont, Linda Kelso, Katharine Reibig, Pam, Sarah Dalziel, Linsey Neale, Sarah Brown, Karen Davis, Taylor Rain, Brenda, Christine Folks McGraw, Terri Roller, Margaret Liddle, Tracy Humphries, Anja Peerdeman, Liz Batton, Allie Copland, Susan Kline, Kate Newnham, Marion Davis, Tina Laws, Sarah Turner, Linda Brain, Stephanie Keller, Linda Locke, Kathryn Davenport, Kat, Sandra Hoff, Karen M, Mary Nickell, Vanessa Rivington, Darlene Riggs, Jill Tatum, Helena George Anne Kavcic, Nancy Roberts, Cathleen Brickhouse and Susan Reddington.

THE "DEATH ON A SUMMER'S DAY" COCKTAIL

In the twenties, the idle rich would swap London clubs for the bars of luxury hotels on the Côte d'Azur on a seasonal basis. The most celebrated bartenders would follow them on that great bi-yearly migration.

Pat MacGarry, the famed mixer at London's Buck Club, is said to be the creator of the **Sidecar**, a mixture of Cointreau, cognac and lemon juice that took the south of France by storm in the early twenties. It became one of the most iconic drinks of its era, shaken in Paris and London's fashionable clubs or at the private cocktail parties that bright young things would throw during the 'années folles'. The drink has since been claimed by establishments such as Harry's New York Bar and the Ritz (both in Paris). Neither had anything to do with its creation, but their continued advocacy ensured its survival in the postwar years, when it almost disappeared. Today, the Sidecar is seen as one of the key drinks in cocktail history —and one of the most pleasant.

45 ml (1 1/2 oz) cognac

20 ml (3/4 oz) Cointreau

15 ml (1/2 oz) lemon juice

10 ml (1/4 oz) simple syrup (optional)

Add all ingredients to an ice-filled shaker, shake and strain in a cocktail glass. Garnish with a lemon twist. The original recipes call for equal parts cognac, Cointreau and lemon juice. This tends to be a little tart. The above version is closer to the current standard. American bartenders usually add a little simple syrup to round off the drink. It's optional, but most people find it a welcome addition.

The idea for our cocktail pages was inspired by my friend and the "Lord Edgington Investigates…" official cocktail expert, Francois Monti. You can get his brilliant book "101 Cocktails to Try Before you Die" at Amazon…

THE IZZY PALMER MYSTERIES

If you're looking for a modern murder mystery series with just as many off-the-wall characters but a little more edge, try **"The Izzy Palmer Mysteries"** for your next whodunit fix.

"A CORPSE CALLED BOB"
(BOOK ONE)

Izzy just found her horrible boss murdered in his office and all her dreams are about to come true! Miss Marple meets Bridget Jones in a fast and funny new detective series with a hilarious cast of characters and a wicked resolution you'll never see coming. Read now to discover why one Amazon reviewer called it, ***"Sheer murder mystery bliss."***

ABOUT ME

Writing has always been my passion. It was my favourite half-an-hour a week at primary school, and I started on my first, truly abysmal book as a teenager. So it wasn't a difficult decision to study literature at university which led to a masters in Creative Writing.

I'm a Welsh-Irish-Englishman originally from **South London** but now living with my French/Spanish wife and presumably quite confused infant daughter in **Burgos**, a beautiful mediaeval city in the north of Spain. I write overlooking the Castilian countryside, trying not to be distracted by the vultures, hawks and red kites that fly past my window each day.

When Covid 19 hit in 2020, the language school where I worked as an English teacher closed down and I became a full-time writer. I have two murder mystery series. There are already six books written in **"The Izzy Palmer Mysteries"** which is a more modern, zany take on the genre. I will continue to alternate releases between Izzy and Lord Edgington. I hope to release at least ten books in each series.

I previously spent years focussing on kids' books and wrote everything from fairy tales to environmental dystopian fantasies, right through to issue-based teen fiction. My book **"The Princess and The Peach"** was long-listed for the Chicken House prize in The Times and an American producer even talked about adapting it into a film. I'll be slowly publishing those books over the next year whenever we find the time.

"Death on a Summer's Day" is the third book in the "Lord Edgington Investigates…" series. The next book will be out in time for Christmas and there's a novella available free if you sign up to my readers' club. If you feel like telling me what you think about Chrissy and his grandfather, my writing or the world at large, I'd love to hear from you, so feel free to get in touch via...

www.benedictbrown.net

WORDS YOU MIGHT NOT KNOW

Scabrous – can mean rough or squalid and once referred to harsh sounds.

Cornish ice cream is quite similar to vanilla but traditionally made with clotted cream. It's delicious!

The expression **"what the deuce?"** is a very mild swear word which is derived from words for the devil but could also mean bad luck in general.

Coot – is a type of water fowl but also means fool.

Milksop predates **Milquetoast**, which is the word I originally wrote but is from American in the 1930s. Both mean weak and wimpish.

"Hasta iver deeked a cuddy loup a five bar yat?" is Cumbrian dialect for "have you ever seen a donkey jump a five-bar gate?" Why the officers would be discussing this is unknown even to me. I noticed a lot of such example sentences when I was researching the dialect and so decided to include it in its entirety. Cumbrian is an ancient dialect with Norse and Celtic influences that shares some words with the Scots language. It was fun learning about it and I hope I haven't made any mistakes – any Cumbrian readers are welcome to get in touch to tell me off if I have!

Cove can be used positively or negatively– a good chap or bad.

Barb originally comes from Latin words for the sharp points of a beard which leant itself to the barb of an arrow and later, metaphorically I suppose, came to mean an insult.

Adelante is the Spanish word for "go ahead". So Chrissy gives the definition without knowing it.

Guttersnipe was originally Wall Street slang for "street-corner broker," though, by 1869 referred to street urchins. It's American in origin, but seems to have made it to the UK by the twentieth century and was commonly used to insult wicked children.

Cogitation means thought.

Gaucheness comes from the French word for "left" (as opposed to right) and means awkward – in Chrissy's case, that's socially awkward.

Freakful is a bit of an anachronism – in the right direction though. It means freakish but is more Victorian than 1920s. I included it merely because it is associated with John Keats who uses it in his poem 'Lamia', and he's rather important to this story!

Inamorata – from the Italian innamorata meaning female lover or sweetheart.

Blotto, you probably all know, means drunk!

Salvo is another word for a volley of gunfire or projectiles. So the opening salvo is the first attack.

Ragging means teasing and comes from student slang. It had originally meant to scold or intimidate.

The metaphorical raising of hackles probably comes from the sight of a cockerel getting angry.

Objet d'art is borrowed from French to mean pieces of art that are not painting or sculpture.

A conflagration is a substantial fire.

"To grouse over spilt milk" is an older spin on the saying. To grouse means to complain and is British army slang.

Ah, deek at that effort, eh? – Cumbrian dialect again to mean, "Look at that (negative) thing!"

Some donnat's made a right maff of it. It's in a gay ole scrow. – Some fool's made a real mess of it. It's in a terrible state.

Cushty barie! – Very good

Mummery comes from mummers who performed silent plays in the middle ages. This came to refer to a ridiculous performance in general soon after.

Sot is an interesting word. It means a fool but can refer to any affected state from drunkenness to excessive romance and gives us the word besotted.

Hurray for words! Aren't they wonderful?

CHARACTER LIST

Toffs etc!

The Most Honourable Marquess of Edgington, Lord of Cranley Hall – I hope you know him by now. He's the main character of this series. Retired Metropolitan Police superintendent, owner of the grandest estate in Surrey and Christopher's grandfather.

Christopher Aloysius Prentiss (Aged sixteen, soon to be seventeen!) – Kind-hearted, well-meaning and somewhat sentimental, Christopher is Lord Edgington's assistant.

Professor Samson Filigree – "The Professor" – Cambridge lecturer and life-long student, he was best friends with Lord Edgington during their adolescence on their summer trips to the north of England.

Robert "Bobbie" Atwell, the fifth Duke of Chandos – the current proprietor of Chandos Grove estate in the Lake District and old friend of Edgington and the Professor.

Ariadne – his wild, adopted daughter.

Philomena Fontaine – "Mimi" – Bobbie's ex-fiancée and a future politician. A powerful woman who is married to the Home Secretary of Great Britain.

Stuart – her son and personal secretary.

Elodie Rous – "Lala" – The last in line of a wealthy family, she was another member of the Chandos Grove gang who spent their summers together.

Morwenna Fairbright – The final member of the Chandos gang. She died in her teens.

Deborah Fisher – The Professor's university research assistant.

Domestics etc!

Todd – Lord Edgington's chauffeur and all-around helper. Mixes a mean cocktail and is always on hand when action is needed.

Halfpenny – Cranley Hall's Footman.

Alice – Cranley Hall's maid and Chrissy's (first) one true love.

Patrick Driscoll – Cranley Hall's head gardener.

"Cook" – Henrietta – Cranley Hall's somewhat experimental cook.

Mabel – Chandos Grove's maid and sole employee.

Jim, Phil and Sergeant Massey – local police officers from the Cumberland region.

CPSIA information can be obtained
at www.ICGtesting.com
Printed in the USA
LVHW091157200222
711576LV00022B/378

9 781838 299262